THE KINGFISHERS

by

ALAN THOMPSON

W & B Publishers

USA

The Kingfishers © 2013 All rights reserved by Patrick Thompson.

W & B Publishers

For information:
W & B Publishers
Post Office Box 193
Colfax, NC 27235
www.a-argusbooks.com

ISBN: 978-0-6159363-14
ISBN: 0-6159363-1-8

Book Cover designed by Dubya

Printed in the United States of America

For my sons, who became men more gracefully than their father

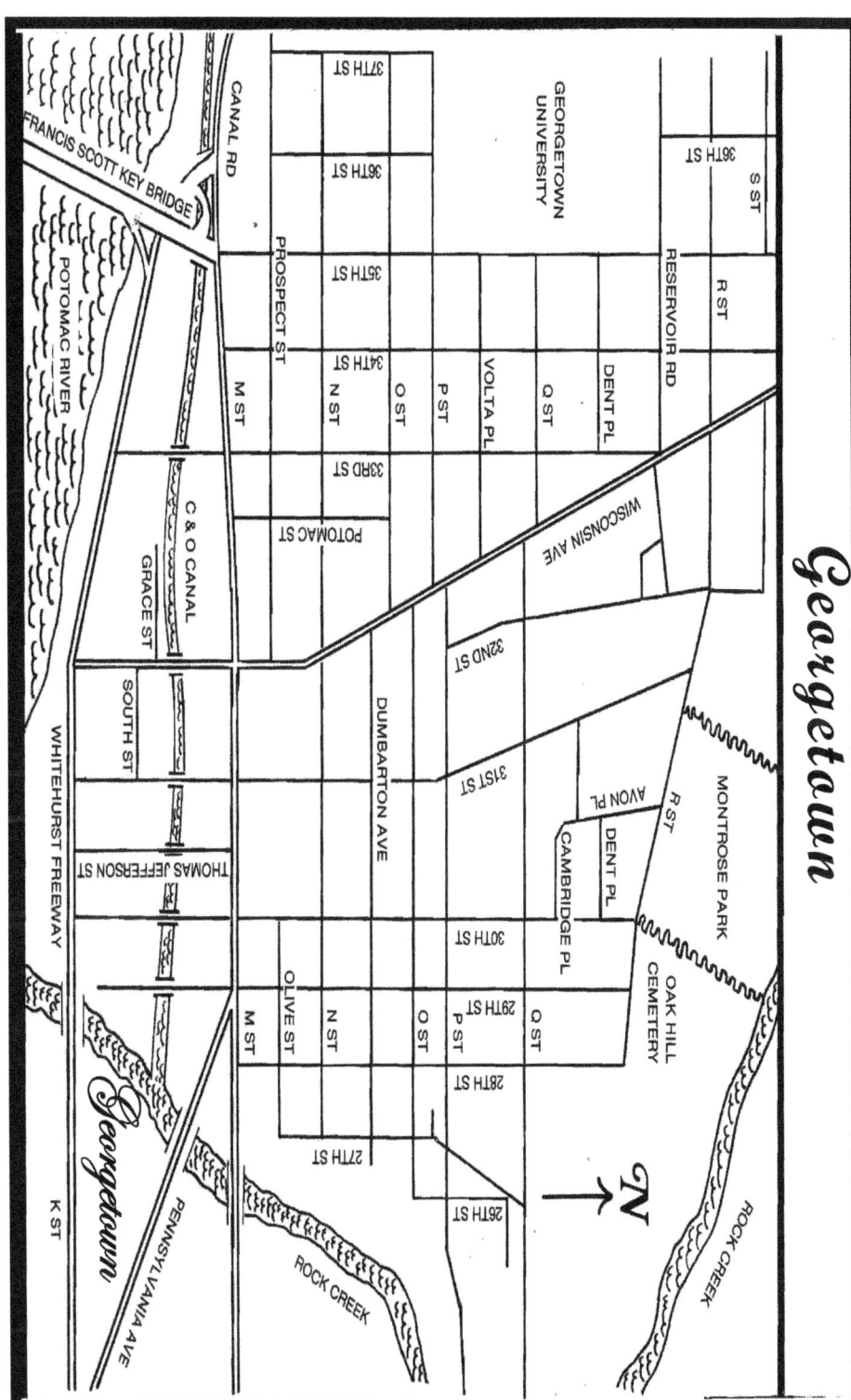

THE KINGFISHERS

THE GREAT cloud of dust drifts aimlessly in the infinite marches of dead, black space. It has no purpose, no reason for being. It merely is. Eons pass . . .

A star dies, and a brilliant light and terrible heat overwhelm the dark for an instant, then begin to recede. Lethal remnants from the fractured star join the dust which gathers and thickens, and forms a whirling, tilted disk that glows in the new darkness. As it turns, the dust and debris draw closer still. The center of the cloud collapses and another star, a yellow one, appears. The outer particles continue to condense and accrete and orbs, still turning around the new sun, emerge. More eons wear on . . .

The third orb from the new sun is bombarded by massive rocks from the depths of space. Chunks of its mantle are thrown off and another sphere, tethered by gravity to the orb, is formed. The orb's surface heats and cools and becomes solid – locking in place the ferocious elements it has carried since its cataclysmic birth – and water and wind materialize from the vapors surrounding it. Animate forms appear. Oxygen is created. Another eon begins . . .

The awful, destructive energy absorbed in the beginning rests within the orb, and the orb itself con-

spires to unleash – at a single, insignificant location for an instant in time – the deadly elements imprisoned in its decaying rock. Water and air combine with the rock to release the unknowable heat and toxins of the broken star from which they come. Unlike the star, the orb is not destroyed – the water that enables the reaction also moderates it and, when the rock is depleted, the reaction stops. The genie is once more inside the bottle, Pandora's Box is closed. Millions of years go by . . .

The orb carries on. Oceans are filled with fish, mountains rise and fall, land is abundant with forests, and the first winged creatures appear. Plants flourish. Dinosaurs dominate and disappear. Horses, monkeys, whales, apes and elephants emerge, and the ice comes and goes. The rock continues to decay, rendering itself more and more harmless until at last it poses no threat to the orb . . .

BOOK ONE

It nests at the end of a tunnel bored by itself in a bank. There, six or eight white translucent eggs are laid . . . on bones thrown up in pellets by the birds.

On these rejectamenta . . . the young are born. And, as they are fed and grow, this nest of excrement and decayed fish becomes a dripping, fetid mass –
......Charles Olson

CHAPTER ONE

THE MAN, not yet a corpse, seemed to hover in the air. His mouth was open but no sound emerged, or perhaps his cry was lost in the noise of his approaching doom. The violent collision – the rending of flesh, the crunch of bones, the spray of blood – was sickening but solitary. Only seconds before, his passage from life to death had been reckoned in decades – now it was over in an instant. The engine of his demise took no notice, but the man who controlled it knew that something was wrong. As he emerged to inspect the remains, a dark figure retreated into the insensible crowd.

THE PLAIN white tablets, thousands of them, sprouted from the rolling green palisades like mushrooms after a heavy storm. I smiled. The imagery was unavoidable. The man beneath the ground before me had lived much of his life in the shade of a colossal mushroom – not one that grew from the ground like Jack's beanstalk, but one that formed above it, destroying everything in its shadow.

I looked at the marker. There was a Christian cross at the top, a symbol that the man had refused to recognize in life and likely would have rejected in death had he anything to say about it. It was there because the government functionary in charge of the cemetery had inquired and my mother, who observed the rituals without taking the time to understand them, had declared him a member of her tribe. I read the words:

ROBERT W. ROGERS
U.S. ARMY AIR FORCES
January 2, 1924 – February 12, 1995
CREW MEMBER, ENOLA GAY

Most of the stones in this vast necropolis on the Potomac River touted wars or battles fought, or decorations won, but his singular achievement – and the legacy he left behind – was to unwittingly participate in the instant slaughter of eighty thousand men, women and children, and the prolonged suffering and death of countless others.

Technically, my grandfather wasn't supposed to be here. The graveyard bureaucrats had a hierarchy of rules equating battlefield valor with time-serving and "government service," and he fit none of the niches that they described. Mother had raised hell with our congressman, and the Army quickly retreated from its initial refusal. In truth, they were glad to have him. He and the others who had flown with him that day gave a human face to the monstrous massacre over forty years earlier, and diverted attention from those who were really responsible. She lay next to him. The stone offered no clues to her life, no hint of the ambition and need that drove her. She was here because her father – and now another man – was here, an irony that she might not have appreciated.

I turned to the third grave, the one that had drawn me to this place today. The iron bouquet of newly turned earth, enriched with the blood of scoundrels and heroes, reached my nostrils, leavened by the smell of new-cut grass and gasoline. I paused for a moment, gazing past the old trees and the whirl of tombstones and the river. On the far side of the bridge I could see Lincoln's temple and Washington's monolith and, further east, the Capitol, gleaming in the late afternoon sun like one of Faberge's jewel-encrusted eggs. The city looked the same from here, but I knew it wasn't. Twenty years was an epoch for a place like Washington. Looking back at the stones, I considered death for a few seconds, then walked down the hill to the car.

MARK SINGER leaned over the table and stabbed at me with a loaded fork. "You should move up here," he said. "Business is booming." He shoved the chunk of bloody meat into his mouth.

"Business?"

"Yeah. The business of government. It's lights out." He paused. "Who was it that said that the business of government is business? Coolidge?"

"That's not what he said. He said that the business of *America* is business."

We were seated on the patio at Mark's favorite place in Georgetown, a bistro called Mr. Smith's. He carved another hunk of steak and pulled it off the fork with his strong white teeth. He ate in the European style – the fork remained always in his left hand and the knife in his right, and neither was laid on the plate until he was finished. I moved my fork back and forth and laid my knife down and, as a consequence, his steak was almost gone and mine barely half-eaten. He sawed off another piece. "Whatever. All I know is that government *is* the business in this town, and the people here are making a killing."

"I thought government was unselfish public service."

"That's for the rubes." I laughed. "If you're not rich when you come here, you're rich when you leave."

"Are you rich?"

He grinned. "Oh, no. I'm just a humble newspaperman."

I laughed again. Mark had been my college roommate. We shared a squalid cell in an old apartment building on New Hampshire Avenue for two years, and I had been an usher at his first wedding. He was the only person from those days that I kept up with. One or the other of us placed a call every three or four months to see what was going on.

He *was* a newspaperman, but neither the "just" nor the "humble" applied. He had started at the *Georgetown Star* as a photographer right out of college, and was now the paper's senior political reporter. He drank with senators and interviewed presidents, and attended the embassy balls and Georgetown soirées. Much in demand by the various charities in town, his current cause, on behalf of the Georgetown Preservation Society, was the restoration of a solitary antebellum mansion situated in the middle of the Potomac River. His three-story townhouse – on O Street just east of Wisconsin Avenue – was often the scene of quiet revelry, and outings on his old red, white and blue trawler – tied up only a few yards away – were legendary. His first wife had divorced him long ago, and the departure of the second four years earlier had confirmed him in his less than sanguine attitude toward women. My divorce from Martha around the same time had inspired a melancholy affirmation of our friendship, and my view of the fair sex was darker than his.

He waited impatiently for me to finish my food, then signaled the waiter. "Bring us two brandies," he said. "And put this on my tab."

"Mark –"

"Don't worry about it." He smiled. "I can write it off." The brandy arrived. "Seriously, I want you to think about coming up here. There's nothing to keep you in New Hope." Later, he walked me to my car. "I'm flying to Vegas for a little R and R tomorrow, but when I get back I'm going to find something for you."

MY LAST few months in Washington, twenty years earlier, had been the best days of my life. When I boarded the train at Union Station on a gloomy day in 1994, I expected to return in a week or two but my grandfather's illness, and Mother's refusal to deal with it, kept me away for two months. When I finally came back, things had changed.

After a few miserable weeks I returned to New Hope and, having nothing better to do, finished the requirements for my degree at the College. I went to law school for the same reason. I didn't want to think and thinking wasn't required – only a point of view was necessary to succeed. Like those who had driven my grandfather from New Hope, the law school faculty was an unquestioning, placid gaggle of conformity. I finished near the top of my class, clerked for a judge at the state capital, and accepted a job at a white shoe firm in Atlanta.

Martha Roberts, my high school sweetheart, had moved on when I first went to Washington but, perhaps sensing that I was sufficiently cynical to succeed in the practice of law, she found me again. I gave no thought as to how it would be, or to the pain I would surely cause her. We resumed the roles we'd started with – cocksure football captain and popular head cheerleader – and it worked for a time, but I had known something more, however briefly. As the years ticked by the things I acquired – a beautiful wife, a successful law practice, a big house in Buckhead – became burdens and drink, which had begun as a macho taboo when I was a boy, became urgent.

The combination of booze and neglect led to painful confrontations, personal and professional, and friends enjoined me to seek help, but I didn't want help. I didn't care about the wife or the house or the career. I was ashamed of my indifference, and mounted a few attempts to overcome it, without result. The chance to rise above the mortality that was every man's due had been snatched away, so I left my prizes behind and returned to New Hope, a place that had never expected much of me to begin with. When Mother died, I moved into the old colonial on Castle Lane and waited for death.

I LEANED back, feet on the desk, and stared out the window of the old stucco bungalow at High Street. The part-time girl was gone and it was almost five o'clock – time for a drink. I dropped my feet to the floor and walked to the refrigerator in the alcove that served as my library. Reaching into the freezer, I withdrew an ice tray and cracked it in the sink. After rinsing out the glass I'd used at lunch, I filled it with ice and poured scotch to the top. As I resumed my seat behind the desk, the telephone rang. I glanced at the clock – it was past five now, after business hours. The rings continued. I counted them – six, seven, eight . . . When I reached twelve, I picked up the receiver to make it stop. "Sawyer Law Office," I shouted into the phone.

"Tommy, doesn't somebody answer your goddamned telephone?"

I relaxed. "Yes, Mark. Sometimes. She's gone for the day."

"Jesus. No cell phone, no computer – it's like trying to communicate with the Pope." He paused. "I've found you that job we were talking about last month."

"*We* weren't talking about a job. You were."

He ignored me. "The work's interesting, not too demanding, and it pays almost $100,000 plus every add-on and benefit a government gnome can devise." He stopped. When I didn't respond, he said, "Honestly, it's right up your alley."

"You've found me a job defending drunk drivers and doing title searches for a hundred grand a year?"

He laughed. "It's Assistant General Counsel at the Nuclear Energy Authority. I had dinner with the Chairman and his wife last night and your name came up."

"Came up?"

"Well, he said that the job was open and I mentioned you. I told him about your sterling record in law school and clerking with the judge and the law practice and all that, and he said he thought you were perfect for the job."

"He did, huh?"

"Well – what he actually said was if you'll apply and jump through the hoops, he'll make sure you get the job."

"What hoops?"

"The usual paperwork that everybody has to submit, and it requires a national security clearance. You're not a spy or a felon, are you?"

"No. What does the Assistant General Counsel at the Nuclear Energy Authority do?"

"The NEA regulates the nuclear power industry. It looks after our bombs, and it oversees commercial nuclear energy plants."

"Why do they need lawyers?"

He laughed again. "Do you live in a cave?"

"Not exactly."

"Everybody hates the NEA. They get sued every day – individual cranks, states, other government agencies."

"Why?"

"Because they have an impossible job. Sisyphus had it easier."

"What do you mean?"

"When we were building the bomb nobody cared about the leftovers. They generated piles of radioactive waste that had no place to go. The people who have it want it gone, and the people who don't are unanimous that it won't end up in their backyard, and we produce a few more tons every day. It's not going away. The radiation in some of it lasts millions of years."

"No wonder nobody wants it."

"Yeah. And it's the NEA's job, among other things, to find a place for it. They used to store it in the ocean, but that was stopped. Then they talked about sending it into outer space, or burying it under the North Pole, but I haven't heard anything about that lately." He paused. "And if we ever start building bombs again, the NEA will be in charge."

We were quiet for a moment. "Why's the job open?"

He waited a beat before answering. "The guy who had it died."

"When?"

"About three weeks ago. The same day you were up here, in fact."

Something in his voice made me ask another question. "How did he die?"

"He committed suicide."

"Why?"

"I don't know."

"Come on, Mark."

"I – really, I don't know. There *has* been speculation among some of my brethren that the job got to him."

"How come?"

"After the big meltdown in Japan a couple of years ago, a court ordered the NEA to do an analysis of the death and damage that a nuclear accident would cause. Your predecessor was in charge of the study."

"Why would he kill himself over that?"

"I don't know. That's what makes the rumors so silly. The report's not out officially, but it's been leaked, and the assessment is pretty mild."

I hesitated. "Why are you doing this? What's in it for you?" As soon as the words were out of my mouth, I wanted to recall them.

There was silence at the other end of the line. I thought he'd hung up, and started to do the same. "You sorry bastard," he said. "You're my friend. I want you to rise from the dead." He paused. "Think about it." The phone went dead.

I poured another drink and put my feet back on the desk. Did I really want something to divert me from the dull, white anger I had tended for so long? The Nuclear Energy Authority was the embodiment of a mind-set that had destroyed my family. Perhaps I could return the favor, or at least inflict a little damage. There was another reason, too, but I didn't dwell on that.

MY MOTHER was raised on a farm in the southeastern corner of the state, about sixty miles from the Atlantic Ocean. There was lots of land and not much money, but her shabby gentility shielded her from the apathy of her peers. She cared about books and the things she studied in school, and she wanted more than the tedious life of those who had gone before her. Her father, a widower who had watched his pretty young wife age and die in the hardscrabble landscape that was all they knew, agreed, and scraped together the money to send her to the Woman's School and on to the College in New Hope.

Before that could happen, though, I came along and, following the dictates of the culture and the times, she married the boy who only wanted to farm the land his family had cultivated for generations. She put aside her dreams and moved in with his parents, awaiting my arrival and his return from a conflict into which he, without the academic aspirations that would have saved him, had been conscripted. I appeared on time. He came back early, maimed and unknowing, and their marriage ended before it began. She left him in the hospital and me on her father's farm, and revived her original plan.

Her pinched childhood had left her vulnerable. Intrigued by the parasitic indifference of the academy – its sophisticated adherents barely acknowledged the reality of the people who wrote the checks – she set out to become a part of it. It was an alternative world where the stated mission was ignored in favor of conversion. Students didn't "learn," they were redeemed, freed of whatever they knew or believed, and the dogma that took its place was uniform. Neither knowledge nor intellect were necessary – only orthodoxy was required, and even that might be illusory. What you said and what you wrote mattered. What you thought, or intimated to your friends, was beside the point. The past – that rickety accumulation of mores and traditions and truth – was past, whatever Faulkner said.

There were nine women professors at the College when she arrived – she would be the tenth. Her course of study depended solely on who was teaching it, and she enlisted in the causes championed by those who would decide her fate. A fetching blonde with long legs and pleasing features, she was popular with the faculty and she chose her companions carefully. Her campaign had all the trappings of success, and then her father and I came to New Hope. When her friends discovered who he was, her future became less certain.

On a warm day in August, 1945, my grandfather had climbed aboard a new B-29 Superfortress and settled in for another bomb run against the Empire of Japan. The mission that day was different, though he didn't know it at the time. The airplane that took off from North Field carried only a single bomb, playfully named "Little Boy" by its creators, designed to loose the planet's most elemental energy and reduce to ashes everything that it touched. The six-hour flight was without incident – they encountered no Japanese fighters or anti-aircraft fire, and the weather was clear. They arrived over the target – a city of 350,000 people left deliberately untouched so that the havoc wreaked by the bomb could be accurately gauged – and opened the bomb bay doors. Forty-three seconds later, at an altitude of 1,968 feet over the city, Little Boy exploded.

The revulsion against nuclear weapons set in immediately. The academics and scientists responsible for splitting the atom and turning it into a weapon repudiated their creation and denounced those who had used it. More than three decades later, Robert Rogers was still a mass murderer in certain circles but, fearful of the reaction among less sensitive elements at the College, that opinion was initially suppressed. She was a fledgling participant in some of those groups, but she had not yet developed the smug hypocrisy necessary to condemn him.

After a few months her friends began to criticize him openly and encouraged their acolytes to do the same. He had plenty of supporters as well. The townspeople, the local newspaper, even a few within the College, noted that *he* was not responsible for the bomb. It was the so-called elites – scientists, professors, politicians – who had poured the resources of the country into the effort without pausing to consider the consequences. He knew nothing about it until he looked down from his perch in the rear of the *Enola Gay* and saw the great mushroom cloud. He was a hero to his advocates, a symbol of the common man doing his duty, and he was never allowed to pay for a drink.

He stood for something else as well. Certain of the virtue of his cause, he had engaged the enemy without second thoughts. There was no temporizing, no question of who was right or wrong. Victory had vindicated him, and he shared the euphoria and release that it produced, but his own special contribution had given rise to an ambivalence that became immutable. A terrible, impersonal death – one that threatened man and the planet he inhabited – had dropped from the sky. Indiscriminate destruction, foreshadowed by Dresden and Tokyo, had become the norm, and the concept of an honorable war was discarded. Never again would there be an objective free of ambiguity.

My father's war was the inevitable result of that lack of conviction. The men who defeated Hitler and Tojo started a splendid little war half a world away confident of quick success, only to find that those drafted to fight it – and, increasingly, those required to pay for it – doubted its necessity. The cohort that followed his, of which I was one, rejected any common obligation, and left the watchtowers to those who wanted or needed to man them. Little Boy's most poisonous fallout was guilt and the paralysis that accompanied it.

What finally mattered, though, was that Mother's colleagues detested my grandfather and the people who supported him. When he realized that he was standing in her way, he returned to the farm, leaving me behind. I was six.

CHAPTER TWO

THE BRIGHT young thing who had introduced herself as my assistant – and whose name I had promptly forgotten – leaned in the door. "The GC wants to see you," she said.

"Who?"

"The General Counsel. Mr. Ames. His office is at the end of the hall on the left."

"Thanks."

The weather in Washington was fine that morning. I had walked from my carriage house apartment on the eastern edge of Georgetown to the nondescript four-story building at 19th Street and Constitution Avenue. The journey was both nostalgic and unsettling. I had walked those same streets many times when I was in college and nothing, on the surface, had changed. Pennsylvania Avenue, the mix of modern structures and ancient townhouses at George Washington University, and Foggy Bottom all looked the same, but the sheer number of people and automobiles was overwhelming. Mark was right. Gold had been discovered beneath the Capitol dome and Washington was a boom town. The monuments and architecture were props, a Potemkin façade that concealed the grubby quest for cash.

I arrived at the NEA just before nine o'clock and – after making my way through a knot of protesters on the sidewalk – introduced myself to the security people who snapped my picture, provided me with an identification "credential" and escorted me to my office on the fourth floor. The elevator had an operator, unnecessary since all he did was push a button, an example of the patronage that had been doled out by the politicians and bureaucrats since the founding of the Republic. As we rose, I asked the guard what the fuss outside was all about. He looked blank for a moment. "You mean the freaks with the signs and stuff?" I nodded. "I honestly couldn't tell you. They're there every day. I've been here two years and so have they."

I left my office and walked down the hall. The brass plate beside the last door on the left read "George K. Ames, General Counsel." I opened the door and stuck my head inside. A striking woman in her thirties, seated behind a desk next to the door, smiled and said, "Can I help you?"

"I'm Tommy Sawyer. Mr. Ames wanted to see me."

She held out her hand. "Welcome. I'm Anne Clark." She gestured to a door behind her. "Go right in."

"Thanks."

George Ames stood up as I entered the room. He was short and round and would have been bald but for the ill-fitting toupee. Despite the fair weather outside and the frigid temperature in the building, large rings of sweat already stained the armpits of his blue dress shirt. The yellow club tie was loose around his neck, and his belly strained against his belt. He came around the desk in short, affected strides that twisted his torso with each step. His hand was moist, and he reeked of cologne. "Sit down," he said. After small talk about my drive from New Hope and my living arrangements in Georgetown, he came to the point. "What do you know about the nuclear power business?"

It was the question I had been waiting for since telling Mark I would apply for the job. Everything I knew about nuclear power was personal, and I had half-expected to be summarily rejected despite Mark's assurances to the contrary. Ames had undoubtedly reviewed my résumé. "Not much, I'm afraid."

He nodded. "Well, that could be a good thing."

"Why?"

He looked disconcerted. "You know, no preconceived notions, no prejudice one way or the other."

I *did* have some pre-conceived notions but kept them to myself. "Prejudice?"

"What we do around here is controversial. People are afraid of nuclear power in spite of the fact that it provides a lot of our electricity." He paused. "A big part of our job is to try to remove that fear."

"Isn't it a good thing to fear something so dangerous?"

He frowned. "I think respect is the right word. Just as you would respect a coal-fired furnace or a hydroelectric dam." He changed the subject. "We have a meeting with the Consortium next week, and we need to get you up to speed."

"What's the Consortium?"

"The trade group for our nuclear power generators. It represents all of the companies that operate commercial plants in the United States."

"What's the meeting about?"

"Waste storage and reprocessing. They're always on the agenda. And we have a new item – plant re-certification."

"I have some idea of the waste problem. What's reprocessing?"

"When we began to generate electricity from nuclear energy, we intended to reprocess the spent fuel like they do in Europe. It reclaims plutonium, which can be used to produce more energy, and it reduces the quantity and – and virulence of the remaining waste."

"What's the problem?"

"The public opposes it because the plutonium might be stolen by some hypothetical criminal or terrorist and used for a nuclear weapon. The scenarios in the media were preposterous, but the process was banned several years ago. We reprocessed at Hanford until we shut the reactors down, but not at the commercial plants. It's cost the operators billions and put a terrible strain on their waste storage capacity."

"What's Hanford?"

"The Hanford Engineering Works in Washington State. It's where we used to produce plutonium for the bombs."

"So what's to talk about?"

"The current administration may lift the ban but with a lot more expense and regulation. We're trying to develop a common approach to the issue."

I pondered that. "Why do the plants have to be re-certified?"

"They are way past the end of their design lives. We've already approved an additional twenty years, and we're discussing twenty more."

"But – if they're only designed to last –"

"They are refurbished and additional inspections are required." He stared at me. "If we don't do it, the nuclear power industry will go under. The electricity they produce will disappear. It would be catastrophic." He looked at his watch and rose. "The Chairman wants to meet you." He turned for the door. "I'll send one of the technical people to your office after lunch. You'll be an expert by next week."

Mark had already filled me in on John Marsh Winslow, Chairman of the Nuclear Energy Authority. Sixty-two years old, he was the descendant of Virginia planters, old blood that was thinning out. After graduating from Yale and the University of Virginia law school, he had worked in government all his life. An aborted run for Congress in the '90's had sidetracked his career for a few years, but he was now the consummate Washington insider, a confidante of presidents of both political parties.

He was exactly what I had expected – tall, silver-haired, exquisitely dressed. There was a long silence as we shook hands, and the appraising stare was unsettling. Unlike Ames, he had no inclination to talk shop. He seemed intent on finding out who I was, and peppered me with questions about my past, especially my time in Washington. "Why didn't you finish school here?" he said. The answer was both complicated and personal, so I mumbled something about my grandfather's death and tried to change the subject. He wasn't satisfied, but allowed the diversion.

As we were running out of pleasantries, the intercom buzzed. Winslow frowned and pushed the button. "Yes?"

"I have Mr. Withers on line one."

"All right." He looked up, the frown still on his face. "I need to take this call. I hope you'll excuse me." Ames stood up and I followed. When we reached the door he called after us, "Mr. Sawyer – Tommy – we're having a small dinner party this Saturday. You're invited. You, too, George."

"I'LL HAVE the crabmeat cocktail and the filet," said Mark. "Rare."

The waiter looked at me. "Just bring me a martini," I said. "Straight up." Mark lifted his eyebrows, but said nothing. I responded anyway. "I'm cutting back. This is the first one today." He nodded. "All that rich food will kill you quicker than booze anyway. *And*, liquor's not as fattening."

"What are you implying?"

"Nothing."

"I'm not fat. I have large bones."

I grinned. In college he had just been tall, four inches over my six feet. Now he was *big*, for whatever reason, and the black hair that he had worn in a ponytail in the old days was shorter, less abundant and streaked with gray. We were seated at a table overlooking 19th Street. Ten blocks north of the NEA building, this was where the city's power brokers lunched, and Mark appeared to be first among equals. He dominated the room – several patrons had stopped by the table to trade news and gossip. There were a few scattered women, but it was a boys' club.

Mark Singer was a peculiar combination of doubt and self-regard. I'd seen him fail many times all those years ago – with girls, books, money – and his first reaction was always a brief withdrawal, as if he were assessing what went wrong, followed by an ever more assertive expression of his own singular worth. Nothing was ever his fault, an attitude everyone, including me, overlooked because of his overwhelming personality. Bullshit was his stock in trade. "How was your morning?" he said.

"Okay. I met the General Counsel, a guy named Ames. He wants me to attend a meeting next week with a group of plant operators, and he's providing me with a tutor so I won't make a fool of myself."

He laughed. "Did you see Winslow?"

I nodded. "For about ten minutes. I'm invited to a dinner party at his place on Saturday."

"It's not really *his* place. His wife owns the house. It's been in her family for two hundred years." He paused. "It's very impressive."

"Where is it?"

"On 28th Street in Georgetown Heights. It backs up to Oak Hill Cemetery."

I closed my eyes – I knew Oak Hill Cemetery. My drink arrived. I took a sip. "Didn't you tell me that the NEA *regulates* the nuclear power industry?"

"Yeah. Why?"

"I got the impression this morning that they don't regulate, they promote."

"That's always been the knock on the NEA. Promoting nuclear power *was* part of the mission at one time, but that was supposed to stop a long time ago. It hasn't."

"Why not?"

"It's like a lot of things around here. The people you were regulating yesterday are now working for you, and vice versa. And the nuclear power industry is very different from, say, brokerage houses or banks."

"Why?"

"Brokers and banks began as private enterprises. Regulation came later. The nuclear industry is a creature of government. Commercial power is an offshoot of the Manhattan Project." His food arrived. The sizzle of seared meat and smell of hot butter, so early in the day, repelled me. I ordered another drink. "The government still owns the weapons facilities, and it subsidizes the technology that private companies can't afford." He paused. "It's probably hard to keep it all straight."

We were quiet while he ate his food and I polished off my second martini. When the check arrived, I plucked it from the waiter's hand. Mark protested. "I'm a well-paid bureaucrat now," I said. "I can afford it."

As we were preparing to leave, he said, "By the way, there's a new wrinkle in your predecessor's demise. It's in the paper."

"What?"

"His widow says that he didn't commit suicide."

"Really? Why?"

"She doesn't say. She just says he didn't kill himself."

"What do the cops say?"

"They still think it was suicide."

"Are you looking into it?"

"Me? No – not in my bailiwick."

"Wouldn't you like to report on something serious every now and then?"

He laughed. "I'm offended at your insinuation that my work's not serious. Nothing's more serious than politics around here." We walked to the door. "Why do you care?"

"I want to know if it's an occupational hazard. I'm the new Assistant General Counsel, you know."

"I'll talk to the young lady covering the story. If she has anything that indicates you may be next, I'll let you know."

"What's her name?"

"Blaine. Regan Blaine." He started to say something else and stopped, then waved down a cab. "I'll see you."

I turned left and walked down the hill toward the river. The gin had smoothed the ripples in my head, and left me tired and sleepy. I grimaced. This wasn't New Hope. This was supposed to be a new beginning, and I would have to change some old habits if it was going to succeed.

I stopped in the lobby and bought a copy of the *Georgetown Star*. There was a man talking to my secretary – Jane Wilson, her nameplate read – when I reached my office. "Mr. Sawyer," said Jane, "this is Gordon Bell. He's Director of our technical division."

He was a few inches over five feet and had a full head of snow-white hair. His grip was firm and his voice loud, as if he were hard of hearing. There was a cell phone on his belt and another one in the breast pocket of his short-sleeved shirt, and the chronometer on his wrist weighed at least a pound. "George Ames asked me to stop by," he said. I gestured toward the inner office and he preceded me through the door. When we were seated he said, "George tells me that you need to brush up on your nuclear power bona fides."

I smiled. "He was too kind. I'm afraid it's more basic than that." He grinned. "I think you should start from the beginning."

"All right. Great. This'll be fun." He leaned back and adopted the voice and demeanor of the academic he had undoubtedly been at some time in his professional life. "Let's begin with the source of the energy then. Uranium is a natural element found all over the globe. The ore reserves in this country are located primarily in Wyoming and New Mexico. It's extracted from the soil by mining or leaching and sent to our enrichment plant."

"Our?"

"Yes. The government owns and operates it."

"What's enrichment?"

"Naturally occurring uranium is no longer able to produce the reaction we need. It has to be concentrated before it can be used – a few per cent for commercial reactors, much higher for weapons facilities."

"Why do you say it's 'no longer able' to do it?"

"Billions of years ago, the concentration of uranium in the earth's crust was far greater than it is today. In fact, about two billion years ago there was a natural nuclear reaction in an ore deposit in Africa that continued for thousands of years."

"Did it explode?"

"No. The process that allowed it to happen also kept it from reaching a critical stage, and when the uranium was depleted, it stopped." He paused. "Anyway, in all the billions of years since the earth formed, its uranium has decayed to a point where it will not react as it is so it must be enriched."

"How does that work?"

He grinned and delivered the movie punch line. "I could tell you but then I'd have to kill you." I laughed out loud. The idea of this little professor killing anybody was ludicrous. "Seriously, it's highly classified because enrichment is the key to the weapons program, too." He paused. "The process of making a nuclear bomb is pretty well-known. The technology needed to do so is still secret."

"Okay. What happens next?"

"The result of enrichment is uranium oxide which is formed into ceramic pellets and stuffed into rods made of zirconium. Typically, about two hundred forty of the rods are configured into a fuel assembly. Spacers separate the fuel rods."

"Why?"

"These things generate tremendous heat – the uranium decays, atoms split, neutrons crash about and so forth. They raise the temperature in a nuclear reactor to more than seventeen hundred degrees Celsius, so –"

"What's that in Fahrenheit?"

He frowned. "Uh – a little over three thousand degrees." He stopped. "The fuel assemblies have to be cooled, usually by water flowing around the rods, or they would quickly overheat and melt. The spacing also permits the control rods to be inserted."

"How do these things actually produce electricity?"

"A typical reactor is very simple. It's really just a boiler, a machine that heats water. Approximately two hundred fuel assemblies are gathered and placed inside a pressure vessel full of water. The amount of energy released – heat created – is determined by the control rods."

"How do they work?"

"Without going into the chemistry or physics of the thing, they control the speed of the reaction occurring within the fuel rods. When the control rods are lowered the reaction slows and the reactor cools down. When they are raised, the pace of the reaction increases and temperatures rise. If the control rods are lowered into the water completely, the chain reaction stops and the reactor shuts down."

"What happens with all this heat?"

"The steam turns the blades of the turbine in an electrical generator, and power is sent to the grid. Just like a coal-fired plant built sixty years ago."

"Without the dirt and emissions."

"Yes. That's one of its main selling points. Clean energy."

We sat without speaking. "But it's not really clean, is it?" I said. I watched him closely. Was the technical division on board the bandwagon?

"No, it's not. Certain things are better than they used to be. In the beginning we released radioactive gases into the air, dumped radioactive water into rivers and streams, and buried contaminated instruments in shallow trenches. We've stopped doing that for the most part. But those things were never as problematic as the waste we produced."

"Meaning?"

"We have different kinds of waste, but most of it is spent fuel from commercial reactors. By the time it's removed from the reactor the radioactivity has been increased a million times. A year later, a human being standing three feet away from it would absorb a lethal dose in less than a minute."

"You mean we *create* the radioactivity?"

"Well – yes. There's radioactivity in the beginning but not nearly as much."

"What causes it?"

"A lot of the waste is still uranium oxide, but approximately five per cent consists of new elements formed in the reactor. Most of them disappear within weeks, but others are long-lasting and very dangerous."

"Why?"

"Some are severely radioactive, and they give off terrific heat that lasts for many years. In others, the severity of the radiation is lower but it lasts for thousands, even millions, of years." He stopped. "We think that the heat dissipates in 1,000 years, and that the worst of the radiation is gone in 10,000 years."

"But some of it lasts much longer?" He nodded. "Are you saying that we actually *make* radioactive waste that lasts for millions of years?" He nodded again. "But why? What's the justification? Surely it's not just because it creates electricity we can get somewhere else."

"Nuclear energy began as a weapon. In the beginning, only the destructive capacity of a nuclear bomb was considered. Little, if any, thought was given to radiation."

"But, that's so –"

"Back then we believed that the country was at risk. If *we* didn't build the bomb, the Germans would." He paused. "After the war, the radiation effects of the bomb became apparent. It's one of the reasons nuclear weapons haven't been used since."

"But we set off little bombs every day in a hundred commercial reactors around the country."

"We generate heat. There's no explosion." He sighed. "The difficulty with the waste wasn't really understood or – or revealed until most of our reactors were already on line."

We were quiet. My grandfather's face appeared before my eyes. "And we're still making this stuff?" I said.

"Each reactor produces about twenty tons of waste a year."

"Why are we doing this?"

His expression changed. The professor's relaxed, detached outlook hardened into the blinkered attitude of the firmly committed. He answered as if by rote. "We have a tremendous investment, public and private, in nuclear energy. Without it, large swathes of the country would be without power indefinitely." He paused. "It really *is* the cleanest, most efficient form of energy we have. If everyone would just act – rationally, we could solve the problems."

"What about wind and solar?"

"Both are decades away from providing a significant portion of our energy."

"So this waste that nobody wants keeps piling up."

"Yes. It's stored on the site where it's created, usually no more than a few feet from the reactor itself."

"And the question is, what happens when they run out of room?"

His countenance had gradually resumed that of the mild-mannered academic. "Yes. That's one of the questions."

"Some of these plants have been closed, haven't they?" He nodded. "What happens to the waste?"

"Nothing."

"Nothing?"

"The waste remains on site. We have some plants where the only thing left is the waste."

"Are you serious?"

"Yes."

"So – a plant is closed and – demolished, and this pile of radiation is left behind?"

"Yes, and many of the facilities are just mothballed because the equipment and structures are also radioactive waste." He looked at his watch and stood up. "That should give you enough to get by next week. Call me if you need anything else."

"Thanks."

I leaned back in my chair and considered the conversation. Gordon Bell seemed to be a serious, rational man, who believed that nuclear power, done right, was good. My skepticism was visceral. The "experts" always sounded reasonable until the next disaster. The steady drip of bad news from Japan, where several reactors had melted down after a tidal wave swept over the plant, reflected their refusal to come clean about the danger.

I picked up the *Georgetown Star* and turned the pages. The story was on the second page of the local section. It was only a few paragraphs, most of which recounted how the man had died beneath the wheels of an approaching train at Union Station. His widow had no idea what happened – she just didn't believe that it was suicide. He had seemed perfectly happy, ebullient even. They had been married for two years and were expecting their first child, and he had a pro-ject in hand that he said was really going to pay off. I wondered at that – "pay off" was not a phrase I asso-ciated with work at the NEA. The dead man, whose name was Charles Martin, had a habit of making notes to himself which he collected in a three-ring binder. According to Mrs. Martin, there was nothing in the notebook that would indicate he wanted to kill himself.

I leaned into the outer office. "Jane, is there a draft of the 'death and destruction' report?"

She laughed. "Yes, but we call it the 'Reactor Consequence Analyses.' RCA for short."

"Of course we do. Would you bring me a copy of it, please?"

The RCA Report was the last "project" that the previous Assistant General Counsel at the NEA was known to be working on. The gist of it was that while the meltdown of a nuclear reactor was very serious business indeed, it was a "once in a million years" event, and nearly everyone would have time to evacuate. That seemed reassuring at first, but what if this were the year? Why were a few deaths "acceptable?" It was electricity, not war. The report was still only a draft. Maybe those issues would be addressed before it was finally released but somehow I doubted it.

I was curious now about Charles Martin, and it had been a long time since I was curious about anything. I picked up the telephone.

"Georgetown Star."

"Regan Blaine, please."

"Please hold." She came on the line a moment later. "Ms. Blaine, my name is Sawyer. I'm a friend of Mark Singer's."

"Yes?"

"I'm, uh, interested in the article you wrote for this afternoon's paper. In the local section."

"Why? Do you know something about it?'

"Um, no. I have the job formerly held by the deceased, and I –"

"At the NEA?"

"Yes. I – there's a reference in your story to a project that was 'really going to pay off.' Do you know any more about that?" She didn't say anything. "Ms. Blaine?"

"Mr. Sawyer, I don't disclose information that I obtain in the course of covering a story."

"But all I – Were those *his* words? Did Martin actually say that it would pay off?"

More silence. Then: "According to his wife, those were his words."

I pushed my luck. "Did you see the notebook you mentioned in the story?"

"Yes."

"Did you read any of it?"

"No."

"Do you think you could get it from –?"

"Mr. Sawyer. I don't know what your interest in all this is, but I'm not going to do *anything* because of your curiosity." She hung up.

I spent the rest of the afternoon pretending to work on the RCA Report. There really wasn't much to do. At precisely five o'clock I tidied up my desk, rose and walked to the door. Jane was already gone. During my passage through the corridors and down the elevator, I tried to make the scarred tile floors, the tired green walls and the utilitarian cage seem sinister, and failed. It was just depressing. I needed a drink.

I took the northerly route home. After walking five blocks up 19th street, I turned left on Pennsylvania Avenue and passed the University's hospital. On the far side of the circle, I turned north again on 25th Street, then west on M, and crossed the creek into

Georgetown. My new place, a renovated carriage house on Olive Street that Mark had negotiated from one of his friends, was only a block north, but I continued west on M Street past the shops and restaurants. The industrial area south of M, once home to dangerous wharves and dingy warehouses, had been gentrified – the past converted to a gentler, more profitable modernity. Small elegant hotels, boutiques and other commercial establishments beckoned invitingly, but I was intent on finding a warm place remembered from my youth. I crossed Wisconsin Avenue and turned into Clyde's, a saloon that I had frequented in college. It was a chain now, of course, but this particular location looked exactly the same. I sat down at the bar. "Double scotch on the rocks," I said.

A few minutes later I ordered a hamburger and another drink. The crowd around me was different from the one I recalled. There were lots of people who were obviously tourists – cameras and name tags and what-not – and the locals all looked alike. Segregated by sex, the men wore three-piece suits and shirts with French cuffs, the women – brittle Ganymedes unsure of their place – suits with pants or long skirts and wide, droopy bow ties. They all sounded like lawyers. I ordered another drink to keep the gloom at bay.

CHAPTER THREE

I STEPPED into the elevator. "Four, please." The morning walk had been less pleasant than the day before. The sky was leaden, and rain fell intermittently. My head hurt and my eyes focused only with an effort, and the tiny spark of optimism had been extinguished. The mindset that had dropped the bomb was still going strong, and it was naïve to think that there was anything I could do about it. I pondered my retreat – better to rot in New Hope, surrounded by people who knew me, than in a place full of strangers. I considered what I would say to Mark.

Jane handed me a pink message slip as I passed her desk. "She's called three times," she said with a wide smile. I dialed the number, a digit or two different from the one I had called yesterday.

She picked up on the first ring. "Regan Blaine."

"Ms. Blaine, this is –"

"Sawyer?"

"Yes."

"Tell me what you know about the Martin case."

"I don't know anything about the Martin case."

"Why did you call me yesterday? Why did you want the notebook?"

Her tone made my head hurt worse. "I was just curious about the project that was going to 'pay off.'

I have the last thing he was working on right in front of me, and it's not the sort of thing that pays off. I thought maybe there was something else –"

"I haven't told the cops about you yet, but I'm going to if you don't tell me the truth."

"What the hell are you talking about?" She didn't answer. "I know nothing about Martin's death. I didn't know his name until yesterday." She still didn't respond. Tired of explaining myself to this woman, I started to hang up.

"Martin's wife was killed last night. By a hit-and-run driver." She paused. "I don't think it was an accident. I think somebody killed her."

"Why?"

"I don't believe in coincidences. A seemingly happy man kills himself, and a month later his wife, who has just stated publicly that she doesn't believe it, is run over in front of her own house. I don't buy it."

"What do the cops think?"

"They haven't made the connection. They probably won't until they read my story." She paused. "I'm going to the house. I want to see that binder you're so interested in."

"That's not a good idea. If you're right, two people have been murdered. Turn it over to the police."

"No. Not yet. This could be a big story." She stopped. "You think so, too, don't you? That's why you called yesterday."

"I don't know. I just don't think you should go to that house by yourself."

"I appreciate your concern, Mr. Sawyer. I can take care of myself. Goodbye."

"Wait. I'll – I'll meet you there. Where is it?"

"In Georgetown. 3423 Prospect Street. I'll be there in an hour." She broke the connection.

I stared at the receiver. God damn it! Why couldn't I keep my big mouth shut? If this – this girl wanted to get in the middle of something she thought was murder, let her. I sat there for a moment, fuming, and walked into the other room. "I have an appointment," I said to Jane. "I'll be back after lunch."

"Woman trouble already?" I ignored her and pushed through the door.

I WAS surprised at the serenity of Prospect Street. There was no sign that two of its recent tenants – one of whom had lain in the narrow, tree-lined road only a few hours earlier – were dead. The uniform facades of the old Federal town houses – large salmon or cherry-colored bricks laid in a Flemish bond, gabled roofs and windows, chimneys rising from either end – were blank. There were no open doors or windows, no children or dogs, no neighbors in the street or on the stoops lamenting their friends. Sudden, violent death – the illusion, if not the reality – was commonplace. Prospect Street had absorbed it and moved on.

I looked at my watch. I was ten minutes early. Rather than loiter, I walked to the end of the block, glancing at Number 3423 out of the corner of my eye. It was smaller than the others, but neat, and clay pots with petunias and daisies and ferns lined the steps beside the curved wrought-iron railing. Turning, I saw a woman round the corner from Wisconsin Avenue. As the distance between us decreased, I could see her more clearly. She was tall and slender, and the short hair that framed her head was the color of burnished copper. She wore a gray skirt and white blouse that draped her hips and breasts without hiding them, and sensible low-heeled shoes. Sunglasses covered half her face.

We met in front of Number 3423. Without speaking, she climbed the steps and, ignoring the iron knocker, tried the door. It swung open – the bolt had been forced. She entered the house and I followed, pulling the door closed behind me. The day was still dark and the curtains drawn, so I flipped on the light switch beside the door. The chaos was shocking in the harsh light. Chairs and tables were tipped over, books strewn on the floor, pictures torn from the walls. Each of the drawers in a secretary on the far side of the room had been pulled out and dumped on the carpet along with its contents.

It was the same story in the kitchen. She pointed to an old roll top desk in the corner. "That's where he worked. The notebook was in the middle drawer." Nothing was in the middle drawer now – it, too, had been taken from the desk and dropped to the floor.

We rummaged amongst the debris, but turned up no notebook or anything else of interest. The bedrooms and baths on the other two floors had suffered the same fate. The destruction and disarray were systematic, as if it were an effort to obscure rather than discover.

Back on the street, I hoped that my ruminations regarding the indifference of Prospect Street were accurate. I didn't relish being called to account for the mess in Number 3423. I turned to her. "I'm Tommy Sawyer."

She smiled. Perfect white teeth showed between full, unpainted lips. "Regan Blaine."

We turned east. At the corner, I said, "Do you have time for a cup of coffee?"

She hesitated. "Sure."

"Good. You'll have to say where. The only place I know is Clyde's and it's probably not open yet."

She laughed. "Nobody goes to Clyde's any more."

At the bottom of the hill we crossed M Street, found an alley that emerged at the river and entered a tiny shop packed with bric-a-brac that looked old and expensive. An air freshener of some kind smelled like money. We had our choice of the three small tables in the window. An elderly woman who seemed to be the only other person in the shop appeared beside the table. We sat quietly until she brought our coffee.

I decided to speak. "Ms. Blaine, I'm not –"

"Call me Regan. We've broken and entered together. I think we can forget the formalities."

"I'm Tommy." I paused. "I'm not sure what that scene was meant to convey."

She pushed the sunglasses to the top of her head. There was something about her that I seemed to recall – the wide brow, the violet eyes, the barely turned up nose – but I dismissed it as wishful thinking. She was easily two decades younger than me, and I was clearly a stranger. "What do you mean?" she said. "Somebody broke in and took the notebook."

"Maybe. But why tear up the whole house? You said the notebook was in his desk. Why not look quietly in the places it would be and go about your business? Why tip furniture over and knock pictures off the wall?" I paused. "They took the book or it wasn't there. I'm guessing that it wasn't there. Either way, having broken into the house, I think they wanted to hide what they were looking for. So they trashed the place."

We drank our coffee in silence. "Do you think it's something at work?" she said.

"I have no idea. The report he was working on is – disturbing, but I don't think it's profitable. I don't know of anything else."

"If the notebook wasn't there, where is it?"

"Search me. I guess she didn't have it with her when she was run over?"

"Not according to the police report."

I finished my coffee. The sun finally came out and streamed through the windows, illuminating the polished gold and crystal objects inside the little shop. It washed over her, too, sitting there in the window. She was lovely to look at. "Have you met the chairman yet?" she said. "John Winslow?"

"Yesterday. He's a very – distinguished fellow."

"He's a jackass."

I had no response to that except to wonder how she had reached her conclusion. I decided not to inquire. "How long have you been working at the *Star*?"

"Almost a year. My mother got me the job after I flunked out of college." She paused. "Actually, I just quit after the first semester. Talk about a waste of time."

I smiled. Her view of the academy matched mine, though it had taken me longer to figure it out. We were quiet again. I wanted to just stay there, looking at her, but little mannerisms – a glance at her watch or cell phone, fiddling with the over-sized sunglasses – showed that she was growing impatient, so I rose and cleared my throat. "I hope you'll let the police handle this now, Regan. It looks dangerous." I paused. "It was great to meet you." She was quiet as I turned for the door.

Back at the NEA, I had a message from Ames. I walked to his office. "How's the RCA Report coming?" he said

"It's finished. You and Mr. Winslow are the last to sign off."

"Great. Ask your girl to bring me the latest draft. I'll take care of the Chairman."

"All right."

"And start preparing your testimony."

"My what?"

"Your testimony on the Hill. Introducing the report. It's what Assistant GC's do." He giggled. "You go up there and let those pompous blowhards bloviate for a few hours while you look uncomfortable."

"But I don't know anything –"

"Keep working on it. Gordon will be with you." He paused. "And remember: They don't really mean it."

"Who?"

"Congress. It's just for show. We've been going up there for sixty-five years and nothing ever changes."

"When is it?"

"Two weeks from today. The House in the morning, the Senate in the afternoon."

Anne Clark appeared in the doorway. "I have the Hanford Patrol Supervisor on line two, Mr. Ames," she said.

He reached for the telephone. I started to rise, but he waved me back down. "Yes, Jack?" he said. After a few seconds, he closed his eyes and turned his chair away from me. He listened for another minute or two, then: "Where did it happen?" He listened again. "All right. Keep a lid on it. I'll get back to you."

He remained still, looking out the window. As I rose to leave, he turned. His ruddy face was pale, and the loose lips were pressed tightly together. "There's been an – accident, Tommy." He looked at his watch and called "Anne!" She stood again at the door. "Check the flight schedule to Richland. Tommy's taking a trip to Hanford."

I STUDIED the RCA Report on the plane – with the charts and appendices, it was more than five hundred pages. A sense of responsibility long ignored, and a reluctance to disappoint my friend, had convinced me to stay in Washington until after my appearance on Capitol Hill. I thought about the young woman I'd met that morning, but refused to admit that she was part of it. Old habits that once marked me a success temporarily reasserted themselves.

The report was full of jargon and acronyms but fortunately a glossary was provided. The introduction touched briefly on the horrendous effects of radiation on the human body and the NEA's progress over the years in providing more and more protection for those working in the nuclear industry. There were frequent references to the early days when, in the haste to produce the bomb, safety measures and environmental concerns were ignored, and much self-congratulation about the things done since to remedy those deficiencies. The report outlined several new "safety" procedures, including a drill designed to immediately remove all workers from the site in the event of a serious accident. What was striking, though, was the unconscious acceptance of an unknowable risk, not just the risk of accident but the peril to people who simply went about their work every day. One of the appendices listed the "minor" accidents – there were dozens of them – that had occurred at the country's nuclear plants, and the loss of power and profit as a result of the ensuing shutdowns. There were broad hints that burdensome safety requirements would eat further into those profits, and that the commercial use of nuclear power – always quantified as "over twenty percent of the country's energy needs"– would decline.

The language became more opaque as the report finally reached the issue it had been commissioned to explain: How many people would die, and how much damage would be done, in the event of a reactor meltdown? It seemed to say that many bad things *could* happen but wouldn't, for reasons I had trouble understanding.

I put the report away and considered my visit to Hanford. "One of our inspectors is dead," Ames had said. "I want you to go out there and – and make sure it's nothing unusual." I raised my brows. "The Hanford Works is a federal reservation. Any crime there is a federal case which might mean FBI, Defense Intelligence and so forth."

"Crime?"

"They think he may have been murdered. We need someone there to protect our interests."

"I don't understand."

"It's our turf. Anything unusual is always used to criticize the mission. I want you to see that there's nothing to criticize."

In 1943 the government had seized the prosperous little town of Hanford, Washington, along with 670 square miles along the Columbia River north of the small city of Richland. Fifty thousand workers descended upon the once tranquil farmland and, thirteen months later, the first plutonium reactor in the world was up and running. Plutonium from Hanford was used in the first nuclear bomb, detonated at the Trinity site in New Mexico, and in the weapon dropped on Nagasaki, Japan that brought World War II to a close. By the mid-'60's there were nine reactors and five reprocessing plants operating at Hanford, all dedicated to the creation of America's nuclear arsenal. All of this was accomplished in total secrecy – in the early days, even the workers had no idea what they were building.

Over the years, some of the country's great corporations had been retained to maintain and enhance plutonium production at the site. Substantial bonuses were paid when quantities exceeded projections. At the height of the Cold War, the reactors were operating around the clock and, by the time the NEA began to mothball the reactors, most of our 60,000 warheads carried plutonium generated at Hanford. The last operating reactor, commissioned in 1963, had been shut down in 1987.

The drive from Richland was just over twenty-five miles. Jack Roller, the longtime Supervisor of the Hanford Patrol, met me at the gate. The Patrol, a division of the NEA, was in charge of law enforcement at Hanford. Roller was a tall, grizzled man with leathery skin and teeth stained by coffee and tobacco. He had been at Hanford, in one capacity or another, from the beginning. After I introduced myself, he spoke, without taking the cigarette from his mouth. "Why didn't they send Martin?"

"Charles Martin?"

"Yeah. He already knows his way around here."

"He's dead."

I waited for follow-up questions on Martin's death and my appearance in his place, but there were none. After the briefest hesitation, he pointed to a black pick-up truck with a gumball on top and said, "Let's go." His office, a low block structure painted white was only a mile or two from the gate.

Once inside, I said, "Who's dead here?"

"A fellow named Jerry Wallace. He's one of Mammoth's inspectors."

"Who's Mammoth?"

He frowned. "How long have you been with the NEA?"

"Three days."

He laughed and shook his head. "Mammoth Engineering Company is the site contractor."

"What do they do?"

"They monitor the site."

"What does that mean?"

"This plant made plutonium for forty-four years. The by-products of that process are still here – in underground tanks, reactor basins, waste trenches and steel capsules. It has to be watched." He paused. "This is the dirtiest place in the world."

"What happened to Wallace?"

"It looks like he drowned in one of the storage tanks. The question is whether or not he was conscious when he fell in."

"Why is that a question?"

"There's evidence of a blow to the back of the head. The autopsy's this afternoon." He leaned back. "It might tell us, it might not."

We sat quietly. "Who else is involved in this?" I said.

"I've notified every jurisdiction and bureau required. So far, no one is interested."

"What about the press?"

"You'll be meeting with them in the morning."

"What am I supposed to say?"

He laughed again. "'No comment.' And, 'It's under investigation.' And, 'We'll get back to you.'"

"But – you could say that."

"We have an understanding here. If the NEA sends a man from Washington to say 'No comment,' they'll accept it and go away. Except for those assholes from Seattle and Portland."

"Who are they?"

"Old hippies with gray hair and granny glasses. Like yours." I laughed. "They claim to care about the flora and fauna and –" he spread his arms "– the *cherished* Columbia River, but I think they just like to cause trouble."

"Aren't the locals concerned about the river? I mean, they live here."

He stared at me. "This place has been the life-blood of these folks for seventy years. When we stopped making nukes, they opened a commercial plant. Nobody wants to look too close at the goose laying the golden eggs." He checked his watch. "Want to see the crime scene?"

"Sure. I guess so."

Back in the truck, I said, "Did Charles Martin come out here a lot?"

He thought for a moment. "He's been here four times over the past year."

"Why"

"Damned if I know. He never *did* anything except wander around and talk to the men."

"When was the last time he was here?"

"About two months ago."

"Did he know Jerry Wallace?"

"I don't know. I wouldn't be surprised."

The "tank farm" at Hanford was a vast collection of giant steel shells that stretched to the horizon. They looked abandoned. The one in which Jerry Wallace died was open to the sky. I sniffed, trying to detect the stench that should have been there but wasn't.

"When were these things built?" I said.

"In the '40's and '50's mostly."

"Are they still used?"

"Not for at least twenty-five years."

"What's in them?"

"Dissolved fuel rods."

"What?"

"Dissolved fuel rods."

"You mean that – that fuel rods from the reactors are *dissolved* and put in these tanks?"

"Yes. Plus the chemicals used in the process."

"Why?"

"Spent fuel rods have to be separated from the plutonium." He paused. "It's mostly liquid, but some of them contain gases and sludge. Sort of like radioactive beach sand."

"How much do they hold?"

"They're different sizes, but altogether there's more than 50,000,000 gallons of this stuff."

It was hard to comprehend. "Is it like commercial –?"

He shook his head. "Commercial waste is bad, but it doesn't compare to the poison here."

We walked back to the truck. "I've never heard of this place," I said.

Roller laughed. "Neither has anybody else."

The autopsy that afternoon was inconclusive, but the coroner thought he might have something more definitive in a few days. I met with reporters from Yakima and Richland the next morning and said 'No comment,' and they seemed to be satisfied. No hippies from Portland or Seattle attended the "press conference." When it was over, I borrowed Roller's truck and drove north to the giant bend in the Columbia River where the reactors were located. Reactor B, Hanford's original reactor, was a museum now, open to the public, but its leavings – the putrid stew festering in aging steel tanks only a few miles away – were the true legacy. Hanford had been "closed" for a generation. How many more would have to deal with it?

CHAPTER FOUR

"DO YOU know anything about Martin's trips to Hanford?"

Jane shook her head. "All I know is that he went out there. He made his own reservations and paid for his airfare and expenses with a personal credit card. There were no memos or correspondence. Nothing."

"Why would he do that?"

"I don't know. I asked him once and he ignored me." I turned away. "Tommy, wait. There *was* something. He used to get a letter with a Richland postmark every month or so. They were all marked 'personal.' He got really mad when I opened one of them."

"Do you remember anything about it?"

"It was seven or eight pages filled with numbers."

"Signed?"

"No."

I entered my office and closed the door behind me. Seated at the desk, I reached for the telephone. After five rings, it switched over to the *Star's* operator and I left a message. She called back an hour later. "I haven't seen anything about the Martin case in the paper," I said.

"There'll be a short piece tomorrow, but I'm still working on it. I plan to pull it all together next week."

"How about a drink after work? You can tell me about it."

"You're sweet, Tommy, but I can't."

"Why not?"

"I have another engagement."

"Oh."

"Maybe we can do it another time."

"Sure. That'll be great." I paused. "What's the piece tomorrow about?"

"The report that Martin was working on is going up to the Hill in about ten days." She paused. "I guess you know about that?" I didn't answer. "It's a pretty big deal. My article describes the background, what the report will say. It mentions how he died and that his wife didn't accept the suicide verdict."

"Is that it?"

"Yes, pretty much."

"Pretty much?"

"Well – there's a paragraph about how she died, too."

I closed my eyes. "Do you think that's wise?"

"Sure. Why not?"

Why not indeed? Who was I to tell her how to go about her business? "Never mind. How do you know what the report says?"

"A draft's been floating around town for weeks."

"What's left to pull together then? It sounds like it's almost over." She didn't answer. "Regan?"

"I have the notebook, Tommy."

"You do? How?"

"It arrived yesterday. She mailed it to me the day she died."

"Did she say why?"

"No. There was no note or anything. Just the book."

"She must have been afraid of something."

"I think so, too. And – there *are* things in his notes that point to something big, something related to his work. It was easy after I found the key, and I think I've –"

"Are you crazy? Please take the thing to the police. Two people are dead already."

"No. It's my story and I'm going to finish it."

"Christ, you're stubborn." I tried to think. "*I'll* go to the cops if you don't. I'll tell them about the house and the notebook and –"

"No!"

"Yes."

"I'll hate you if you do that."

I smiled. This girl had become important to me, and she seemed to know it. Any emotion was better than the callow indifference shown so far. "Well, I'll just have to live –"

"Tommy, listen." She stopped. "Give me a week. I'll be careful, I promise. If I don't have the story by next Friday, I'll give it all to the police." She stopped again. "Please."

It was her life and she wanted to succeed, and she obviously believed that this was her big chance. I wanted to tell her how fleeting it all was, how infinitesimally small her achievement would be, but I didn't. She was too young and too ambitious to believe me. "I'll tell you what," I said. "I think that book's dangerous." I paused. "You have a courier service over there, don't you?"

"Yes."

"If the notebook is in my hands within the hour, I'll give you the week. If not, I go to the cops tomorrow."

"But –"

"Take it or leave it." There was a brief silence before she slammed down the telephone.

Forty-five minutes later, Jane knocked on the door. "I have a young man out here from the *Georgetown Star*. He has something to give you *personally*." I signed his receipt, and he handed over a large envelope.

The small black binder was stuffed with multi-colored sheets of paper, some filled with a dense, crabbed handwriting, others with only a line or two. There was a note as well, without salutation or signature. It was written in green ink.

> *We have a deal, you bastard, and you'd better not renege on it. Just so you know, I've copied the pages I need.*

I shook my head. The loss of the book wasn't going to stop her, but it might shield her from the people who had ransacked the house on Prospect Street. Except for Regan, my own interest in the Martin case had waned. In a couple of weeks, I was retreating to the academic backwater where I had been raised, and murder and machinations at the Nuclear Energy Authority would be something I could read about in the papers. A comic Achilles without sword or armor, my world would be reduced to me again, and everything else could go to hell. Still, people were dying because of this book, and Regan seemed to know why. Maybe I could help her before I left.

It was a black six-by-nine three-ring binder. The first part of it consisted of thirty-five or forty pages of brief, handwritten notes in reverse chronological order. The one on top, dated the day that Martin died, read "Baldwin – Union Station, 7:22 P.M.," followed by a telephone number with a New York area code. Many of the older notations appeared to concern the RCA Report – I recognized chapter headings and timetables. The rest of the book was split into sections by red and blue dividers. There were twelve of them, each with someone's name on top – Allen, Carlisle, Joseph, and so on. None meant anything to me. There were two or three pages after each name filled with numbers and letters that were equally meaningless.

The Carlisle pages were different from the others. There were seven sheets with three columns of numbers written in someone else's hand, and the date at the top was ten days before Martin was killed. Just under the date was a notation, "177/177," and there were 177 separate lines of numbers. I removed the pages from the book and carried them to Jane's desk. "Do these look familiar?"

She flipped through them. "I don't know if I saw these exact pages," she said, "but they look like the ones from Hanford."

Back in my office, I returned the pages to the notebook. A chart toward the back seemed to be a summary. Except for Carlisle, the same names were listed down the left-hand margin, followed by five columns headed by the same letters: PEF, PEI, PDC, PD and V. The rest of the chart was filled in with numbers except for the "V" column, which contained only check marks. I glanced through my copy of the RCA Report, but found neither the names nor the letters. Carlisle was by itself at the bottom of the summary, followed by "177/177 – 21,730,000 (41 % GW)." I puzzled over that for a minute, then gave it up.

The next-to-last page contained a list of NEA regulations – reference to RCA confirmed that they were safety requirements for the country's nuclear power plants. There a number, the same number, beside each provision – 104. Several local telephone numbers were written on the last page.

I turned back to the front of the book. There was a map of Cuba in the pocket inside the cover. I unfolded it. There were four circles around places in the mountains at the eastern end of the island. All but one of them had been marked through.

I looked at the notes again. They were suffused with NEA nomenclature that I was still trying to learn. Another acronym – CRAC – was sprinkled throughout, though it did not appear in the RCA glossary. Bureau of Labor statistics describing employment and economic growth in parts of the country were included. The output of energy from dozens of power plants – coal, oil, nuclear and even hydroelectric plants – was set forth in minute detail. There didn't seem to be any overall purpose. What was it that Regan had said? Once she had the key, the rest was easy. I could detect no key. The nearest thing was the summary. I jotted down the New York number and removed the summary and the other telephone numbers from the notebook.

About to close the book and put it away, I noticed a pocket inside the back cover sealed by a plastic zipper. I slipped a finger inside, fished out a small unsealed envelope and emptied its contents – two strips of negatives containing three images each – onto my desk. I went to the window and held them up to the light, but it was impossible to discern what they depicted. I slipped them back into the envelope and put it in my pocket.

I opened the map once more. The region Martin had marked was the least populated, least accessible area of Cuba. I noticed more marks on the reverse side, a smaller scale map of all of Central and South America. Martin had drawn three long arrows from the eastern end of Cuba. One led to Columbia, one to Venezuela, and the third to Peru. Each of them carried another acronym. One had been in the news recently – a terrorist group in Venezuela called the National Liberation Army.

It was almost noon. I was trying to lay off the booze, and I wasn't hungry, so I decided to get some exercise. Outside on 19th Street, I turned left, then left again onto Constitution Avenue. On the far side of the Mall, I stood for a moment in front of the Capitol, then walked northeast on Louisiana Avenue. After five blocks, I passed under the massive Roman arch at Union Station and entered the great gold and white vault that served as its main waiting room. A kiosk straight ahead of me contained schedules for the various railway lines that passed in and out of the station – the local subway, Amtrak, the Virginia Railway Express and the Baltimore and Ohio Railroad. I found the tables for Amtrak's Northeast Regional Corridor. A train from New York City arrived each evening at 7:22 P.M. and disgorged its passengers onto Platform 17.

I crossed to the far side of the train shed. Platform 17, and the tracks running parallel to it, was empty, but it was easy to see how someone could hurl himself – or be pushed – beneath the wheels of an oncoming train. The barriers were designed to prevent accidents, not intentional acts.

Back in my office, I stared at the phone like a newly-minted broker about to make his first cold call. I picked up the receiver. A woman's voice came on the line: "Doctor Baldwin's office."

"May I speak to Doctor Baldwin, please?"

"I'm sorry, he's not available. Who's calling?"

"My name's Sawyer. I'm with the Nuclear Energy Authority in Washington. I'm calling about my – colleague. Charles Martin."

There was a short silence. "Oh, yes. Of course." She was quiet again. "Doctor Baldwin is out of the country. He'll be back tomorrow evening."

"Would you ask him to call me as soon as he can?"

"Certainly."

I gave her both numbers. "Thanks."

I pushed the button down and started to dial Bell's extension, then thought better of it. I called Ames. Anne picked up the phone. "I need to talk to George. Can he see me?"

"Hold on. I'll check." She returned a few seconds later. "He has five minutes if you come right now."

"Great. I'm on my way."

Ames, coat on and tie pushed up to his neck, met me in the outer office. "What's up?" he said.

"I've been going back over the attachments to the report and there's a reference to some program or something that I don't understand. What's CRAC?" He looked puzzled. I spelled it for him.

He hesitated. "I don't know." He looked at Anne. "Ever heard of it?"

"No, sir."

He turned back to me. "Sorry." He started for the door.

"What about the number 104? It seems to have some significance I can't figure out."

He looked around. "I don't know how it's used in the report but the number 104 is very important around here. Isn't it, Anne?" She nodded. "That's how many commercial reactors we have." He paused. "And all we're likely to have, too." He passed through the door.

I smiled. "That was a short five minutes."

She shrugged. "He's a busy man." We laughed.

My office came furnished with a complete set of NEA regulations. I opened the big book on my desk and looked up the ones detailed in Martin's notebook. Each dealt with a specific element of a nuclear plant – reactor core, pumps, waste storage facilities – the degree and frequency of their inspection, and the consequences in the event an inspection failed, mostly fines and reactor shutdowns. The last line of each regulation was identical: "The Chairman or his designee may, in the exercise of his discretion and taking into account the energy requirements of the United States of America, waive any and all of the provisions set forth herein for whatever duration he deems necessary." Given the affinity between the NEA and the operators, it was unlikely that the specified penalties were ever assessed, but why had Martin included the regulations in his notebook? The RCA Report analyzed an accident caused by outside forces, not everyday wear and tear.

I withdrew the summary from my inside coat pocket and studied it more carefully. The numbers were large, and the PD at the top of the fourth column had a dollar sign next to it. The numbers in that column were by far the greatest – the lowest was $92 billion, the highest more than $1 trillion. Perhaps PD stood for "property damage." One of the minor components of the RCA Report was an estimate of the damage that might be caused by a reactor meltdown, but even the worst scenario didn't approach $92 billion. What, then, did these dollars represent?

I put the summary away and turned my thoughts to the empty evening that stretched before me. Most of my evenings for the past few years had been empty, but they had been blurred and shortened by alcohol. I was trying to do something useful, and I knew I would fail if I didn't stay sober. Still, maybe cold turkey was too much to expect. Maybe I could ease my way into it.

GEORGETOWN, ONCE part of Maryland, was named after the country's last successful monarch, George II. The commercial sector had always been situated on or near the Potomac River, and the earliest residences were large, isolated houses built in the northeastern corner of town known as Georgetown Heights. Later, Federal-style row houses sprang up further south, closer to the river, and the newest housing stock was clustered around M Street and west of Wisconsin Avenue. Due to the abundance of high-quality clay in the area, brick was the building material of choice.

East of Wisconsin Avenue, once the old town's High Street, the "skyline" created by the houses was unusual because the rigid grid of the streets – designed to tie into L'Enfant's plan for the rest of Washington – had been cut into the sloping bedrock long after the houses were built. Accordingly, many of them, especially those in Georgetown Heights, were located well above the public roadways, small isolated fiefdoms set apart from their neighbors. The estate where John Winslow and his wife Charlotte lived was one of those places.

It was only a few blocks from my carriage house and the evening was cool, so I decided to walk. I had taken the same path many times, though back then my journey carried me beyond the wrought-iron gates that led to the house. As I reached the corner of Olive and 28th Street, two limousines cruised past me, undoubtedly bound for the same destination. Dinner at the Winslows was a highly-prized invitation.

The gatekeeper, surprised by a guest on foot, had to come out of his gatehouse in order to affirm that I was, indeed, on the list. A line of cars waited patiently while he concluded his examination, and I stayed well off the macadam driveway as they drove slowly past. The pavement gave way to a cobblestone courtyard that ran right up to the front of the house. Rather than enter immediately, I turned to look back down the hill – past the pools and fountains and obelisks, across the rest of Georgetown and the river – to

Mason's Island and, beyond that, the Northern Virginia shore. It was a remarkable vista to encounter inside the busy sprawl of Washington.

The house was a palace of rose-colored brick surrounded by acres of lawns and gardens encircled by walls ten feet high. The front of the two-story façade had a single wide door topped by a light within a white Roman arch, and vertical glass down the sides. There were four double-hung windows down and five up, three gables jutting from the roof, and four chimneys. Giant wisterias wrapped around the corners, partially obscuring substantial wings that had been added since the original house was built. The door was open and John Winslow stood just inside. He extended his hand. "Tommy, thanks for coming." He gestured to the woman standing next to him. "This is my wife, Charlotte."

"Welcome to our home, Mr. Sawyer," she said.

I turned in her direction and looked into her face, and the world skidded to a halt. Blood raced to my head and, just as quickly, drained away. I looked back at him, desperate to conceal the shock. It seemed incredible, but she didn't know me. There had been no recognition in her eyes – the lids didn't even flicker. Twenty years were gone. I was different. My hair was shorter, the unfortunate red beard long since shaved away, and wire-rimmed glasses had become necessary. I stifled the overpowering impulse to touch her, to tell her it was me. How many times had I imagined this meeting? Had I ever stopped imagining it? Her image had tormented me and made me hope and now the bored, unknowing greeting had ended whatever dreams I had left. I struggled to face her. "Thank you, Mrs. Winslow."

I found a bar and ordered scotch. A few seconds later, I asked for another one. If she removed the makeup, pulled the golden hair back into a ponytail, and slipped into jeans and a turtle-neck sweater, she was the same girl. The face might be a little fuller, but the wide-set purple eyes, narrow nose and generous mouth had not changed. Her body was artfully concealed by a low-cut evening gown, but the perfect breasts, slender hips and long shapely legs beneath it had been in my brain for two decades.

Then, inevitably, the shock was replaced by the familiar madness. I spent the rest of the evening avoiding her. She didn't remember me, and now I didn't want her to. Her presence in this house, *her* house, meant that she was never the girl she had pretended to be. One of the wealthiest women in Washington, she had married Winslow when she was only twenty years old, and yet she had celebrated her twentieth birthday in a tiny apartment on New Hampshire Avenue, and I was the only guest. The idyll that I had cherished for so long was false from the beginning.

For some reason, Winslow was intent on introducing me to everyone there. I met a Supreme Court justice, the Director of Central Intelligence, and two cabinet secretaries. The chairmen of both of the committees before whom I would testify in a few days were in attendance. I drank far too much but the usual loss of sensation didn't set in – I was intensely aware of everything and nothing. Dinner was easier – her chair was empty. Winslow announced that she wasn't feeling well, but would rejoin us later. Determined not to chance another encounter, I fled as soon as the meal was over.

The tumult in my head was undiminished and, after passing through the gate, I turned up the hill rather than down. A few steps brought me to another gatehouse, this one guarding the entrance to Oak Hill Cemetery. Mausoleums, crypts and markers of every shape gleamed in the light of the moon. I hurried past the Gothic chapel and ornamental gardens, crossed the lawn, and plunged down the familiar serpentine pathway. The implacability of the old burial ground was reassuring. When I came to the bottom of the incline, I turned my head to the right and looked up. The granite vault stood where it had always stood, casting a shadow against the brick wall that I had never paid much attention – it was just an anonymous boundary that separated the eternal silence of the graveyard from the noisy world beyond. Now I knew better. It was actually *her* wall, a barrier between us that she had never confessed.

I left the path and climbed the hill, leaving footprints in the damp grass. The old vault was the color of blood in the moonlight. Its steep gabled roof, oversized archway and peculiar ornamentation – gargoyles at the corners and a finial at the top of the roof that resembled a misshapen birdhouse – created a sinister impression. The name etched into the stone over the doorway gave me pause. Like the wall, the family that rested inside the chamber had been meaningless until now.

There was a gate in the wall that I had forgotten. A rusty chain and padlock denied access to unsanctioned visitors. I gazed through the iron bars, past the temples and gardens and statues, to the bright lights of the house I had left a few minutes before. The enormity of the ruin, its truth and – perhaps more important – its revelation, settled over me.

I stood there for a time unmeasured, then turned away. Uncertainty had leavened the bitterness all these years, but knowing now added to the foul brew of my emotions. I paused again at the entrance to the vault. Small arched windows had been cut into the granite on either side, and the ledges beneath them were hollow. The top of the ledge on the left was loose. I pushed the stone cap aside and withdrew a rubber envelope from the cavity. The zipper didn't want to give way at first, but I finally coaxed it open. There was a piece of paper inside, a message from someone written long ago. A brief notation, in a different hand, had been added to the end: "I'm sorry."

FOR ONCE, I was thankful to have something to divert my attention from myself. The meeting with the Consortium was set for Tuesday, and my testimony on Capitol Hill was a week later. As soon as that was done, I would return to New Hope to nurse my wounds and marinate in booze and lost opportunity. I ran into Bell in the hall. "Are you going to the meeting tomorrow?" I said.

"With the Consortium?" I nodded. "Yes."

"Do you know who else will be there?"

"Sure." He followed me into my office. "Ames and the Chairman, of course. Attendees from the Consortium vary, but the two who will certainly be there are Eli Withers and Amanda Bliss."

"Who are they?"

"Withers is the Chairman and CEO of Mammoth Power and Light. It's the biggest producer of nuclear power in the country." He paused. "He also owns Mammoth Engineering."

"The contractor at Hanford?"

"Yes." He hesitated. "Mark Singer's a friends of yours, isn't he?" I nodded. "He and Withers almost came to blows at a White House event a couple of years ago."

I laughed. "And Amanda Bliss?" I had heard that name recently but couldn't dredge her up.

He smiled. "Amanda plays several roles. She will be here tomorrow as President of the Nuclear Power Workers of America."

"A union?"

"Yes."

"I didn't know the industry was unionized."

"It's about fifty per cent and growing. They have some kind of presence at every plant in the country, and they have a lot of support on the Hill."

I considered that. "But isn't that dangerous? What happens if they go on strike?"

"Fortunately, we haven't been required to find out. They have a no-strike contract."

"Why would the head of the union attend a meeting between owners and the NEA?"

He laughed. "Do you think we're adversaries?"

"We're not?"

"Not at all. It's a very cozy relationship."

The telephone rang. I reached for the receiver. Bell rose and left the room. "Hello."

"Mr. Sawyer?"

It was Winslow's secretary. "Yes."

"The Chairman would like to see you."

"When?"

"Now, if possible."

"I'll be right there."

I took the elevator to the third floor and entered the large corner office where I was immediately ushered into the inner sanctum. "Come in, Tommy, come in," he said. The room was not the usual government cubicle. A few compulsory items were on display – flags, scattered photographs of the Chairman and various dignitaries, a framed picture of the President behind the desk – but the antique furniture and oriental rugs didn't come from a government warehouse. He indicated a chair. "I missed you after dinner the other night."

"I was beginning to have too much fun, and I didn't want to embarrass myself."

He laughed. "Very wise." He held up a piece of paper. "Have you seen the agenda for tomorrow's meeting?"

"No, sir."

"Take mine. I don't need it." He pushed it across the desk and leaned back in his chair. "Tell me about your trip to Hanford."

I described the autopsy and the meeting with the press. "The coroner's waiting on results from the crime lab before making a final decision."

"Was there any talk about who might have struck him? Or why?"

"No." He nodded. "Jack Roller said that Charles Martin was at Hanford several times recently. Did you know that?" He shook his head. "Why would he go there?"

"I have no idea." He paused. "How are you coming with your visit to Capitol Hill?"

"Okay. I've been through the report and –"

"All of it?"

"Yes, sir."

He looked surprised. "All those graphs and statistics?" I nodded. He laughed again. "Don't go overboard. The committee is used to non-answers from our lawyers. They expect it." He paused. "Let Bell dazzle them with details. That's what he gets paid for."

"Well – sure. All right."

"Your testimony is really just a cover letter. It's better not to wade into something you're not really familiar with."

I hesitated. "Yes, sir."

He stared at me for a moment. "What did you think of it?"

"The report?"

"Yes."

"It's very thorough. Everything you'd want to know about the history of nuclear power. The protective measures taken over the –"

"What about the conclusions?"

"The dead people?" He nodded. "Well, as you say, I'm no expert, but the estimates seem reasonable given the assumptions."

"Assumptions?"

"Yes, sir. The selection of an earthquake and loss of power as the critical event means that the meltdown would be – orderly." I paused. "It allows for twenty hours to evacuate."

"So?"

"If the problem were more immediate, that time period would be much shorter."

"How could that happen?"

"I – I don't know, but –"

"So you're just speculating?"

"Well – yes. Of course. But –"

"What else?"

I felt like a hostile witness under cross-examination. "The evacuation rate assumed in the report is high, and the idea that the people will immediately take the anti-radiation tablets seems optimistic. Also, the report assumes stable weather which limits the range of the radiation."

He was frowning now. "Is any of this – hypothesizing in the report?"

"No, sir."

"Then I don't expect to hear any of it when you testify. Your job is to introduce the report. Let the experts debate the fine points."

"Yes, sir."

He hesitated. "Did you know Charlotte when you were going to school here? You're about the same age."

I forced my face to remain set. Had she said something? No good would come from a truthful answer, so I lied. "No."

After a moment, he nodded. "Do you have any questions about the meeting tomorrow?"

"No." I stopped. "Well, there is one thing."

"Yes?"

"A woman named Amanda Bliss will be here. I feel like I've heard the name before, but I can't –"

He laughed. "You *were* having too much fun. You met her at the party. She was with Senator Bright." He paused. "The tall, dark woman in the – revealing dress." He laughed again. "She's hard to forget."

Returning to my office, I pondered the decision to stay in Washington for the hearings. Anybody could just *deliver* the damned report. I was sorry I'd wasted my time. And his curiosity about the past was disturbing, though I couldn't say why.

I picked up the phone. A minute later, Mark came on the line. "I was just going to call you," he said. "How was the dinner party?"

"Fine. It's quite a place."

"Did you meet Charlotte?"

"Yes."

"She's a looker, isn't she?"

"Yes."

"She's got brains, too. And she does a lot of good things around here that people don't even know about."

I was unwilling to learn more of her virtues. "Great. Listen, what did you tell Winslow about me?"

"I said you were a good guy, a fine lawyer – you know. Why?"

"Did you tell him that I'm an unmotivated slacker who will do as little as I can get by with?" Even as I spoke the words, I realized how apt the description was.

He burst out laughing. "Of course not. Did he say that?"

"No, but that's apparently what he expects. I'm supposed to –"

"Hold on a second, Tommy." I heard voices in the background. "I have to go," he said to me. "Something's come up here that I need to pay attention to."

"Okay."

"I'm having some people over tomorrow night. Can you come?"

"Sure."

"Good. Seven o'clock." He hung up.

I picked up the agenda that Winslow had given me. A single sheet, the list of attendees was at the top. There were six men representing the Consortium, four from the NEA and the President of the Nuclear Power Workers of America. The agenda included the items that Ames had mentioned a week earlier plus one more – the RCA Report. Sharing it with the people it was intended to evaluate, before presenting it to the court that had ordered it or the Congress that would debate it, was troubling but, like everything else, it seemed to be part of a team effort and we were all on the same team.

CHAPTER FIVE

"LET'S GET started," said Eli Withers. "You can fill him in later." Dressed in black except for a white shirt with a round collar and a red string tie, Withers looked like a character out of a Gothic novel. He was at least six and a half feet tall and gaunt as a cadaver. Straight black hair hung nearly to his shoulders, and the wide-open dark eyes burned like failing stars. When he spoke, his lips barely moved. The thin, rasping voice seemed to come from somewhere else, like a ventriloquist's.

"We can't conduct this meeting without the Chairman," said George Ames.

"Of course we can," said Withers. "He and I have already discussed these things. We're in total agreement."

Ames frowned, and turned to the stenographer at the end of the table. "Don't take that down. I'll tell you when to start." He looked at Withers. "It doesn't matter what you and Winslow agreed to. These issues are subject to public and congressional scrutiny, and we have to proceed in accordance with the law."

Withers laughed, and started to respond. The woman next to him interrupted. "Eli, be patient." She put a hand on his arm. "I'm sure that John will be here shortly." The silence interspersed with small talk resumed. Withers and Amanda Bliss were seated on a leather love seat between two windows in the Chairman's office. The rest of us sat at a round mahogany table on the other side of the room.

Winslow had been right about her. It spoke to the extent of my distraction that I had been unable to recall her image. Her features were attractive – raven hair that fell past her shoulders, large black eyes, plump painted lips – but it was her body and its presentation that was unforgettable. Her appearance this morning had refreshed my recollection. The black dress she wore at the party had indeed left little to the imagination. The plunging neckline displayed her full breasts, and what wasn't immediately visible could be discerned through the fabric. Her smooth back and strong thighs were bare, and the neat calves and ankles were showcased by the patent leather pumps on her feet. The implication was obvious, the invitation inclusive – she was theoretically available to everyone in the room. Walter Bright, the Chairman of the Senate Energy Committee, had been the lucky man Saturday night. I considered that. Was it one of her "roles"? Was it her responsibility to cater to the needs of the highest elected official charged with oversight of her industry, the industry that employed the members of her union? Perhaps the incest wasn't limited to the Consortium and the NEA.

Her work clothes differed from her evening attire only by degree. Her breasts, encased in a tight yellow sweater, were twin beacons that held the attention of every man in the room, and the long tan legs that extended from the short black skirt caused a stir each time they were crossed. When Ames introduced us, I managed to keep my eyes on hers, and the smile there reflected her recognition of the effort.

Anne Clark looked in the door. "Mr. Ames, could I speak to you for a second?" Ames rose and left the room.

He returned a moment later. "I'm afraid we'll have to call this meeting off. The Chairman is unable to be here. I'm sorry."

Withers leaped to his feet. "God damn it, George, you can't do that. Things are coming to a head. When that report is issued we have to have –"

Ames cut him off. "Eli, it can't be helped. The regulations require that the Chairman be here." He looked at the stenographer. "We won't need you today, Mary. Thank you." He walked to the door and looked back. "I'm sorry. I'll try to set up a conference call or something." He closed the door behind him.

Withers was losing control. "God damn it!" he shouted to the room. "This is bullshit. We don't have time for this crap. We have to be ready –"

Amanda stopped him this time. "Eli, shut up." She softened her words with a smile. "Everything's going to be fine." She took his arm and walked him through the door. Everyone else gathered their pencils and notepads and briefcases, and followed them. I began to assemble my things in the quiet of the empty room.

"Tommy." I looked up. She was standing in the doorway, leaning against the jamb. "Would you help me with one of these?" Amanda said, pointing to two briefcases she had carried in by herself.

"Sure." She bent to retrieve one of them. Free of her eyes, I took in the view. I had not been very interested lately, but this woman could arouse a corpse.

We were on the sidewalk before she spoke. "I'm parked on F Street." I nodded, and we turned north. When we reached her car, a black Mercedes convertible, she opened the trunk. Fat rolls of blueprints were stacked neatly between boxes of thick books and binders. "My homework," she said. She moved some things around to make room for the briefcases, then unlocked the driver's side door and opened it. "I'm sorry about that outburst back there. Eli's under a lot of pressure."

"Why?"

"He has millions of dollars tied up in Mammoth. He's made a huge bet on commercial nuclear power. Every little dip in the stock price rattles him. The next week or two will be critical."

"How come?"

"The RCA Report –" she paused "– *your* report will be made public next week. It's not as forthcoming as it might be, frankly, and we expect trouble. Not from the politicians – they're in it with us – but the agitators will have a field day."

"Why not write a better report?"

She shook her head. "John and Eli won't do it. We've been downplaying the problems for years, and everyone is heavily invested in the status quo."

"Including you?" She didn't respond. "Do you really believe they're agitators?"

"There may be some who oppose us on principle, but most of them have an agenda. Their research is funded by our competitors. It's all about economics." She stopped. "Everything's for sale."

"Even the planet?"

"Of course." She stepped closer. Her scent was exotic, and she wasn't as young as she appeared. A hint of the lines disguised by her makeup was visible at close range. The black eyes were pools that drew mine in as if she were trying to see what lay behind them. She touched the back of my neck. "You're not an agitator, are you?" she said softly, moving closer still. The heat from her body raised the temperature in mine. The appeal was primal, a throwback to the time – before education and culture and convention – when females relied on allure to secure themselves and their children. Had she lain across the hood of the car and offered herself at that moment, I would have taken the proffered flesh without hesitation. "Are you?" she said again.

Her voice broke the spell. Shaken, I took a step backward. "No. No, I'm not."

She laughed again, convinced only of her power to compel the answer she wanted to hear. "Good." She slid into the bucket seat, deliberately allowing the skirt to ride up her hips. "I'll see you next week."

I lifted my eyes. She was smiling again. "What's the occasion?"

"I'll be sitting at the table with you. I'm testifying, too."

I loitered on my way back, considering the new characters in this foray beyond myself. Rather than stop at my office, I walked a few more steps and pushed through the door into the chambers of the General Counsel. "Is he free?" I said.

"I'm sorry, Tommy," said Anne Clark. "He's already gone for the day." She was standing next to her desk sorting small stacks of paper into larger piles. No more than an inch or two over five feet, the heels of her shoes made her seem much taller. The jet-black hair was short and swept back over her head like a man's, and her breasts – concealed by a black turtleneck sweater and short leather jacket – were high, firm and large. The hollow cheeks were lightly pocked and the wide blue eyes, highlighted by dark make-up, were both hard and inquisitive. "I saw Amanda commandeer your services. What do you think?"

I felt the blush on my face. "She's, ah – formidable."

She laughed. "That's one word for it, I guess, but don't let the sex fool you. She's very bright, too."

"Really?"

"She was one of Bell's prize pupils at Hopkins."

"She's a physicist?"

"Nuclear engineer. She knows more about the actual generation of nuclear power than anyone in that room except Gordon."

"Speaking of that, what happened to our meeting?"

"You haven't heard?" I shook my head. "The Chairman's daughter is missing. They think she's been kidnapped." She fished around in her waste basket and pulled out a section of the *Star*. "Here. You can read all about it."

"Thanks." I turned away.

"Tommy?" I looked back. "Mark tells me that you'll be at his place tonight."

"Yes. Are you going?" She nodded. "How do you know him? I thought he'd sworn off women."

She laughed again. "We go back a long way." She stopped. "We had a little fling a few years ago, but I'm just one of the gang now." Her tone was light, but her expression seemed to belie her words. Mark had never mentioned her.

I returned to my office and spread the newspaper across the desk. My mind was still on Amanda Bliss, and it took a few seconds for the picture on the front page of the *Georgetown Star* to register. The photograph was attributed to the staff of the *Green Gate*, the yearbook of the most exclusive girls' school in Georgetown. The exhausted irony that infected the rest of the world had not yet penetrated the brick walls and iron gates of Georgetown Visitation. She wore the traditional white sweater and pearls, and there was a phrase beneath the name intended by the yearbook's editors to characterize her place among her classmates:

Regan Thomas Winslow
A Different Drummer

I stared at the name under the picture. Regan Winslow, alias Regan Blaine, was the Chairman's daughter, and that made her Charlotte Winslow's daughter, too. She used Blaine, her mother's maiden name, professionally, but that's not what caught my attention.

SHE WAS "Charly" and I was "Tom." She had always insisted that that was enough. Even after we fell in love she said that who we were before was unimportant. It was make-believe, but we were still children and still capable of ignoring the world around us. We pretended concern for the issues of the day but, in truth, we were searching for each other and when the quest was over there was really nothing else.

I had remained in Washington the summer before my senior year in college. The initial idea – my mother's – was summer school, but when Mark went to work at the *Star* and moved out, money became more necessary than school. I didn't want to spend those last days of freedom in class anyway, so I took a job assisting the groundskeeper at Oak Hill Cemetery. It was a Victorian garden planted with people.

The plateau just inside its monumental gateway was the highest ground in Georgetown, and from there the property fell and rose through forests and stone outcroppings until it reached Rock Creek. Vaults and mausoleums and plain worn tablets covered in moss marked the people at rest, overshadowed by the great trees – beeches and oaks and poplars, and conifers of every variety – some more than three centuries old. Stone steps built into the slopes provided access to grave sites situated on high mounds and knolls.

The work was hard but satisfying. I mowed grass, clipped hedges and weeded flower beds, and quickly came to know every square foot of Oak Hill's twenty-two acres. The individual graves were notionally the charge of the families left behind but, in practice, we made the little repairs that we could. I secured loose finials and urns, replaced broken bricks and tiles, and set the older stones upright when they fell. Often the engraving on them was illegible. The first occupant had been interred 170 years earlier.

One morning in early September, a week before the beginning of school, my boss – a garrulous man in his seventies – laid out the chores for the day. At the end of the list, he said, "The last thing is the Blaine vault. You know where that is?" When I didn't answer immediately, he said, "It's the funny one right next to the west wall. It's red granite, has a weird little birdhouse on top –"

"Oh, sure. I know the one you mean."

"The ledge under the window on the left is loose. Take some mortar up there and seal it."

"Okay."

It was well past quitting time when I climbed the hill to the red vault, but I didn't mind spending extra hours at Oak Hill, and I wanted to begin with a clean slate the next morning. The overwhelming green of summer was just beginning to give way to the red and pink and bronze of sourwoods and hydrangeas, and the smell of earth and fresh cut grass made me smile. The old tomb blazed in the late afternoon sun. As I approached with my trowel and bucket, I noticed a female form seated on a stone bench in front of the vault. I tried never to interrupt prayer or contemplation, so I did an about-face and started back down the hill. Her voice reached me. "Sir! Come back. You won't bother me." I looked around. She was standing now, beckoning to me. When I hesitated, she called again. "I'll be leaving in a few minutes." By the time I reached the tomb, she was seated again, looking up at me. "I thought you were the old man who works here."

I removed my cap. "Nope. Just the summer help." She was about my age. The jeans and thin cotton sweater didn't hide the creamy skin and delicate features, and the slender fingers – now sweeping the hair from her face and re-tying the ponytail – were elegant. I turned away to examine the window ledge, my own fingers suddenly clumsy and stiff.

"Summer's almost over," she said.

I looked around. "I'll be back in school next week."

"Me, too. Do you go to school around here?"

I abandoned the window ledge. Tomorrow would be soon enough. "Yes. What about you?"

"Yes."

I sat on the bench across from hers and we began the conversation that served as an introduction among our contemporaries. We scorned the polite rituals of the past and, as a result, we were forced into inquisitive, less polite, rituals of our own. It was somehow easier this time, and the questions and answers less important. She, too, was a senior. Her Jesuit university was located twelve blocks west of my own secular institution. She lived in a dorm on campus and seemed interested in my place on New Hampshire Avenue. She was apparently a native, but avoided details of her history.

I told her whatever she wanted to know. The words flowed easily. The agonizing pauses, the struggle to present myself so that she would approve, were missing. It wasn't that I didn't care. In a few short minutes her approval had become very important to me, but the stress was absent. She listened and laughed and responded, her eager words sometimes stepping on mine. It was the first time in my life that conversation was a joy rather than a chore.

The chimes from a nearby church interrupted. She waited until they had finished. "Is it really seven o'clock?" she said.

"I guess so."

She rose. "I have to go."

"I'll walk you to the gate."

"No – no." She seemed uncertain. "I still have – something to do here."

"Okay. Well –" The easy talk was over. "Well, how about dinner some time? Or – or a movie?" She smiled, but didn't answer. I grew desperate. "Or we could just talk."

She laughed. "Maybe. I'll think about it."

"How can I get in touch with you?"

"You'll be here for the rest of the week, won't you?" I nodded. "I'll get in touch with you."

That was highly unsatisfactory, but better than an outright rejection. She extended her hand. The fingers were warm in the chilly twilight. "I'm Charly."

I waited for more, but there was none. "Tommy. Tommy –"

"Tommy's enough. I'll call you Tom."

I still held her hand, and she did nothing to withdraw it. Finally, unable to justify the continued contact, I let it go and walked down the hill. When I reached the bottom, I turned and looked back. She was gone.

THE ORIGINAL entryway to Mark's brick townhouse was on the east side, through a two-story porch with round columns and balustrades on each level. When it was built, the grounds extended north to P Street and east to 30th, taking up more than half a city block. It was hemmed in by other houses now, and the public entrance was by way of an undistinguished door in the south façade, but friends still used the porch. It was less than four blocks from my carriage house, so I trudged up the hill, turned into the drive from 30th Street, and climbed the steps.

I was still thinking about Regan Blaine. The kidnappers – if that's what they were – had left no note. The police and reporters were certain that a ransom demand was coming. She was the only child of wealthy, powerful people and the price for her freedom, and perhaps her life, would be high.

I believed it was something else. Her apartment on 31st Street had been rifled, an unnecessary invasion if kidnapping were the objective. The Martins were dead, in part because of the notebook in a locked drawer of my desk, and Regan had apparently been within days of revealing the details. She had been taken because those who committed the murders and dismantled the house on Prospect Street didn't want that story told, and they seemed to know that she had the book. They didn't find it because she'd given it to me. Did they know that, too?

I had strongly suggested that she take it all to the police and threatened to do so myself, but now I was unsure. How much did she really know? If she had pieced it all together she was probably dead. One more murder was nothing to the people who wanted the book. If, on the other hand, Regan had not yet tumbled to the truth she could still be alive and the notebook, unknown and unexamined by the authorities, might purchase her life. Any hint of its existence, and the possibility that its secrets might be exposed, could be deadly.

But who was I to make that decision? I knew that I should take the whole thing to Winslow but something nagged at me. I couldn't shake the feeling that Martin's work at the NEA was part of the plot. The tedious statistics in his notebook had to mean something. If that were so, how would Winslow respond? Yes, Regan was his daughter, but if something was amiss at the NEA, he might hesitate to make it public. That was probably unfair to him, but that's where it stood.

Anne Clark answered the door. She had changed into jeans and a white oxford-cloth shirt with the sleeves rolled up, but the casual clothing did nothing to soften the chrysalis that she occupied. The hair was perfect and the make-up fresh. She was barefoot, and the wide raspberry mouth smiled up at me. "Mark's still at the office," she said. "I'm playing hostess until he gets here."

I looked at my watch. "It's past seven. I thought he was a big shot over there."

"The Blaine kidnapping has caused a bit of turmoil. He's meeting with the publisher to decide how the story should be handled."

"Why?"

"Regan works at the *Star* and Mrs. Winslow is a substantial shareholder. That raises some – ethical issues." She gestured toward the kitchen. "The rest of the crowd's in there. I'll introduce you."

A few minutes later, I had met the men who were Mark's real friends. One was a sportswriter, another a coach, a third the headmaster at one of the local boys' schools. I poured some scotch and listened to the conversation, all about Regan's disappearance. They, too, were sure it was a kidnapping, and they were handicapping the ransom demand. Five million dollars "– a lot of money, but not enough to give Charlotte Winslow heartburn –" was the consensus.

I stepped down into the little study off the kitchen where Anne was sorting through Mark's CD collection. He insisted that music from vinyl transmitted to the highest quality disc was better than that downloaded from the Internet, and he had a state-of-the-art machine – and super audio CDs – that did just that. When the mood struck him, he would collect record albums from friends and strangers and record his own music for hours. His collection was eclectic – the next song was always a surprise.

I crossed the room to the window. From there I could see a summerhouse on the far side of the lawn. It was gray frame with white trim, and a cupola topped by a copper weathervane rose from the roof. A rotary lawn mower leaned against the wall next to the door.

The study was like Winslow's office without the phony décor. Pictures of Mark with celebrities and politicians were scattered about the tables and shelves, and the walls were covered, haphazardly, with plaques and framed newspaper clippings that attested to his stature in the journalism world. Here and there were pictures that he had taken during his early years as a photographer at the *Star*. A scarred desk stood in the corner, littered with manuscript pages, magazines and bills – he'd never been able to manage money. The envelope on top of the pile, from a local branch of Bank of America, was marked "Urgent!" An electric typewriter sat amongst the debris. "Does he still use this thing?" I said.

"He says he does."

"I'd swear it's the same one he had in college." Her glass was empty. "More wine?" She nodded. When I returned, she was sitting on the sofa, eyes closed, listening to the music. Mark's beloved bulldog, Bo, lay beside her, his head in her lap. I sat down on the other side. "How long have you been at the NEA?"

She took the glass. "Five years."

"What did you think of Charles Martin?"

She turned appraising eyes toward me. "He was – young." She paused. "And he was ambitious, and much too sure of himself for someone so new to this place. Naïve, almost."

"Did he have access to everything at the NEA?"

"Everything within his security clearance. Just like you."

"Did the RCA expand that?"

"What do you mean?"

"Did he get into areas where he wouldn't ordinarily go?"

"Probably. He was a lawyer, not an engineer."

"Did you know that he made several trips to Hanford over the past year?" She shook her head. "Have you read Regan Blaine's stories? In the *Star*?"

She nodded again. "Do you know any reason why someone would kill him?"

"He was nowhere near as important as he thought he was. I think that's very unlikely."

"His wife was killed by a hit-and-run driver a few days ago. Did you know that?"

The blue eyes stared. "No. I didn't."

"Do you think Regan was really kidnapped?"

She seemed startled. "Of course. Don't you?"

"I'm not so sure."

"Why not? It seems obvious." She stared at me, seemingly provoked at my refusal to accept the common wisdom.

"You're probably right." I leaned back against the leather cushion. "Is there anything unusual about the RCA Report?"

She took a moment to answer. "No. The RCA Report is very much business as usual."

I tried a different tack. "Does Ames like his job?"

"Are you pumping me about my boss?"

"Well – yes."

She laughed. "I'd be offended if there were anything to tell." She stopped. "George Ames is a career bureaucrat. He's been in and out of every department and agency in town. His only goal is to serve out his time without trouble. He'll retire in less than a year and pull down a hundred thousand dollars per annum for doing nothing." She stopped again. "That meeting didn't *have* to be canceled this afternoon. That was just George making sure that no one who mattered – Winslow, mainly – could object."

"Is he married?"

She almost choked on her wine. "George?"

"He seems pretty gung-ho about nuclear energy."

"Only because the NEA is officially gung-ho about nuclear energy. Winslow and Bell are the true believers."

"Winslow? He doesn't seem to believe in anything but Winslow."

"He was appointed head of the agency two years ago. It's been in turmoil ever since."

"Why?"

"He's determined to push the industry's agenda. George is scared to death that he'll upset the apple cart."

I rose and looked out the window again. The master of the house was walking up the driveway. Seconds later I heard the greetings, and Anne and I returned to the kitchen. Mark waved to us from the doorway. The others were clamoring for news. He shook his head five or six times, then raised his hands for quiet. "I can tell you one thing," he said, "and that's only because it'll be in the *Post* first thing tomorrow morning. After that we talk about something else. All right?" He registered the grudging nods. "We received the ransom note this afternoon. It came to my office." The tumult rose again. "That's it." He accepted a glass from Anne. "What're the Redskins' chances Sunday?"

The card game started a few minutes later. Intermittent questions were posed about the kidnapping, all of which Mark ignored. Finally, the headmaster introduced a new subject. "How's the house on Mason's Island coming along?"

Mark laughed. "It's one headache after another. I was over there yesterday meeting with the contractor. The Preservation Society wants to put in central heat and air. He said the entire electrical system will have to be replaced."

"Why?"

"It was installed a hundred years ago. The circuits and wiring can't take the load." He paused. "Any modern appliance, even the wrong kind of lighting, could cause a problem."

The coach spoke up. "Every time I see that place at night, it's lit up like a Christmas tree."

Mark laughed again. "There are six different decorators trying to get the contract to furnish the house. Each guy has a room or two to show his stuff, and every one of them is packed with new rugs and furniture. And you've never seen so many extension cords in your life. They pop two or three fuses a day."

"Sounds dangerous," I said.

"It probably is. That's another reason we're changing out the wiring."

"Is someone staying over there?"

"Not yet. We're trying to hire somebody."

The conversation drifted to the usual topics – football, politics, women. Anne was fully engaged but, after a few hands, rose and announced that she was going home. I stood up. "I'm leaving, too, before you vultures pick me clean." I caught up with her in the kitchen. "I'll walk you home."

She smiled. "Let me get my coat. I'll meet you on the porch."

I stopped for a minute to cash in the chips of what was left of a $100 bill. When I reached the porch, she and Mark were speaking in low tones. He turned his head toward me.

"How much money do they want?" I said.

"Money wasn't mentioned. And it wasn't really a note. It was a compact disc. From Regan."

"So she's alive."

"Yes. When she made the disc."

"What did she say?"

"I'm sure that she was reading whatever they put in front of her. She said that the cops should back off and, if they did, there would be further communication." He paused. "Charlotte told the Chief to stop what he was doing. He agreed, but there wasn't much to go on anyway. The FBI's waiting for instructions." Anne wrapped a bright red scarf around her neck and slipped into a pea coat. We started down the steps. "You'll be happy to know that the *Star* has assigned its best reporter to the story," he called.

"Who?"

"Me. I'll be the point man until the cops take over again."

Anne and I were quiet as we walked down the hill. Fifty yards short of the Potomac, we turned onto a sloping brick path that ran alongside the Chesapeake and Ohio Canal. The mist rising from the canal cloaked the trees and the buildings, and made the carriage light at each place seem a detached, anonymous destination even though her townhouse was one of several fashioned from an old tobacco warehouse. The miasma was a mixture of fish and diesel fuel. When we reached her door, she said, "Would you like to come in?"

I was surprised, but pleased. "Yes, I would. Very much. But not tonight." I paused. "I hope you'll ask me again."

She surprised me again with a kiss on the lips. "You have an open invitation."

Mark's news had not changed my view of Regan's abduction, but it had relieved my conscience about Martin's notebook. It *was* a kidnapping and Charly – as I always thought of her – had told the police to stand down, but the book was still the key. Regan, with the confident skepticism of the young, had declared coincidence unworthy of belief. I knew that it happened all the time, but I was also certain that serendipity had nothing to do with her disappearance. She had been on the verge of discovering the truth. Perhaps I could finish the job and, more importantly, maybe I could find her.

CHAPTER SIX

THE *GEORGETOWN* *Star* had nothing new. Mark's story, below the fold on the front page, was a rehash of what he had written before, plus a catalogue of the law enforcement agencies – all of which might have jurisdiction over the kidnapping of the child of a high-level federal official – awaiting further word from the kidnappers. Their impotence would have amused me had I not cared so much for the victim, and I had a growing conviction that Regan was more to me than that. I gazed at her picture again, sorting out the possibilities.

I dropped the paper into the trash can. The martini at lunch had not cured the headache, nor provided the usual balm for my emotions. I was as helpless as everyone else – more, maybe, because I had custody of a giant clue that somebody might decipher. I had read and re-read every note in Martin's book, and nearly memorized the words and statistics, to no avail.

Jane looked in the door. "Anne Clark's on line one."

I picked up the receiver. "Hello."

"Tommy, it's Anne. What are you doing for dinner tonight?"

"I have no idea."

"I'm making spaghetti. The recipe's way too much for me and my freezer's full. I need help."

"I'll bring a bottle of wine."

"Don't bother. I have plenty." Hanging up the phone, I wondered at the invitation. I retained a measure of vanity, but it was tempered by experience and the cynicism that afflicted the rest of my life. Her attention, which I had encouraged without much hope of success, was a little jarring.

Jane, who had remained in the doorway, was smiling. "What are you grinning at?" I said.

"I just like to watch her work."

"Meaning?"

"Anne treats every new man as a challenge. She's especially partial to Assistant General Counsels." She turned away.

A moment later, I stopped beside her desk. "Are you saying that she and Martin had an affair?" She smiled but didn't respond. "Come on, Jane. He was married. His wife was expecting."

"Anne's not particular about the details. She almost got fired a couple of years ago."

"Why?"

"She was dallying with Eli Withers. He was married then, too."

I hesitated. "What about Mark Singer?"

"They used to be *very* close. She says the split was mutual, but I don't think so." She paused. "It's a sensitive subject."

I left the building and hailed a cab. "Where to?" said the driver.

"The *Georgetown Star*. R Street."

Mark was sitting at his desk, talking on the phone. He lifted his eyes and motioned to a ragged blue couch on the far wall. I sat down and waited. He wrapped up the conversation hurriedly and laid down the receiver. "What brings you here?" He looked at his watch. "Still office hours. You haven't quit, have you?"

"Not yet." I paused. "Do you still have the CD from Regan?"

"Yes."

"Can I listen to it?" He raised his brows. "It's not idle curiosity. I – I have a reason."

"Which is?"

"I think I know why she was kidnapped. It's not for money."

"Would you care to share it with me?"

"I will. Soon. I need to think it through a little more." I paused. "Can I hear it?"

He reached into his pocket and withdrew a set of keys. Selecting one, he opened the middle drawer of his desk, and produced a compact disc. I examined the blank jewel case as he inserted the CD into a computer. The words "MARK SINGER, *GEORGETOWN STAR*" were scrawled across the plastic. "Was this delivered directly to you?" He nodded. "Why?"

"I don't know. The Winslows are friends, I work at the paper . . . I don't know. Maybe they wanted instant publicity." He pushed a button. Regan spoke in her usual voice, unafraid or trying to seem so. Her message lasted less than a minute, and when it was over Mark extended a finger to extract the CD.

"Can I see that?" He hesitated, then handed it over. After a moment, I gave it back. "Thanks."

He pushed the disc into its case and returned it to the drawer. "Does that help your investigation?"

"I don't know."

"Be careful. These people aren't very nice."

"I know."

I KNOCKED on her door. Anne answered it and, smiling, took the wine I offered. "Dinner's almost ready," she said. "Can I fix you a drink?"

I hesitated. "No. I think – maybe just a glass of wine."

The preliminaries went well – the food, the conversation. A Pennsylvania native, she had come to Washington right out of high school to intern for a newly-elected Walter Bright. The internship lasted only a few months but she remained, working at various places within the great bureaucracy. Never married, she liked men – powerful men, it seemed – but she named no names. She *was* sensitive about Mark. When I joked about his winning ways with women, she defended him, an edge in her voice. "He's just picked the wrong women. And they're draining him financially. He's paying alimony through the nose."

When the leisurely meal was over I helped her with the dishes. The unspoken intimacy of two people standing at the same sink was rare for me – I had avoided it for years – but I was exhausted now, and empty, ready to try something else. If Anne Clark wanted another scalp, she could have mine.

Her long black gown tied at the waist. It covered her completely while intimating that she wore nothing underneath it, a hint that was confirmed a few minutes later. I had almost forgotten how to please a woman, but she helped me remember. She acquainted me with her body the way a sommelier presents a bottle of wine – the vessel first, then the bouquet, then the molten texture and taste.

For her part, she left nothing undone. Her attentions were business-like, and she refused to allow me the perfunctory, self-indulgent gratification I had cultivated for so long. The eruption in my head, when it finally came, almost rendered me unconscious, and I slept hard and undisturbed for the first time in years.

I OPENED my eyes and looked at the clock – 8:15. I would be late for work. There was a note on the bedside table.

> *Tommy –*
> *Coffee's made. Please turn it off when you leave. There's juice in the refrigerator. See you soon.*
> *A*

My clothes were folded neatly over a chair. I smiled as I put them on, trying to recall the last time I had donned yesterday's clothing in someone else's bedroom. It had been a pleasant interlude. Could it be something more?

The bright yellow sun had not yet cleared the trees when I stepped outside, made sure that her door was locked, and turned east. A freshening breeze damped the smell of the canal and the river. The carriage house where I lived was built in the same Federal style as the big brick house on the other side of the driveway. Gabled, with fanlights over the doors, it stood in the midst of a garden rapidly losing its color. Clipped broadleaf evergreens and conifers screened it from the main house, and a path made of pea gravel led to a stone terrace and pool in the backyard. The unlikely privacy was a pleasant contrast to the busy street only a few paces away.

Inside, I picked up the telephone and called Jane. Having reported my tardiness, I decided to prolong it. I slipped on a pair of shorts and a sweater and returned to the warm sunshine. The redwood bench outside my door would ordinarily be shaded by the hornwood tree beside it, but most of its leaves now lay on the ground around me. I sat down and gazed across the drive to Olive Street, pondering again an escape from the past. A tall, slender woman dressed in blue crossed the street and turned into the driveway. The past returned abruptly – only the ponytail was missing. "Hello, Tom."

"Hello, Charly."

We had been the only people in our make-believe world. In the beginning, I wondered at her insistence that we be alone but soon found the isolation intoxicating. Each time I saw her it was as if I had been swept from Kansas to Oz – my black-and-white life turned to technicolor. It was always like the first time we met, and we took pains to insure that no one interfered. Like Peter and Wendy, we pretended to be grown up, but we always remained on the island. The real world never distracted us. The only expectations that mattered were our own, and neither of us failed the other until the end. My faith in her was perfect, and her betrayal had made me a cripple.

We left messages for each other at the cemetery. The day I left for New Hope, I composed a note asking her to tell me how to find her when I returned. Two months later, almost overcome by anticipation, I climbed the hill to the red granite vault and extracted an envelope from the cavity beneath the window.

> *Dear Tom,*
> *I'm sorry about your grandfather. I*
> *wish I could be with you. I'll be at Oak*
> *Hill every Sunday at noon until you return.*
> *I love you.*
> *Charly*

I left her a note and waited at the vault every Sunday for five weeks. She never appeared. After the second Sunday, I abandoned our world and haunted the buildings and walkways at her college, and roamed the streets of Georgetown. I never found her. On the fifth Sunday, I checked the envelope again. My note was still there, but this time there were other words appended to it: "I'm sorry." Confusion became a white-hot rage banked, but never extinguished, by time. That evening I boarded another train for New Hope.

I had come to Washington again with the implausible notion that I might find her and I did, but my success was pyrrhic. Instead of the unaccountable mistake that I dreamed of, she had played me false from the start. She was a wealthy woman married to another man, a union consummated even before my grandfather's death. Struggling to come to terms with the past, I resented the intrusion. "What do you want?"

She flinched as if I'd struck her. I thought for a moment she would turn away. Instead, she took a piece of yellow paper from her pocket and handed it to me. It was the receipt for the notebook I'd signed a few days earlier. "You've met my – Regan, haven't you?" she said.

"Yes."

"How?"

I bit back the anger. We had been over and done with for years, but Regan was part of the here and now. "She was working on a story about the man who used to have my job. She called me about it." I paused. "I'm sorry. I like her very much."

She tried to smile. "You should. She's your daughter." The fury that I had nurtured for so long – the rage that had *sustained* me for two decades – became less certain. The sense that Regan was more than a girl I had met a single time was confirmed. "I went to your apartment the day I saw my doctor. I was happy and I wanted you to know. You weren't there, so I walked to the cemetery." She stopped. "And I was there every Sunday for the next four weeks. You never came. I felt so alone, and then –" She stopped again.

"What happened?"

"My mother found out that I was pregnant. She was furious." She looked away. "She gave me an ultimatum – marry John Winslow or I was on my own. No money, no home, nothing. I could have the baby in the emergency room." Her expression hardened as she remembered. "I told her to go to hell. She said I should think about it. And then I made a mistake."

"What?"

"I told her about you." She paused. "I thought she might understand that I was in love and leave me alone. I was wrong."

"What did she do?"

"She said she was going to have you arrested. That she would tell the police you raped me."

"But that's ridiculous. She could never prove that. All you'd have to do –"

"You didn't know my mother. She was a big deal in this town, and she had very influential friends. She wouldn't have to prove it."

"She didn't even know who I was. How could she find me?"

"She knew where you lived and where you went to school, and she knew about the job at Oak Hill. Believe me, she would have found you."

"Why didn't *you* find me? I could have –"

"I tried at first. I saw your name on the mailbox and talked to the caretaker at the cemetery, but when she threatened you I gave in. You were gone, and I was pregnant and alone and I didn't know what else to do." She took a deep breath. "I was sorry then that we'd hidden from each other so well."

"Why did we do that?"

She hesitated. "Because I didn't trust you. The importance of money, *our* money, had been drilled into me since childhood. Any boy who got too close was suspect. *She* would choose, and it had to be someone just like me." She paused again. "I didn't want you to know who I was because of the money, and I didn't want Mother to find out about you." Her eyes glistened, but she restrained the tears. I wrapped my arms around her. "I knew by then that you loved *me*, but it was too late. The man I married cared only about the money." She stepped back. "I'm sorry, Tom. I was afraid."

"I'm sorry, too." Ashamed of the bitterness now, I was wary of what might take its place. I opened the door and followed her inside.

"When you came back, I could see you from my window. I think I would have killed myself if not for the baby." She paused. "It's been that way ever since. Every time I looked at Regan I saw you. The pain was fresh every day, and I welcomed it."

"Have you told her?"

"No. I should have. I spoiled her rotten because of you."

We stood together in the middle of the room for a long time. The years fell away and we were alone again. Finally, we sat down at the kitchen table. "When Mark Singer told John about someone named Tommy Sawyer, I wondered if it was you. I was a basket case before that dinner party, and I almost fainted when you came through the door." She paused. "I couldn't let him know who you were." I nodded. "But he already knew. Mother told him before we were married. He's using you to get at me."

"How?"

"He brought you here because he wants a divorce and a lot of money. He thinks he can embarrass me, and he – he threatened to tell Regan about us." She looked out the window. "I decided to tell her myself, but she disappeared before I could." She turned back to me. "We're not as close as we used to be. She spends money like water, and when I refused to give her any more, she moved out. That was a year ago. Things have been better lately, but money's still a sore spot."

"Where did you get the receipt?"

"At her apartment. I was looking for anything that might help me find her. It was with her laundry."

"Let me tell you how I got involved." I told her everything I knew. "The receipt was for the notebook," I said at the end.

"Where is it?" I pointed to my briefcase next to the door. "What's in it?"

"Lots of things that don't mean anything to me. Regan said there was a key that made it make sense, but I can't figure it out." I paused. "I'm turning it over to the police."

"I – let me see it first. It might be something I would know."

"It's been bad luck for at least one woman. And Regan. I'm not sure –"

"I'll be okay. Nothing's going to happen." She withdrew a thick gray envelope from her purse. "I'll trade you."

"What's that?"

"Did Regan tell you about John's Mammoth stock?" I shook my head. "While she was working on the Martin story, she found out that Eli Withers has been giving John Mammoth Power stock for several years."

"Giving?"

"Yes, and Eli has sold a lot, too. It's tripled in price since John went to the NEA. Regan said that Eli's money goes directly to an account in Cuba." She pushed the envelope across the table. "That's her evidence – copies of the trade confirmations and some other stuff."

"Why'd she give it to you?"

"She hates John. She wanted me to use it so that *I* could divorce *him*."

"Do you know what's going on in Cuba?"

"No."

"What about Venezuela or Columbia."

"John goes to South America every year. He still has friends there from his State Department days. He was posted to Cuba, too."

"Does he go alone?"

"He used to. He took someone with him this year."

"Who?"

"Eli Withers."

I laid the envelope on the table. "Did Winslow know that Regan had these things?"

"I don't know."

I retrieved the book and gave it to her. "I think we need some help. Is there someone you can count on, unofficially?"

"Well – Mark, maybe. He already knows most of the story."

I hesitated. She was right. In fact, Mark probably knew *more* than anybody else. That disturbed me for some reason – jealousy or selfishness or something – and I balked at sharing my secret with him. Another thing was percolating in my brain, a coincidence that I was not yet ready to confront. In any event, *I* would be the knight errant, not him. "Isn't there somebody else?"

She tilted her head and smiled at me. "What's the matter with Mark? He's your friend, isn't he?" I nodded. "Then why not ask him to help?"

"I – okay." We agreed to meet again that evening at Regan's apartment, with Mark if he was available. She would return the notebook and tell us what she had gleaned from it, and I would examine the wreckage as if I knew what I was doing. I watched her walk down the driveway to the street and resumed my seat on the bench. I had made a cautious, risk-free life where upset – emotion, strain, engagement – was kept at arm's length. When I took the job at the NEA, I knew that might change, but I never imagined the magnitude of the change that had occurred over the past few days. I was a boy again with an old man's wounds, and I wasn't certain I was up to it.

Winslow's prying was explained. He wanted to use me to plunder his wife, but I had the whip hand now. That Mammoth stock, and maybe a "project" in Cuba, was going to bite him somehow. I heard the telephone ringing just inside the door. "Hello."

"Mr. Sawyer?"

"Yes."

"Jim Baldwin."

"Yes?"

"I'm returning your call."

"Oh. Of course. I'm sorry, Doctor Baldwin. I called about Charles Martin. Am I correct that you were working on something together?"

"Yes. I rode down to Washington a few weeks ago to meet him and deliver my report. I was on the train that ran over him."

"What kind of doctor are you, Doctor Baldwin?"

He laughed. "I'm a Ph.D. in Economics. I teach at Columbia. What kind of bureaucrat are you?"

I laughed, too. "I've taken Martin's place at the NEA. I have to present the report he was working on when he died. What did he ask you to do?"

"He wanted me to analyze the economic impact of a hypothetical loss of power in a single region of the country. As he put it, 'What would happen if the lights went out?'"

"When you say a loss of power, what do you mean?"

"He asked me to assume that the local power plant was shut down indefinitely."

"What conclusion did you reach?"

"What would *you* do if you had no electricity and no hope of having any?" He paused. "Seriously, the impact on the people affected is horrific."

"Did you discuss your findings with him?"

"Yes."

I paused. "Would you send me the report, Doctor Baldwin? I need it as soon as possible."

"Of course. I'll overnight it to you."

"Great. Tomorrow's Saturday, so send it to the house."

On my way to work I tried to separate the personal revelations from the mystery surrounding Regan, and couldn't. She was no longer just a friend. Her face, and images of her mother past and present, occupied all the space in my head.

When I reached the office, I forced myself to think of other things. Charly's news about Winslow's Mammoth stock explained his relentless boosterism – the greater the government's commitment to nuclear energy, the higher the stock would go. The rosy report I would deliver to Congress on Tuesday – and its unquestioning acceptance there – would probably do the same. Was there something in Martin's notebook that would create trouble for Winslow and Withers? Baldwin's analysis had obviously been done for the "property damage" portion of the RCA Report, but the numbers in the book were much greater than those in the report. Why would Martin downplay the economic disaster that a meltdown would cause?

Gordon Bell looked in the door. "You wanted to see me?"

"Yes. Thanks." I picked up the RCA Report and waved it at him. "I want to make sure I understand the scenario *and* the end result before I testify next week."

"All right."

"The 'accident' is an earthquake. When it hits, all outside power to the plant is lost. Right?"

"Yes. The hypothesis assumes that the earthquake disrupts the external source of power somehow

– lines down, transformers lost, maybe even the destruction of the plant that provides it – for a considerable period of time."

"Okay. That shuts everything down, and batteries at the nuclear plant come on-line to power certain facilities."

"Yes, for those plants that have them. Some don't."

"But they only last a few hours?"

"Right."

"And unless some other source of power is provided, the various cooling systems and so forth won't work."

"Yes."

"Including the pumps that run water through the reactor."

"That's correct."

"What happens to the water in the reactor when the power's shut off?"

"It begins to boil and dissipate, uncovering the fuel assemblies. The reactor starts to overheat."

"How long does that take?"

"The fuel assemblies would be totally exposed after about eleven hours."

"Then what?"

"An hour or two later the nuclear fuel will have melted completely and dropped to the bottom of the reactor vessel. From there it will melt or burn its way through the various barriers in the containment building."

"And then it's Katy bar the door."

"Yes. The fuel will start fires and hydrogen gas will cause explosions, and radioactive materials are discharged into the atmosphere."

"Killing lots of people?"

He stared at me. "Maybe."

We sat quietly. I broke the silence. "You know, the power at my place in Georgetown went out this morning."

"Yes, and the people at the power company worked hard to turn your power back on. So would all the people at our hypothetical nuclear plant." He paused. "It takes nine hours for the water in the reactor to reach the top of the fuel assemblies. And that report mentions other measures, like on-site diesel generators and diesel-driven pumps that can provide auxiliary power."

"Are any of those in place?" He shook his head. "Too expensive?" He didn't answer. "Isn't the waste stored on these sites also cooled by water?"

"Yes. Mostly in large concrete pools lined with steel."

"The water loss there would be the same, wouldn't it?"

He nodded. "Spent fuel isn't as hot as reactor fuel. It would take ten days for the water to boil away, unless the pool contains fuel taken recently from the reactor." He stopped. "In that case it would be about a day."

"And cause the fire and explosions and so forth."

"Correct."

"Could the water be lost some other, quicker way?"

"Sure. Puncture, valve malfunctions, outside attacks."

"Isn't there a better way to store it?"

"Not while it's hot. After it's cooled for five or six years it can be kept in dry storage."

"What's that?"

"The fuel rods are placed in steel casks and loaded into concrete silos."

"Are we doing that?" He shook his head. "Why not?"

Bell grinned. "Too expensive."

"The spent fuel isn't mentioned in the report, is it?"

He leaned back in his chair. "I believe our task was to evaluate a *reactor* meltdown."

We were quiet again. "Tell me about the casualties," I said.

BOOK TWO

The world began without the human race and will certainly end without it – Claude Lévi-Strauss

CHAPTER ONE

I CHECKED my watch. Charly was late and so was Mark. I stood up as he pushed through the door into the lobby. The ubiquitous sound of sirens came through the open door. "Where's Charlotte?" he said.

"She's not here yet."

He smiled. "You didn't explain how you developed this – relationship in such a short period of time."

I smiled, too. "It's actually a very *long* story. I'll tell you about it sometime."

"Tell me more about the notebook." I related the story about the Martins, and Regan, and described the contents of Martin's book. "Is she bringing it with her?" I nodded. He looked at the clock over the elevator. "Why don't you give her a call? Maybe something's happened."

"I don't have the number."

"I do." He took an address book from his coat, flipped to the W's and handed it to me.

"Why don't you call her?"

He hesitated. "Okay." I paced the lobby as he murmured into a cell phone. "They say she left the house nearly an hour ago. It's only about ten blocks." He paused. "Was she going anywhere else?"

Panic was setting in. "I don't know, but she was supposed to be here half an hour ago." I felt in my pocket. "She gave me a key but we decided to meet you in the lobby. I'll make sure she's not upstairs." No one answered my knock and, uneasy about entering without her, I returned to the lobby.

We left Regan's apartment building and turned north. Two blocks ahead of us an ambulance, its siren blasting again, pulled away from the curb. A policeman in uniform was speaking to another cop in plain clothes. Mark stopped beside them. "What's up, Blake?"

The plainclothes man turned his head. "Jesus Christ, Singer. How'd you get here so fast?"

Mark laughed. "Teleport." Blake frowned. "Seriously, I was just meeting my friend –" he gestured toward me "– down here. What happened?"

"A woman's been assaulted. Struck on the back of the head." He paused. "Charlotte Winslow."

I fought to keep my face expressionless. As soon as I saw the ambulance I knew it was her, but I didn't want to get involved with the police until *I* decided to. Mark didn't mention our rendezvous, either – instead, he played the role of reporter. "Is she badly hurt?"

"She's unconscious and she's lost a lot of blood, but she was still alive when they put her in the truck."

"Which hospital?"

"George Washington."

"Robbery?"

"Looks like it. Jewelry's gone. There's no wallet in the purse."

"What was she doing down here?"

"How the hell should I know? I've only been here ten minutes." He paused and looked south. "She may have been going to her daughter's apartment."

"Do you think they're connected?"

"I don't know. We might find out if they'll let us." Blake turned away.

Mark called after him. "Have you told Winslow?"

"I'm going to do that right now if you'll shut up and leave me alone."

While this interrogation was ongoing, my eyes had cautiously surveyed the scene – the street, the sidewalk, the inside of the police car. I didn't see the notebook. It *wasn't* robbery, not in the ordinary sense. "I need a drink," Mark said. We turned right at M Street and stepped into the small, elegant lobby of the Latham Hotel. In the bar he chose a table near the piano, silent at the moment. "Order me a brandy," he said. "I have to call the office."

I nodded. "Do me a favor." He looked back. "Call the hospital. See what you can find out."

"All right." He walked back outside. I waited, trying not to think. He returned twenty minutes later. "She's still unconscious. It must be pretty serious. They've put her in intensive care." He picked up his glass. "Don't you want a drink?"

"I've had enough to drink."

The walk home passed unnoticed. She was still a wealthy woman married to another man, but that didn't matter. And there was something else now – my fears for the bearer of the notebook had proved out again, and Mark was the only person who knew that Charly had it. I tried to concentrate. Was that true? It was barely possible that she'd mentioned it to someone after leaving me earlier in the day. I needed to know.

I CONTEMPLATED the telephone. The people at the other end of the line might have the means to identify the caller, and I didn't want whoever it was to know it was me. Then I recalled that the phone wasn't in my name. All that would show up on the screen was my landlord's name and number. The possibility that someone might inquire further seemed slight.

The first number was familiar. *"Georgetown Star."* I put down the receiver, and made a note on the list. Had Martin been in touch with Regan before he died? She'd never mentioned it, but why would she? No one picked up at the second number. A woman's voice answered after the first ring at the next one: "Anne Clark." I hung up and wrote her name down. The voice on the end of the line at the fourth number also seemed familiar. I pinched my nostrils and said, "Bill Smith, please."

"You have the wrong number," he said.

"Are you sure?"

"Of course I'm sure, you fool!" He hung up. It was Winslow. He wasn't the type to answer his own telephone, even on a Saturday afternoon at home. I found the phone book. The number for the Winslows on 28th Street was not the number that Martin had kept in his notebook, and there was no separate listing for John Marsh Winslow. It was probably an unlisted number that he used at home. I wrote his name beside the number.

There were two more. I dialed the first one. It rang three times before another, different dial tone began. After a few seconds, someone picked it up. "Anderson." Who was that? I hung up and noted the name. The last number had an extension with a name beside it: Roberto Gomez. The lightly accented voice at the end of the line said, "Cuban Consulate."

"Extension 452, please."

"Just a moment." The telephone rang for a full thirty seconds before a cultured female voice came on the line. "Tourism and Commerce."

"Mr. Gomez, please."

"I'm sorry, he's unavailable. May I take a message?"

"I'll call back, thank you." I replaced the receiver in its cradle and made a note. Was Martin planning a trip to Cuba, or had he already been? The maps in the notebook suggested more extensive travel. And, of course, Withers was doing something in Cuba.

I looked through the phone book again and dialed another number. "George Washington University Hospital."

"Charlotte Winslow, please."

A pause. "I'm sorry. Mrs. Winslow is not allowed any calls."

"Is she still in intensive care?"

"I'm sorry, sir. I can't give out that information."

Stymied, I looked at my watch. The single question that I wanted to ask her would have to wait. The urge to do *something* consumed me despite the fact that I had so far bungled everything – Regan kidnapped, Charly attacked, the notebook lost.

I sat down at the kitchen table and gazed at Martin's summary again. Along with the telephone numbers, it was all that I had salvaged. Should I go to the police? I didn't have the courage. I would have to tell them about the book that I had lost, and the woman who was in intensive care because of it. I wanted to give it to Mark. He already knew the story and, if he condemned me, he would do so silently. But I couldn't, not until Charly told me what I had to know.

I stepped outside, locked the door and dropped the key into my coat pocket. As I did so, my fingers touched an envelope I had placed there three days earlier. I looked at it, almost weeping in frustration. Three days! I examined the negatives again in the sunlight, and was again unable to make anything of them. Mark and the summary forgotten, I hurried down the hill to the drugstore at 30th and M. "How long will it take you to develop these?" I asked the girl behind the counter.

"I can have them for you Monday morning."

I thought of Mark again. Somebody at the paper could produce the photographs much faster. I almost ran back up the hill and climbed to his porch. He wasn't home. I turned north again, to the *Star's* offices three long blocks away. He wasn't there, either, and they didn't know where he was. Defeated, I returned to the drugstore where I was assured I could pick up the pictures first thing Monday morning.

I walked slowly back to Olive Street. A large gray envelope leaned against the door of the carriage house. I withdrew the stack of paper, sat down at the table and flipped through the pages, the bulk of which made the mind-numbing passages in Martin's notebook seem entertaining. Baldwin had selected an anonymous economic region served by a single power plant and then analyzed the extent of its dependence on electricity which, not surprisingly, was overwhelming. The verdict at the end was catastrophe. His conclusion was almost lyrical compared to the rest of it:

> *Since mankind harnessed electricity more than a century ago, it has been the fundamental ingredient for everything since. Locally, that is, among those whose electricity is actually turned off, modern life would quickly grind to a halt. There would be no electric lights, no*

heating or air conditioning, no refrigerated food, no kitchen appliances, no televisions, none of the everyday things we take for granted. Automobiles would be cumbersome to fuel, operate and maintain. Elevators, in four-story hotels and forty-story office buildings, would be inoperable. Water and sewage treatment would stop. Schools, hospitals, businesses and industries would close. In short, a hundred years of progress would be wiped out in a few days. Those who could go would leave, those who remained behind would cope or die, and the cities, villages and towns would be left to those who thrive in the dark.

However, because our power grid is an interconnected thing that serves people far outside the region in question, this scenario is unlikely. Power from elsewhere would be allocated to the affected area although it would be interrupted continuously, and rationing of electricity, for a time at least, would be necessary. The existing grid is fragile and overextended, and new infrastructure faces opposition due to aesthetic and environmental concerns. If the power outage spread, and continued for more than a few days, a large segment of the country's economy would be at risk and more would be degraded. The absence of electricity in any significant degree and duration would make the Great Depression, an era when the country was far less populated and connected than it is now, seem like child's play.

According to Baldwin, the apocalypse was only a power outage away. Why had Charles Martin asked for this analysis? Nothing so dire was included in the RCA Report, and even the numbers scribbled in his notebook didn't seem to represent the economic destruction that Baldwin predicted. I looked at Martin's summary again, and shuffled through Baldwin's report, but found nothing in either one that connected the two.

I turned to the phone again. He answered it himself. "Jim Baldwin."

"Tommy Sawyer, Doctor Baldwin."

"Hello. Did the report get there okay?"

"Yes, thank you. Do you have a few minutes?"

"Sure."

"Did Martin tell you why he wanted this study?"

"No. The critical thing for him was the timing. He was presenting his own report to Congress, and he had to have my work before then."

I considered that. Perhaps Baldwin's analysis *was* related to Martin's report. "Did he mention any of the following names?" I read from the summary.

"Not that I recall."

"Did he ask you to consider the likely response to the situation? What the government and the power company would do?"

"We talked about it. It's my opinion that if we were starting from scratch the damage would be irreparable."

"But you wouldn't be starting from scratch. You could just fix whatever was wrong and turn the switch back on."

"Yes. If that happened quickly, it wouldn't be a problem. If it took a day, it would be expensive and inconvenient, but bearable. Every day beyond that would add to the cost, and the quality of life in the affected area would deteriorate. At some point, things would begin to break down."

I hesitated. "This is just a generic power plant, isn't it?"

"Yes."

"Would it make any difference if it were a nuclear plant?"

"It might. It would take longer to fix the problem because of the toxic environment at a nuclear plant, and probably prolong the power outage."

I thanked him and hung up. It was five o'clock and the ritual appetite for alcohol demanded satisfaction, but I pushed it away. It lingered on the edge of my conscious, ready to renew its call as soon as I provided an opening.

I tried to summarize the issues that confronted me. Two people were dead, one abducted and one attacked. A man on the other side of the country may have been murdered. I was convinced that the three women were targeted because of the book, and that Jerry Wallace died because he was mixed up with

Charles Martin, but Martin's death was still murky. There was a project that was going to "pay off," evidence of which someone apparently believed was in the notebook. What was it? Baldwin's report and Martin's notebook were mostly dry statistics from which I could glean no "project," profitable or otherwise. Where was the payoff? And what did the Cuban Consulate and arrows pointing to South America have to do with it?

I needed someone to talk to. I dialed Anne's number and let it ring. She wasn't there. Restless, I left the house and walked to the cemetery. Seated on the bench where I first met Charly, my troubled mind slowed down. I had been on the verge of finally condemning her to the past and now she was in my life again – a full-blown participant, the mother of my child. Was she something more? Was she again the woman I had almost resolved to forget? For a few moments I had entertained the thought that I could make a life with someone else.

The other side of the coin was that, despite Regan, Charly might be a stranger. We had spent an emotional hour or two together, but when the emotion wore off the years would still be there along with all the baggage that we had acquired. The money and the lies would have to be overcome. I refused to believe that either woman would die. What would we do when Charly left the hospital and our daughter returned? The only sure thing was that life would change, and the course of that change would be dictated by the fate of my daughter and her mother.

Surprisingly, I had come to terms with father-hood quickly. When Martha raised the prospect of children, I had refused, and undergone surgery to make sure it didn't happen. An abominable act of unparalleled selfishness, it was the effective end of our marriage, but I never regretted it. There would be no children to disappoint or abuse. I wanted no part of me left behind, and now it was what I wanted most.

I had been at Arlington a few weeks earlier to bury my father. Horribly wounded in Vietnam, he had spent my entire life in a hospital. He learned who I was, and he remembered his wife and her father, but he was unable to handle the day to day chores of living without help. Mother never went to the hospital. Her single visit, shortly after his return, left her so distraught that she never went back.

I called him my father, but that was true only in the biological sense. My grandfather went to see his son-in-law once a month and, when I was at the farm, he took me with him. After a couple of years I, too, refused to go, and our estrangement was – perhaps unknown to him – complete at last. I didn't grasp the magnitude of my self-absorption until later.

My last visit as a child was still vivid. That morning at breakfast my grandfather had announced: "We're going to see your dad today. Take a bath and put on some nice clothes."

We made the trip in silence. It was a warm, sticky day, and the horizon over the pavement shim-mered in the heat. The old man, who never wore anything but an open-collared shirt and khakis, had on a coat and tie. His best hat, the one with the green feather inside the band, lay between us on the seat. I had no tie, but my cleanest white shirt, tucked into my best cord pants, was buttoned to the throat.

The high brick wall at the hospital seemed to go on forever, but at last we turned through an open gate flanked by brick pillars. A black marble panel, inset near the top of the column on the right, was engraved "Veterans Administration 1935." We continued on a narrow asphalt road beneath oaks and poplars that shaded the grass and the walkways and the identical brick structures, and stopped in front of a building identified by a blue metal sign as "BUILDING C."

Inside was a small lobby with wicker furniture and old magazines and a waterless plastic vase containing dusty plastic roses. A painting, without texture or life, hung on one of the walls. It depicted a woman in a white dress with long sleeves and cuffs, and a frilly white cap that tied under her chin. She was ministering to a man prone on a stretcher as bayonets flashed and cannons roared. It seemed singularly unsuitable, even to me.

On the far side of the lobby was a wide corridor that ran the length of the building. Halfway down the hall, we stopped and waited for the elevator. The operator, a one-armed black man, let us out on the fourth floor. We walked to Room 444. His name, behind a strip of yellowed plastic, was on the door.

The room was dark and still, and the hospital smell irritated my nose. The curtains at the open window stirred but only because of a stale breeze from the fan that rotated on a table next to the bed. The man in the bed, clad in bright red pajamas buttoned to the top like my shirt, was sitting up, leaning on pillows stacked against the metal headboard. His eyes were closed.

"Tom?" the old man whispered.

The blue eyes opened. He saw my grandfather and lifted a hand in greeting, his lips forming a smile. The old man looked down at me, and my father's eyes followed. The smile remained, but there was no greeting, not at first. Then he remembered who was coming to visit that day and said, in a voice halting from disuse, "Tommy. It's good to see you. How's your mother?"

Thirty minutes later the old man said it was "time for us to go." His relief was evident, but he said, "Don't go yet. There must be things we haven't talked about." And, of course, there were. We had discussed the weather, and the football team's prospects, and how the corn and tobacco needed rain, and the food, and the thunderstorm expected later that day. That was all the old man, and the man with the empty blue eyes, and I, could say. We were strangers, finally. Blood was not enough. I gave him the magazines my grandfather had handed to me when we left the pickup truck. He flipped one open and stared at it for a moment, then let it slide from his grasp. "It's been good to see you," he said.

I was a child that day, and perhaps the self-pity was understandable. Later, when I was searching for an excuse, he was a compelling, and convenient, explanation for my shortcomings. I made decisions that he might have made and suffered the inevitable consequences, sure that I was right and everyone else was wrong. My mother was always a girl around me, unable to tell me the truth. There was no one to impose limits, to suggest or demand a different course. Even when I was right, I couldn't avoid the feeling that it was fortuitous, a random card drawn in a game that I had never learned to play. When he found out somehow that Mother had died, he sent me a note. Stunned and ashamed, I went to see him, only to find that he was dying. His one wish was that he be buried next to his wife.

I never condemned her. She had herself, and me, to look after, and their marriage was only a brief convention. I was all they had in common. He and I, on the other hand, shared blood and genes – my eyes were blue and my hair was red – and I had abandoned him because he could do nothing for me. Regan would know me and she, too, would have to decide who I would be.

I walked past the miniature Italian villa that served as Oak Hill's gatehouse and continued west to the *Star's* office. Mark still wasn't there, so I helped myself to a copy of the paper and started for home. His story, this time on the third page, had a new angle – the attack on the victim's mother. There was no word from the kidnappers, and Charly's incapacity had stirred up the law enforcement people. Without her around to restrain him, there were hints that Regan's "father," John Winslow, might turn them loose. I had mixed emotions about that. It was four days since the first and only communication from the kidnappers, and their silence didn't bode well. On the other hand, if the cops disregarded their wishes, and those of her mother, an unnecessary death might result. Mark's story didn't mention the notebook.

I considered Winslow again. *He* certainly had a scheme that would pay off. I turned to the financial pages. The value of Mammoth Power and Light stock had climbed steadily over the past two years, and there was a blurb to the effect that "nuclear stocks" were expected to "strengthen significantly" as a result of the report I would present to Congress next week. I took the pages from Charly's envelope and made a rough calculation – his stock was worth more than $5 million. Winslow obviously had an incentive to suppress bad news, and the RCA Report was fashioned to do just that. Had Martin reached the same conclusion? Did Winslow have something to do with his death? What about Jerry Wallace? Once more, I stared at the summary. It was still just a bunch of letters and numbers that I didn't understand, hardly sufficient to call out the Chairman of the Nuclear Energy Authority. Still, he was a felon dealing in the stock of a company that he was supposed to be regulating, and Mark had mentioned some trouble years ago. Maybe there was something there.

CHAPTER TWO

ON SUNDAYS Georgetown resembled the small Southern village that it used to be. The white people dressed up and walked to church, greeting friends and neighbors along the way. There were more churches now, but the select still attended services at Christ Episcopal on the corner of 31st Street and O. The black people wore their best clothes, too, but they no longer walked to Mt. Zion Methodist Church on 29th Street. Forced out of their homes and neighborhoods by the economic segregation that comes with exclusivity and gentrification, Mt. Zion's parishioners were now scattered throughout the District of Columbia and beyond, but they still made their way to Georgetown for a few hours on Sunday mornings.

I climbed the steps and rang the bell. When Mark didn't answer, I tried the door – it was open. Bo greeted me, his curly tail twitching. As I crossed the threshold Mark appeared on the landing above me. "Hey."

"Hey." I looked at my watch. "I'm sorry. I thought you'd be up by now."

"It's okay."

I followed him into the kitchen. Two champagne flutes stood on the counter next to the sink.

"Celebrating something?" I said, looking back at the stairs.

He grinned and took a jar from a cabinet. "Coffee?"

"No thanks." He stirred some coffee into a mug filled with water and crossed the room to the microwave. "Is the *Star* open today?"

"No, but there's always somebody there. Why?"

"I'm curious about a couple of things. I'd like to get into the morgue."

He nodded. "I'll call. Someone will let you in."

"Thanks." I paused. "Have you heard anything about Char – Mrs. Winslow?" He shook his head. I started for the door and stopped. "I read your piece in the paper yesterday. Is Winslow turning the cops loose?"

"He's meeting with the Chief this afternoon."

"Will you be there?" He nodded. "They have the book now. Maybe they'll let her go." I stopped. "I want you to mention it. Tell them the whole story if you have to." I stopped again. "I might get fired or thrown in jail, but I don't want something to happen to Regan because the police don't know."

The *Georgetown Star* had been in business for more than a century. Its morgue, a repository for everything that had appeared in its pages over all those years, was in the basement of the building. I signed the visitor's log, and the young man who admitted me provided a quick tutorial on the index and the machine – it was all on microfilm – and left me alone.

The entries for John Marsh Winslow numbered in the hundreds. After a brilliant turn at Virginia, he had entered the diplomatic corps. Postings in several South American countries followed and, just as he was about to reach the ambassador level at the age of thirty-seven, the President asked him to serve as Assistant Secretary of State. A year later, he was appointed Chairman of the Securities and Exchange Commission and, when a new administration took office, he returned to the State Department, this time as Chief of Protocol. He was forty-one.

During this period, the record was peppered with speculation about a run for Congress. Winslow had been born and raised at The Orchard, a plantation on the Chesapeake Bay in Northumberland County, about eighty miles southeast of Washington. As each election season came and went, the *Star* reported that he was being touted as a challenger to the long-time incumbent, a man named William Jackson. It wasn't until Jackson died, however, in 1994, that Winslow threw his hat in the ring. The *Star* had at least one story a week about him in the run-up to November.

The newspaper's enthusiasm was easy to understand. John Winslow was the darling of Georgetown's cocktail circuit, a social autocracy ruled with an iron hand by Charly's mother, Alison Blaine. Mrs. Blaine also owned a large stake in the *Georgetown Star*. Winslow's name was never absent from the society pages for long, even when he was in Peru or Venezuela, and there were dozens of pictures of him, always accompanied by a different woman, at the Red Cross Ball or the Cancer Benefit or the Celebration for Catholic Charities.

The microfilm ended with a breathless interview, complete with pictures of Winslow standing in front of his ancestral home, three weeks before the election. The next roll began with a one-paragraph announcement of Winslow's marriage to Charly three months later. I checked all the film in the small metal box, including the rolls I'd already seen, and couldn't find the missing months. I found the young man and asked for help. He, too, was unsuccessful. "Do people check these things out?" I said.

"They're not supposed to. If they want something, they're supposed to ask for a copy of it."

"Is there a backup for this?"

"No."

When he was gone I picked up the visitor's log and examined it. The first name I recognized, inscribed two years earlier, was Eli Withers. The second, written less than a year ago, was Charles Martin.

I worked my way through the rest of the Winslow stories up to his appointment to the NEA. They were fewer, and the tone was different. There were references to his withdrawal from the congressional race two weeks before the election, but no explanation why. He disappeared completely from the society pages for almost ten years – the next picture showed him with Charly at his mother-in-law's funeral. After that, he was mentioned occasionally, but always as Charly's husband. Something had happened during those few weeks twenty years before that lowered the value of his stock. A man destined for great things had been relegated to the background. He was still somebody, but not the person he was poised to become.

I returned to the film before and after the lost months and examined them more closely. After the wedding announcement, Winslow's name appeared only once on the second roll. He had been attacked by a man outside the State Department on C Street. The man, whose name was Arthur Mottrom, was unshaven and drunk at the time, and the police put it down to panhandling gone wrong. Winslow had declined to press charges. The last line of the story listed Mottrom's address as Wicomico Church, Virginia. I went back to the first roll and found the pre-election interview. It had been conducted at Winslow's boyhood home, The Orchard, "amongst the rolling hills and woodlands of Virginia's Northern Neck, near the tiny town of Wicomico Church." How many panhandlers journeyed from Wicomico Church to Washington to ply their trade? My guess was zero.

VIRGINIA'S NORTHERN Neck, bounded by the Potomac and Rappahannock Rivers and the Chesapeake Bay, was an isolated part of the state served by one two-lane road – State Highway 3 from Fredericksburg to the bay – down its entire fifty-mile length. Wicomico Church was a mile from the water and a mile from The Orchard. I stopped at the plantation before driving into town. The Georgian house, isolated on high ground above the bay, was a three-story cube of red brick with white trim. It had two entrances, one on the road leading back to Wicomico Church, the other overlooking the Chesapeake. Each one had a two-story portico and columns supporting a pediment. The hipped roof was interrupted by dormers on all sides, two large brick chimneys and, in the middle, a white pedestal topped by what appeared to be an overturned pineapple. Several outbuildings framed the main house.

John Winslow was the last child to know The Orchard. He had sold off the property and given the house to the State of Virginia, which maintained it at taxpayer expense as a "place of historical significance." I considered the import of its history – natives destroyed or forced out, slaves chained to the walls, class and privilege invoked to the bitter end – and wondered at the generosity of the taxpayers. Couldn't they find a past more worthy of their money? Strangely enough, it reminded me of my grandfather's farm, a tedious outpost where the only option was escape. The Orchard, perched on its hill looking down at the bay, also stood for a solitude that, in our ever more connected world, was fast disappearing.

The church that gave the little town its name was a narrow white frame building with a red door, a sharply sloped roof and a tall steeple so out of proportion to the rest of the building that it looked like it might tip over. The signboard planted in the yard offered a cheerful homily and welcome from the pastor, John Mottrom, which seemed providential. I had come to Wicomico Church knowing only that it was a very small place where I might find Arthur Mottrom or someone who knew him. It seemed likely that Reverend Mottrom could help.

The parsonage, also a white frame structure, was next-door. I knocked and waited for a moment, then knocked again. A man rounded the corner of the house. "Can I help you?" he called.

He was tall and slightly bent, probably in his sixties. "Yes, sir. I'm Tommy Sawyer. I'm looking for someone named Mottrom." I pointed to the sign. "I saw your name."

He opened the door and we stepped inside. "Can I offer you something? Water? Iced tea?"

"No, thank you."

We turned into a small study furnished with books and hard mahogany furniture. He sat down behind the desk, and I took a seat on the bench in front of a bare window. "We have lots of Mottroms around here." He smiled. "Which one are you looking for?"

"His first name is Arthur."

The smile disappeared. "Arthur Mottrom?" I nodded. "I'm afraid I can't help you, Mr. Sawyer. Arthur died years ago." He gestured toward the church. "He's buried in our cemetery."

"Were you related?"

"He was my brother."

Something in his voice told me that his brother was a painful subject, but I pushed ahead. "I wanted to ask him about something that happened a long time ago. In Washington." His face remained blank. "He had an – argument with a man outside the State Department. The police –"

He stood up. The conversation was over. "As I said, I can't help you."

"But –"

"Mr. Sawyer. I don't mean to be rude, but I don't wish to discuss it further."

He moved toward the door and I followed. "Did he have a wife? Is she still –?"

He shook his head. "Mary's gone, too. Just a few months ago."

He watched me from the porch as I crossed the churchyard to the parking lot. When I reached the car I looked back. He was gone. I continued past the car to the cemetery on the other side. It was much larger than the usual country graveyard, probably because of its antiquity – some of the stones dated from the 17th century. The dying grass beneath the ancient oaks and poplars was newly mown, and the tributes to the dead – flowers, wreaths, carefully trimmed shrubbery – added color to the canvas of brown and gray.

I found Arthur Mottrom on a knoll overlooking a rushing creek, and sat down on the stone bench beside him. He had died in August, 1995, five months after his encounter with John Winslow. The grave next to his was not yet fully healed. Mary Mottrom had passed away the previous June.

There was one more stone, this one on the other side of Arthur Mottrom:

JAMES BELL MOTTROM
OCTOBER 20, 1976 – OCTOBER 20, 1994

The boy's middle name gave me pause. I thought about returning to the parsonage and decided against it.

Winslow's interview with the *Georgetown Star* had been conducted on October 18, 1994. Two days later a young man died on his eighteenth birthday. News of John Winslow, who had withdrawn from his race for Congress two weeks before Election Day, stopped. The young man's father attacked Winslow in March and died a few months later. The archives that might have explained it all were missing.

The sun was low in the sky. As I passed the church once more, I noticed a plot enclosed by a wrought-iron fence situated directly beneath a window depicting the Resurrection. A marble obelisk rose from the ground, the family name carved in the stone: "WINSLOW." At least thirty monuments of various shapes and sizes surrounded it. It didn't seem to be as well-kept as the rest of the graveyard. There were weeds instead of grass, and several of the markers had toppled over.

I walked past the car again. When I reached the road, I turned toward the single block of storefronts on each side of the street that comprised the commercial district, deserted now, of Wicomico Church. The diner that I was hoping for was at the end, but the sign inside the door said "CLOSED." Peering through the glass, I saw a young woman pass the counter and approach the door. When she noticed me, she smiled and opened it. "I'm sorry, we're closed."

"I'm starving. I have money."

She laughed and opened the door wider. "You don't look like you're starving."

"I am. I haven't eaten all day." I paused. "I'll take leftovers."

She laughed again. "So if you die on an empty stomach, it'll be on my conscience."

"Yes."

She hesitated. "If you're serious about the leftovers, I guess I can feed you." She stood aside. "The church crowd didn't leave much. There's spinach and mashed potatoes and – a piece of fried chicken, I think, and some cornbread. Maybe peach cobbler."

"Perfect."

She pointed at a booth. "Sit down. I'll have to heat it up."

There was a copy of yesterday's paper on the seat. The *Northumberland News* – published twice a week – reported that, with the exception of a potential late-season hurricane, things were slow in Northumberland County. She sat down across from me. "It should be ready in about five minutes. I found a piece of country ham, too."

"Great."

She extended her hand. "I'm Alice Poole."

I took it. "Tommy Sawyer. I really appreciate this. No kidding."

She nodded. "We don't get many visitors around here, especially on Sunday afternoons."

"I came to see a man named Arthur Mottrom."

I watched for a reaction and saw none. "We have plenty of Mottroms but I don't recall hearing about an Arthur."

"How about Bell? Do you know any Bells?"

"No."

"Are you a native?"

She shook her head. "I'm from the southern part of the state. South Boston."

She was small and fine-boned, and the short blonde hair framed her face. She wore no makeup or jewelry – the only color in her face were large green eyes under dark brows. "What brought you to Wicomico Church?"

"A man." She looked out the window. "He's gone and I'm still here." She rose and went into the kitchen. Seconds later she reappeared, carrying a large plate of hot food and a smaller one with lettuce leaves and tomatoes and two little tubs of French dressing. She set them down in front of me. "What do you want to drink?"

"Do you have any milk?"

She nodded. When the carton of milk had been delivered she resumed her seat and watched me eat in silence. As the last bite of cobbler disappeared, she said, "Where are you from?"

"North Carolina. I live in Washington now." I put down my napkin. "That was very good. My compliments to the chef."

"I'll try to remember to tell him. I only work here on weekends."

"What do you do the rest of the time?"

"I'm a nurse. And –" She picked up the newspaper, folded it to the second page and handed it to me. The headline read "Pot Farmers Indicted," and the byline was "Alice Poole." Another reporter. "I'm also the Wicomico Church correspondent for the *Northumberland News*."

"All the news that's fit to print?"

"Don't laugh. Small towns aren't what they used to be. Pot farms, dope labs, the occasional home invasion. You'd be surprised."

I nodded. Small towns had horrors of their own, but rampant criminality had once been tamped down by the judgment of neighbors. Now villages like Wicomico Church were infected with the same noxious norms – a product of the one-note clamor for unremitting self-gratification that our so-called "culture" demanded – as everyplace else. Their tiny populations made it worse. The picture on the front page was *always* the man next door. Norman Rockwell had morphed into Hieronymous Bosch, and there was no place to go. "How long has the *News* been in business?"

"I don't know. A hundred years? I've been there five."

"Does the paper maintain any kind of archive – microfilm, past issues, things like that?"

"We keep past issues bound in big canvas books."

"How far back do they go?"

"1942, I believe. They started keeping them during World War II."

"So the ones for, say, 1994 and 1995 would be there." She nodded. "I'd like to see them. Do you think we could –?"

She shook her head. "The office is in Heathsville, which is thirty miles away. It's closed and I'm tired." She paused. "You could go up there tomorrow."

I hesitated. I needed to be at the NEA tomorrow, and I wanted to pick up my pictures at the drugstore. "I think there may be something important in those old papers. If I'm right, it'll be a big story. It's yours if you'll help me."

IT WAS eight o'clock when I turned into the driveway off Olive Street. Anne Clark was sitting on the redwood bench. She stood and raised her hand. I met her at the door. "Hi. What brings you up here?"

"I'm always lonely on Sundays. I thought I'd see if you were, too." She thrust a bottle still in the bag toward me. "I brought your wine."

"Thanks." Inside, I searched for a corkscrew, trying to cover my confusion. Charly had reappeared, and the uncertain resolutions I had reached a few days earlier were muddled. I poured a glass and handed it to her. "I need to call Mark. Do you mind?" She shook her head. As I dialed the number, a tiny alarm went off in my head that nearly caused me to hang up, but it subsided when he came on the line.

"Hello."

"Mark, Tommy. What happened at the meeting?"

"Nothing. Charlotte came to this afternoon and everything was deferred." I closed my eyes. The weight that I had carried unconsciously for the past two days lifted. My pleasure at this news confirmed what I had refused to acknowledge, that nothing had changed. She was more to me now than ever. Mark continued: "They won't let anybody see her, not even Winslow, and he won't do anything she might hold against him later, especially where Regan's concerned."

"Any word from the kidnappers?"

"No. Did you find what you needed at the morgue?"

"Sort of." I paused. "Do you know when she can have visitors?"

"It'll be at least a couple of days."

"Did you tell them about the book?"

"Yes."

"And?"

"The Chief said he'll want to talk to you when the investigation cranks up again."

"What about Winslow?"

"He didn't say anything."

"Okay. Thanks."

Anne was sitting in the kitchen. She lifted her glass. "Aren't you having any wine?" I shook my head. "Who do you want to visit?"

Flustered, I avoided the question. "I was just asking about Charlotte Winslow. Did you know that she was attacked Friday night?" She nodded. "She's regained consciousness. They weren't sure that she would." I stopped, searching for further justification. "I know her daughter." I sat down at the table.

"What have you been doing all weekend?" she said.

Most of my activities would sound pretty silly to her unless I divulged the reason for them, and that was a long story I wasn't ready to tell. "Not much. I talked with a fellow in New York who was writing a report for Charles Martin. Do you know anything about that?"

"No. What was it?"

"It's an economic analysis. What would happen if part of the country lost power."

"It must've been for the RCA Report."

I hesitated. "Remember when I asked Ames about CRAC?" She nodded. "Are you sure it doesn't mean anything to you?"

"Yes."

"I came across some information that might be related to Hanford. Was Martin working on a project out there?"

Her expression changed for an instant and I thought a bell had rung. "No. Not that I know of."

Her features were back in place, but somehow the answer didn't ring true. Something *was* going on at Hanford, and she knew it. Why not say so? She had another glass of wine, and we talked for a few more minutes, but the mood in the room had shifted. Whereas before she had seemed ready to settle in for the evening, she now wanted to leave and was trying not to show it. When she finally rose to go, her movements were slow, almost exaggerated, but once through the door she all but ran down the driveway. I was relieved, and pondered where she was going in such a rush.

CHAPTER THREE

I SPREAD the six black-and-white photographs on the counter. They were virtually identical – a crowd of people standing in front of a building I knew well – except for the dates imprinted in the lower right-hand corners. In addition to the Renwick Chapel, a Gothic structure located near the entrance to Oak Hill Cemetery, each picture had something else. Two men stood slightly apart, facing each other, one with his back always to the camera. Each man extended a hand toward the other, as if they were about to shake hands. The images were too small to make out the features of the man facing the camera. The other one always wore a hat and raincoat with the collar turned up, so he was completely anonymous. I was disappointed. I had imagined that these pictures would answer questions instead of raising others. Someone was waiting behind me so I scooped up the photos and stepped aside.

A moment later I approached the man behind the counter. "Can these pictures be enlarged?"

He shuffled through them. "Yes."

I pointed. "Would they be big enough to see this face?"

"Yes." He looked again. "They were shot with a zoom lens. You might lose some resolution."

"When can they be ready?"

"The best I can do is Wednesday afternoon." I would be on Capitol Hill all day tomorrow. Wednesday would be soon enough. "Okay. Thanks."

On my way to work, I considered the dates on the pictures. They had been taken at seven-day intervals from July 19 to August 23, and I was certain that each date was a Saturday. Sight-seeing tours were conducted at Oak Hill every Saturday beginning at 4:00 P.M. The chapel was one of the attractions, and the crowds shown in the photographs looked like tourists. It seemed unlikely, however, that the two people I was interested in had joined the tour six weeks in a row just to see the sights.

I spent the morning working on the prepared statement that I would read to both committees tomorrow. It was as innocuous as the RCA Report itself, and I resented the part I was playing in Winslow's scheme, but absent any evidence that it was fraudulent rather than just optimistic, I didn't see a choice. I considered whether or not to mention his recent stock acquisitions and decided against it. I would wait for Regan and Charly, and do what they wanted to do.

After lunch, I called the hospital again and was advised that Mrs. Winslow was still not taking calls or seeing visitors. I was expecting her husband to raise hell with me about Martin's notebook, so when Jane knocked on the door and announced a visitor, I was pleasantly surprised to find that it was Amanda Bliss. The blue suit she wore covered her completely and was neither especially short nor tight, but it didn't matter. A suit of armor couldn't blunt her appeal.

She sat in the chair in front of my desk and crossed her legs. I decided to look. If she wanted to tease me, I would be teased. If, for some reason, it was more serious than that – temptation, maybe – I would be tempted. The neurons were snapping inside my head, and my conscience was nowhere to be found. "I want to coordinate what we're going to say tomorrow," she said. I nodded – we were teammates. "Has the report been delivered yet?"

"Yes. It went to both committees this morning."

"Were there any changes to the one I saw last week?"

"No."

She handed me three typed pages bound by a staple. "That's my statement. Can I see yours?" I pushed it across the desk and began to read. I was surprised to see a few criticisms of the NEA, but marked it down as a lukewarm pretense to the traditional antipathy between union and management. My statement, which had already been approved by Ames, criticized no one. She looked up. "You catch on pretty fast."

"We aim to please."

She stared at me. "You've never done this before, have you?" I shook my head. She looked at her watch. "I'd like to go over the whole process with you, but I don't have time right now. Why don't you come by my place after work and we'll talk about it?" Thus did Circe extend her invitation and I, without sword or potion or advice from the gods, accepted it.

When she was gone I crossed to the window and looked down at Constitution Avenue. I compared Charly to the woman who had just left my office. Her sexuality was every bit as powerful as that of Amanda Bliss, but she kept it under wraps. Accustomed to the prim capitulation of girls like Martha, Charly's abandon and almost greedy desire had surprised me but they were contained, reserved for those she selected. Amanda, too, could pick and choose, but her task was harder because no man who saw her doubted that she would choose him. I shared the common optimism, but wondered at the benefits.

The phone behind me rang. "Hello."

"Tommy?"

"Yes."

"It's Alice Poole. I've found the things you wanted."

"Good. Can you fax them to me?"

"Sure."

"Terrific." I gave her the number. "Thank you, Alice. I'll be in touch."

I went to Jane's desk and stood by the fax machine. After a moment it came alive, and a minute later it began to push out sheets of paper. I plucked each one as it emerged. They were all from the pages of the *Northumberland News* – three obituaries and news stories from July, 1994 to August, 1995.

I arranged them in chronological order. The first story, dated July 5, 1994, recounted a campaign swing by John Winslow through the Northern Neck, followed by a description of his participation in the area's Fourth of July celebrations. There was a picture of Winslow with one of his local volunteers, a smiling young man with large eyes and delicate features named Jimmy Mottrom. Another man in the photograph looked familiar, but I couldn't place him.

A week later, Jimmy Mottrom was in the news again. He was going to Washington to work at Winslow's campaign headquarters. There was none of the usual reticence of a teenage boy beginning a great adventure. I could feel his excitement from twenty years away. "I almost passed out when Mr. Winslow called me," he told the reporter. "I'll just die if he doesn't win."

There were more campaign stops in August and September, and young Mottrom often accompanied the candidate. Another picture appeared with the account of a speech given in Chesapeake Beach, a few miles east of Wicomico Church, on the first of October. The change was startling. There was no smile, and the sunken eyes that stared into the camera resembled those of a wounded animal begging for peace. I read the caption and story more carefully to be sure it was the same kid. Another article that day reported the arrest of Arthur Mottrom for public drunkenness and disorderly conduct. The Sheriff had been called by someone at The Orchard, where Winslow was staying. There was no mention of Jimmy Mottrom.

An account of Winslow's interview with the *Georgetown Star* was front-page news on October 21, and Jimmy Mottrom's obituary appeared a few days later. I shuffled through all the pages again. There wasn't a word, anywhere, about how he died. I picked up the phone. "Alice, it's Tommy."

"Hi."

"None of this stuff says how James Mottrom died."

"I know. I went back and looked again. There's nothing in the *News* about it."

I hesitated. "Is anyone there who was around back then?"

"No. The paper changed hands about seven years ago."

"Do you know who owned it in 1994?"

"Yes. It's in the banner on the editorial page of these old papers."

"What's it say?"

"It says, '*The Northumberland News*, a *Georgetown Star* publication.'"

I considered. "Do you get another paper down there? A bigger one?"

"The closest big paper is the *Richmond Times*. Some people take the *Norfolk Tribune*."

"Can you –?"

"I have friends at both papers. They use my stuff sometimes. I'll check with them."

"Thanks."

I started to hang up. "Tommy?"

"Yes?"

"The guy that looks after these books told me that I'm the second person in the last two months who was interested in Jimmy Mottrom."

"Who was the first?"

"He couldn't remember his name, but he worked at the Nuclear Energy Authority."

"Ask him if the name Charles Martin rings a bell."

She was back a moment later. "You were right. It was Charles Martin."

Martin's actions were becoming clearer. The microfilm missing from the *Star's* morgue, probably stolen by Eli Withers, had set him on the same path I had taken. "Thanks."

I turned back to the boy's obituary. It was short and largely dedicated to his family and his church. There was no mention of his work on the Winslow campaign.

The rest of the news articles detailed the precipitate decline of Arthur Mottrom. He was depicted as a dangerous drunk, maybe a lunatic, even though he had never been in trouble before the incident at The Orchard. He had farmed his family's land for twenty-five years before his son went to work for John Winslow. The *Northumberland News* was a rural newspaper that treated the members of its community gently when they erred, except for Arthur Mottrom. His obituary was shorter than his son's. They were the last of their branch of the family except for the preacher at the church. According to her obituary, Mary Mottrom was also survived by a brother.

Jane knocked on the open door. I looked up as she placed two faxes on my desk. One of the cover sheets was from the *Norfolk Tribune,* the other from the *Richmond Times*. Both of the stories were essentially the same and the photographs were identical – a young man hanging by the neck from the limb of a large live oak. The building in the background was unmistakably the main house at The Orchard. Jimmy Mottrom had died by his own hand. There was no note.

I picked up the phone again. "Alice? I need one more favor."

RICHMOND VIA I-95 was just short of two hours away. The *Richmond Times* was housed in an old brick building a few blocks east of the James River. Alice's friend led me to the morgue, also located in the basement. After finding the microfilm for the period in question, and making sure I could work the machine, she left me alone.

I moved quickly through the final months of the campaign. The coverage was not as lavish as the *Star's,* but the editors and reporters at the *Times* clearly believed that John Winslow was the man for the job. There was a reprint of the *Star's* October interview, including the photographs, and an editorial endorsement the same day. A rally planned for the following evening was canceled with no explanation.

I read again the report of Jimmy's death – it was just a few paragraphs. Winslow and his staff had returned to Washington right after the interview, leaving Jimmy behind. An "unnamed spokesman" for the campaign said that he planned to rejoin them "for the final push" after a few days with his family. Five days later Winslow withdrew from the race, citing exhaustion and trouble raising money. Neither excuse seemed likely. He had radiated confidence, and talked at length about the generosity of his campaign donors, in the interview with the *Star*.

The announcement of his withdrawal was the end of the *Times'* coverage of the Winslow campaign. I was surprised and disappointed again. The *Star's* missing microfilm had convinced me that the end of the campaign had something to do with Jimmy Mottrom's death, something that might help unravel my own mysteries. I turned back to the withdrawal story. There was a grainy photograph with it – Winslow at a podium flanked by three unidentified members of his campaign staff. The face of the man immediately to his left was partially obscured, but I thought I recognized him. I flipped through the fax pages that Alice had sent until I found the picture of Jimmy Mottrom, the happy one. The same face appeared in that photograph, looking over the boy's shoulder. His hair was thin and combed over his head, and the eyes were recessed behind folds of fat, but the photo was so bad that I still wasn't certain.

I leaned back and closed my eyes. Even if my suspicions were true, it was just another irrelevant, uninformed, factoid like those in Martin's notebook. I knew no more about the connection between Jimmy's death and Regan's disappearance, if there was one, than I did before.

I looked back at the index and checked for more stories about Mottrom. There were none for "Jimmy," and one for "James" – a brief account of the inquest dated October 28, 1994, by Zack Collins, the same reporter who'd written of Jimmy's death. The verdict was suicide by hanging, and the only thing out of the ordinary was a request by the Mottrom family doctor to testify, which was denied.

I climbed two flights of stairs to find Alice's friend, an attractive young woman named Barbara. "I'm finished downstairs. Thank you."

"Did you find what you were looking for?"

"Well – not exactly. Do you know someone named Zack Collins?"

"Yes. He's our Managing Editor." She pointed to a large cubicle in the corner, topped by frosted glass. "That's his office."

"Thanks." I turned in that direction.

She stopped me. "He's not there. He won't be back until Friday."

I hesitated. "Would you give him a message for me?"

"Sure."

I wrote a short note and handed it to her. "Thanks again. I appreciate it."

AMANDA OPENED the door. "Hi, Tommy. Come in." She wore a long red dressing gown, and her perfume was subtle, vanilla or maybe tea olive. "Would you like a drink?" I shook my head. "Sit down. I'll be right back."

I crossed the elegant room, pushed the sliding glass door open and stepped onto her balcony. Despite the hour, traffic was still heavy in both directions on the Francis Scott Key Bridge. Looking south, I could see the Kennedy Center awash in spotlights though the building itself was dark. Between them the primitive gloom of Mason's Island, its thick hardwood forest black against the artificial illumination beyond, was an isolated reminder of what had been everywhere a few hundred years before. The marina was busy. Pleasure craft and fishing boats crowded the river. Immediately beneath me, people passed to and fro on the boardwalk, and mingled at the outdoor cafes. When she stood beside me, I spoke, still staring across the river. "What can I do for you, Amanda?"

"I'm sorry?"

"What can I do for you?" I turned to face her. "I don't want you to go to any trouble. Just tell me what you want."

She smiled. "It's really no trouble. In fact, I was looking forward to it."

"So was I."

"What made you change your mind?"

"I'm not sure." I paused. "I stopped making decisions a long time ago. If a choice was offered, I refused it. I accepted a status quo that was only changed by somebody else."

"Somebody like me?"

I grinned. "Well – I won't pretend that there were many like you." I looked down at the marina again. "After a time all the little changes changed everything. There was a new status quo, and the process repeated itself." I turned my head. "I guess I've decided to stop that. You're the first choice."

She took my arm. "Let's sit down." We walked into the living room. "I really *was* looking forward to it. If you change your mind, let me know." I nodded. "Are you sure you won't have something to drink?"

"No, thanks." I sat down in a chair next to the fireplace. "Does Gordon have a sister?"

"Yes. Or he did. She passed away recently."

"Where did she live?"

"I'm not sure. Somewhere on the Virginia coast."

"You know him pretty well, don't you?"

She nodded. "I wouldn't be here without him. He found me in a shack in Mississippi and got me into Hopkins, and made sure I graduated from college and grad school. And my first job in the nuclear power business was his doing."

"Why?"

She smirked. "Not for the reason you think." She paused. "Gordon's a saint. He believes we're on the verge of calamity, and he blames John and Eli and – Walter Bright."

"Whose side are you on?"

It took her a moment to answer. "I haven't decided."

"How long has Gordon been at the NEA?"

"This time around? About two years. He came back to the agency right after John became chairman."

"Did they know each other before?"

She hesitated again. "I don't know. Why?"

"No reason." I paused. "Do we really need to talk about the hearings? Isn't the fix already in?"

"Yes, it's in, but we have to do it anyway. It's part of the game. We pretend to do the people's work, and they pretend to believe it."

"Why?"

"Why do they pretend to believe it?" I nodded. "I don't know. I guess it's too much trouble not to." I nodded again. No one wanted trouble, including me. As soon as the thought crossed my mind, though, I realized that it was false. I'd come to Washington to *cause* trouble, and so far I'd come up short. Rather than stick my finger in Winslow's eye, tomorrow I would foster more of the corruption that I claimed to despise, and enrich him in the process. The search for Regan, completely unlooked for when I came here, was all I had left.

Ten minutes later, she walked me to the door. Standing in the open doorway, I said, "Was a complete power failure ever considered while the report was being drafted?"

Her face, animated seconds before, was blank. "How complete?"

"No electricity at all for an extended period of time."

She seemed to force a smile. "No. That scenario was never a part of it."

IN AN earlier incarnation, I always arrived ahead of time to check the lay of the land. Sometimes it was a conference room or a council chamber, but most often it was a courtroom. I wanted to know what the place was like without the people who belonged to it. They were comfortable there. To the extent that I, too, could become acquainted with the battleground, their advantage was diminished.

The hearing at the House was scheduled to begin at 10 a.m. It was 8:30 when I climbed out of the cab at the corner of Independence Avenue and South Capitol Street. Membership in the House of Representatives had been frozen at 435 since 1929 but, like the rest of Washington, the growth of empire there had continued apace. The Longworth Building was one of three office buildings erected south of the Capitol to contain the ever-expanding apparatus of "the People's House." Its architecture was Neo-Classical. Because of the sloping site, the granite foundation varied from two to four stories, and the façade was the ubiquitous white marble. It had five porticos, all with columns supporting a broad beam. Four of them were topped by a frieze and cornice and the fifth, through which I entered, was crowned with a pediment.

I consulted the directory for the Assembly Room. Ordinarily the lair of the Committee on Ways and Means, it had been borrowed for today's hearing to accommodate the crowd. The door was locked. I found a nearby policeman who let me in. The Assembly Room was typical of Washington – banal symbolism gone to ruinous excess. Molded swags of ribbons and foliage, and plaques and classical masks, adorned the walls. Gilded stars encircled the ceiling, and four monumental eagles – framed by plaster sunbursts and cornucopia overflowing with flowers and fruits – surveyed the room from atop a marble platform. The upper and lower rostrums, where the committee and its helpers would sit, were made of walnut, barely visible behind more eagles, wreaths and stars. Portraits of past worthies looked down from places designed especially for them. Despite the pretense, it was still a government building, and the dominant smell was disinfectant.

I toured the room, sitting in the Chairman's seat and the one that I would occupy – behind a table in front of the marble balustrade that separated the participants from the onlookers – before dropping into a chair at the back of the gallery. The committee staff began passing in and out, arranging microphones and glasses and water pitchers. They saw me, but didn't speak. Photographers started to assemble their lights and tripods, and the first spectators, anxious to secure a good seat, drifted in.

My brief career in Washington was coming to a close. I would remain until Regan was found and Charly decided, and be guided by whatever they did. However that turned out, beginning tomorrow my participation in the gold rush was over. I had been in shambles for a long time, but it was an honest disarray. At that moment, I wished for a hand grenade, even though it was certain that someone in this town would profit from the destruction.

THE CONGRESSMAN from Ohio – the next-to-last solon to speak, and maybe get his picture in the papers back home – droned on. I had read my statement and answered a few perfunctory questions from the Chairman, and then it was Amanda's turn. After that, each member of the committee read *his* prepared remarks – utterly predictable depending upon which side of the nuclear divide he stood – and asked a few more questions, most of which I passed on to Gordon Bell, who was sitting between me and Amanda. The tedium was relieved by occasional heckling from the audience. Each protester was allowed to unfurl his banner, shout out his objection to the proceedings, and have his picture taken before being ushered from the room. The gallery was full at the beginning, but there were gaps now. Winslow remained in his seat in the second row, and Withers sat directly behind us.

"Mr. Sawyer?" I struggled to re-focus. The speaker was a woman from Kentucky who, I recalled, was doubtful about nuclear power. She was seated on the lower rostrum in the last chair on the left. "Mr. Sawyer?"

"Yes, ma'am?"

"I'm concerned about these waste pools. There's nothing about them in this report, is there?"

"No, ma'am."

"Why not?"

"We were told to analyze a reactor meltdown." I smiled.

"But won't that impact the waste pools?"

"I'm – not sure."

She frowned and looked at Gordon. "Mr. Bell?"

"The same loss of power could affect the waste pools, Congresswoman."

"How?"

"The pools would boil off like the reactor, only slower."

"What do these pools look like?"

"They are mostly rectangular, like large swimming pools, and between forty and fifty feet deep."

"How much waste do they hold?"

"They are designed to hold approximately two thousand spent fuel assemblies."

"Designed?"

"Many of them now hold twice that many."

"Why?"

"There's no place else to put them."

The Congresswoman from Kentucky hesitated. "Isn't that – dangerous?"

Bell shook his head. "Not as long as adequate precautions are taken."

"But if something did happen?"

It was Bell's turn to pause. "Because the fuel assemblies are much more densely packed than we would like, a loss of power – really a loss of cooling water – would be more serious than otherwise."

"They would melt down and burn and explode just like the fuel in the reactor?"

"Yes – slower."

She shuffled through the paper in front of her. "These pools are not inside a containment building like a reactor, are they?"

"No. They are protected by conventional structures."

"Structures more likely to be damaged if a problem arose? Like an earthquake?"

"Yes."

"And more likely to permit contaminants to escape?"

"Yes."

She stared at him. "The pools at Hanford are even worse, aren't they?" she said softly.

I felt Bell stiffen beside me. He turned his head toward the Chairman who was speaking in low tones to the ranking member. "Congresswoman, I'm not sure I should –"

"Answer my question, please."

"We – we don't really have waste pools at Hanford."

"Storage tanks, then. There are 177 tanks full of the worst –"

The Chairman's gavel cut her off. "I'll remind the gentlewoman from Kentucky that she's treading on classified ground." An aide whispered in his ear. "Your time has expired, Madam."

She didn't even turn her head. "Just another minute or two, please." She looked at me. "You're a lawyer, aren't you?"

"Yes, ma'am."

"When a judge orders you to do something you do it, don't you?"

"Yes, ma'am."

"Do you have a copy of the order that required you to prepare this report?"

"I'm sorry, I –" Bell slid it in front of me – I'd never seen it before. "I have it now."

"I'm on page twenty." She waited for me to find it. "Paragraph fifty-five says, and I quote, 'The analysis shall include the Authority's best estimate of peak early fatalities, peak early injuries, peak deaths from cancer and property damage.' Did I read that right?"

"Yes, ma'am."

"I find none of those things in your report."

I considered denying actual authorship of the RCA Report, but Bell saved me from that ignominy. "Congresswoman, the data don't permit us to make those estimates," he said. "We were given a deadline. This was the best we could do in the time we had." She began to argue with him and I tuned back out. Minutes later, the Chairman thanked us, the audience, the press and his committee members "on both sides of the aisle," and gaveled the hearing to a close.

Amanda leaned across Bell and said, "Tommy, you were great. Let's have lunch."

I shook my head. "I'm not hungry. What time are we due at the Senate?"

"Two o'clock."

"You go ahead. I'll see you there."

I remained in my seat as the room emptied. What I really wanted was a martini, but something was nagging at me. As I started to rise, a young man approached. "Mr. Sawyer?"

"Yes?"

He handed me a few sheets of paper. "That's a copy of the protocol that will be followed this afternoon and a seating chart of the senators." He paused. "I'll be in the hearing room a few minutes early if you have any questions."

"Thanks."

I flipped idly through the pages. The diagram showed a single curved rostrum with twelve names arranged around it: Mr. Allen of Florida, Mr. Carlisle of Washington, Mr. Joseph . . . Mr. Carlisle of Washington? I removed Martin's tattered summary from my pocket and stared at it: Twelve names beginning with Allen, Carlisle and Joseph. And PEF, PEI, PDC, PD, and V. The judge's order was still open to page twenty. I looked again at paragraph fifty-five: Peak early fatalities, peak early injuries, peak deaths from cancer, and property damage. Martin's "project" was now obvious. Someone at the NEA, probably Bell, *had* performed the required analysis and it wasn't pretty, and the only nuclear plant in Washington was Hanford.

At that moment I lamented my refusal to carry a cell phone, but I found an ancient pay phone in the hall – change came slowly to Capitol Hill, too. The rough voice answered: "Roller."

"Jack, Tommy Sawyer."

"Hey, man. You must be a mind reader. I just got off the phone with the coroner."

"What did he say?"

"Wallace was unconscious before he drowned."

"Murder?"

"It looks like it."

Another killing confirmed. "How many storage tanks do you have out there, Jack?"

"What?"

"How many of those storage tanks do you have?"

"One hundred seventy-seven."

"Thanks." My wish had been granted. I shoved everything into my briefcase and raced down the stairs. A cab pulled up to the curb to let its passengers out. "19th and Constitution," I said to the driver. "Hurry."

WALTER BRIGHT smiled down at us. "We appreciate you folks from the NEA coming up here today. I know you've already been examined thoroughly by our friends on the other side of the Hill –" a few titters from staff and audience greeted this sally "– so we'll try to get you out of here early."

I rose. "Thank you, Mr. Chairman." I picked up a sheaf of paper. "There was an error in the document we sent up yesterday. I have the correct information here. If you'll permit me?"

"Of course, Mr. Sawyer. Go ahead." Bright turned in his chair and began speaking to one of the staff.

"Thank you, sir." I left the table and handed each senator the pages that Jane had finished typing a few minutes earlier. Bright's copy was unchanged. I gave the extras to the reporters sitting to the right of the rostrum. Mark, smiling, got the last one. I glanced at Winslow and Withers, both now seated behind us, as I returned to the table. They were frowning. I sat down and began to read my statement. There was a flurry in the ranks of the newspapermen, and several of them left the room. The senators, too, began to stir. One of them – Mr. Carlisle – interrupted me.

"Mr. Sawyer, excuse me." He held up the new pages. "Are you saying that this is now part of the NEA report?"

"Yes, sir."

"But – this is impossible. This says that millions of people could die in a nuclear accident."

"Yes, sir." I saw Bright out of the corner of my eye, frantically shuffling through the report. "That's our best judgment of the deaths, injuries and damage that would occur in the event of a meltdown. And we believe that almost half the waste at Hanford has leaked into the groundwater." The murmurs that had started when Carlisle mentioned "millions of people" became louder, and the senators spoke to one another and tried to join our conversation. Bright rapped his gavel repeatedly, with no result. People rushed from the room.

Carlisle continued: "Why haven't we been told about this before? It can't be new –"

I felt a rough hand on my shoulder. "You son of a bitch!" I turned. Eli Withers, his face contorted, was pointing a gun at me. "You bastard. I'll –" I lashed out at his arm as the gun exploded. It fell to the floor and was lost under the chairs behind him. He disappeared through the door before the stunned room could react. Winslow, too, was gone. I stood still for a second, trying to decide if I'd been shot. When I turned around, Amanda lay on the floor. A vile red stain spread across her breast, and blood bubbled from her lips. Bell knelt beside her, clutching her hand, tears coursing down his cheeks. The room, so frenzied a moment before, was quiet.

I GAZED out the window of the cab as we drove past the White House toward Georgetown. I had remained until the medics wheeled Amanda's body from the room, half-expecting to be arrested for something. When I finally rose to go, I noticed her briefcase – the one I had carried to the car a week before – lying beneath the table. I picked it up and walked to the door. A Capitol policeman noted my name, address and telephone number, but I was otherwise unimpeded.

"You might want to get out of here for a few days," said Mark. "Why don't you go home until all this settles down? Everybody in town will be after you."

"I don't think so. I'll manage."

"Suit yourself. How did you find out about that report?"

"I found the key to Martin's notebook."

"What was it?"

"The senator's names." I stopped. "Anybody else in Washington would have seen it immediately. Regan did." I paused again. "And the judge's order confirmed it." All of that was true, but I didn't really *know* I had it right until Withers tried to kill me – stock in Mammoth Power and Light would undoubtedly be toast in the morning. We stopped for a light by the hospital. I tapped the driver on the shoulder. "Pull over here." I turned to Mark. "What's her room number?"

"Four eleven. But they won't –"

"I'll see you later." I crossed the street and pushed through the revolving door. There was a florist's shop in the lobby. I bought all the yellow roses he had and took the elevator to the third floor. I walked up and down the hallway, noting the location of the stairwell, Room 311 and the nurses' station. If I was lucky, the nurses and Room 411 would be in the same places on the fourth floor, and I could take the stairs and reach her room unobserved.

I was lucky. I stepped into the dark room and closed the door. Charly was asleep. She was pale and drawn, but the care in her face was gone for the moment, and she was again the girl in our make-believe world. I welled up and fought the tears until I realized that they were for Amanda. *We* still lived and so, hopefully, did our daughter. We had a future, whatever it was, something I had despaired of before I came here. Amanda was going home to Mississippi in a box.

I stuffed the roses into an empty pitcher and filled it with water. After one last look, I turned for the door. Her voice reached me. "Who is it?" I grasped the knob. "Tom?"

"Yes." I returned to the bed. "Don't talk, Charly. Please."

"Regan?"

"She's fine. Don't worry."

"Good." I bent to kiss her. "The notebook. I –"

"Don't worry about that, either." I hesitated. "Did you tell anyone that you had it?"

"No, but –"

"Don't talk, Charly." I reached the door. "Go back to sleep. I'll see you in a day or two."

"Good."

I took the stairs all the way to the lobby and stepped out onto the sidewalk. In truth, I was terribly afraid for Regan. Winslow and Withers and – and maybe Mark – were the kidnappers. She had been taken because she knew what the notebook contained. Their scheme had been thwarted, and Regan's silence was no longer important. Rational kidnappers would let her go, but Withers was out of control. He had already killed in the presence of several hundred witnesses, in an area thick with cops of every variety. It seemed likely that Jerry Wallace was another casualty of his ambitions. Other questions remained – the photographs, for example, and Baldwin's report – but I didn't care about that. All I wanted was to find Regan and whatever future was left. Arriving at the carriage house, I glanced at my watch. It was only five o'clock. It seemed like years since I had climbed the steps to the Longworth Building.

CHAPTER FOUR

MUCH AS I wanted to wash my hands of everything but Regan, it was impossible – Martin's notebook remained at the center of her disappearance, and much of it was unexplained. Odd things in the notebook had not been answered by the revelations on Capitol Hill – the map of Cuba, for instance, and the telephone number. Baldwin's analysis might or might not have been commissioned for the real report, but its apocalyptic predictions had not yet been disclosed. And who knew what the photographs might reveal tomorrow?

I sat down at the kitchen table and opened Charly's envelope again. The yellow receipt from the *Star's* courier service was on top. I sighed. Was it another example of my inept interference? Would Regan have been taken if she had the notebook to bargain with? The remainder of the envelope's contents, except for the last three pages, dealt with the transfers of Mammoth stock. The three legal-sized pages in back appeared to be a deed written in Spanish. Private property in Cuba was abolished after Castro's revolution, and the better chunks had been doled out to the Communist faithful. The rest was controlled entirely by the government. I had just enough Spanish to decipher the transaction – it was a grant to the Mammoth Land Trust of a one-half interest in real estate located in Santiago de Cuba Province. The grantor, or seller, was the Cuban Ministry of Defense. Someone, in a pencil parenthetical, had helpfully translated the property description: five hundred acres in the heart of the Sierra Maestre Mountains.

The same pencil had been used to scribble a note on the last page:

> *Regan – This is all I could find. It is for your head only. Do not mention its existence.*
> *B*

An envelope was stapled to the deed. There was no addressee and no stamp, but the return address was "Consulate of Cuba, 2630 16th Street, N.W., Washington, D.C."

The Mammoth Land Trust, presumably a creation of Eli Withers and maybe John Winslow, was co-owner with the Cuban Defense Ministry of considerable property in a remote, isolated corner of the Republic of Cuba. Given the state of relations between the United States and Cuba, ownership alone was probably illegal. There was no conceivable legitimate purpose for such an arrangement, and there was a good chance that it was more consequential than a stock swindle. Martin's map had been marked up in the same location. Was that really why he was killed? More to the point – had Withers discovered that Regan had the deed?

Against all odds, Eli Withers had disappeared. He'd been traced to Reagan Airport where he boarded his private helicopter, lifted off the ground and climbed into the clouds. Apparently, he was still there. John Winslow was missing, too, but the search for him was more leisurely. His crimes were not yet known, but his stewardship of the National Energy Authority had been called into question. The senators and congressman were flabbergasted – shocked – at the dangers posed by nuclear energy, and they wanted answers. The vast scale of the pollution at Hanford was outrageous. The iron rule of politics – first, find someone else to blame – had been invoked in spades. Winslow's absence made the finger-pointing easier. Walter Bright, in particular, was furious about the "cover-up" at the NEA, and promised a thorough investigation by his committee. There was some speculation about how Withers had managed to get the gun through the elaborate security in the Longworth Building, but the political debacle crowded everything else out. Amanda's death was almost lost in the posturing.

Mark had called the night before to renew his suggestion that I hide out in New Hope, and I had again declined. The conversation turned to Regan. "It has to be Winslow and Withers," I said, looking for a reaction. "She knew something and they had to shut her up."

"The CRAC Report?"

"Maybe. Maybe something else."

"What?"

"I'm not sure."

He hesitated. "So Winslow kidnapped his own daughter?"

Already accustomed to thinking of Regan as *my* child, I didn't understand him at first. "What?"

"Are you saying that Winslow kidnapped his own daughter?"

"Uh – yes. I don't think there's a lot of love lost there."

He sounded doubtful. "Well – if you're right, what happens now?"

"I don't know. If it was the stock deal, that's over. Why not let her go?"

He changed the subject. "Are you going to work tomorrow?"

"I don't think so. It'll probably be a firestorm over there. Ames might shoot me." He laughed and hung up.

I pushed the newspaper away and rose to pour another cup of coffee. I was in limbo until there was some word about Regan. My eye fell on Amanda's briefcase, so full it barely closed. Was she part of it? She seemed to be the only one with any influence over Withers. I unfastened the metal clasp and stacked the contents on the table.

Hundreds of typed pages were divided into four categories: "Inspection Reports," "Reactors," "Safety Procedures" and "Triggers." I looked through them. The "Triggers" pages were brief. A different nuclear power plant was listed, followed by one, two or three names, depending on the number of reactors. I counted – there were seventy-nine plants and 104 reactors.

"Safety Procedures" were forms detailing the drills that each plant was required to perform periodically, all completed within the past few weeks. "Inspection Reports" were just what they seemed – more forms prepared within the last fifteen days detailing the condition of the equipment at all seventy-nine plants. They were split into components: reactors, pumps, generators and so on. All reflected deficiencies, some described deterioration as "dangerous" or "unsustainable." I closed my eyes and tried to recall the list of regulations at the back of Martin's book, all with the number 104 beside them.

"Reactors" reverted to inexplicable jargon. I selected one and read a single paragraph over and over again without any understanding of what it meant. I flipped through the others – they were equally unintelligible. No one outside the nuclear fraternity would know what was being communicated. The pages for each reactor included several diagrams with panels and buttons labeled with numbers or colors. They were connected with solid and broken arrows that doubled back on themselves, and the final sentence for every reactor estimated an "elapsed time" of three, four or five days. The end result, if there was one, was beyond me.

I found my own briefcase in the living room and examined again the items I had removed from Martin's notebook. The summary had been explained, but one of the telephone numbers required further examination. I looked at Martin's list and dialed the number. "Cuban Consulate."

"Extension 452, please."

"Just a moment."

The female voice answered again. "Tourism and Commerce."

Who would I be – Winslow or Withers? I tried to pitch my voice. "This is Eli Withers. Let me speak to Gomez."

Another voice came on the line. "Eli, where are you?"

"I –"

"Wait. Don't tell me. I don't want to know. Every policeman in town is looking for you." He paused. "I'm still waiting for the money and the last compact disc. We can't finish the cascades without them."

I spoke through a pretend cough. "I know."

"Our clients are anxious for progress. I'll expect your man at the usual place this week." He hung up. Despite the fact that Eli Withers had killed Amanda Bliss and fled, the Cuban Consulate's Mr. Gomez still needed money and disc to finish the cascades – whatever they were – and he expected Withers to provide them. I stared at the telephone. Another trip to the morgue at the *Georgetown Star* seemed to be in order.

An hour later I peered into the film reader again. I had only glanced at John Winslow's early diplomatic career during my initial visit to the *Star's* archives. His first posting was to the U.S. Interests Section in Cuba, in December, 1980, but he seemed to spend more time in Washington than Havana. Early on, Winslow's name appeared in the paper only once or twice, but it was during this period that he met Alison Blaine. After that, he was mentioned often in the *Star*, and the pictures with Mrs. Blaine and her party always depicted him wearing a tuxedo and holding a martini glass. I scoured the pages for Roberto Gomez, and didn't find him.

Charly had mentioned Winslow's recent trips to South America. In the course of his career he had become an expert on the region, posted to Peru, Columbia and Venezuela between 1984 and 1991. His good press continued, and he received his share of accolades from the host countries and the State Department. A significant promotion loomed.

About to move on to the film for 1992, when Winslow returned to Washington, I came across a series of stories that weren't included in the index. Various armed groups, espousing some flavor of Marxism and terrorizing city and village alike, had tormented the South American continent for years. One of those, with cells inside Columbia and Venezuela, was called the National Liberation Army. It was closely aligned with the regime in Cuba, and its favorite tactic was to kidnap a prominent member of the favored class and hold her hostage, not for money but for recognition, particularly from the world's media. They were rarely disappointed. Each time the terrorists put out a photograph or press release, news-papers, magazines and television networks fell all over themselves publicizing the group and its "griev-ances." It became theater – even the hostages seemed to play a role.

A few weeks before Winslow was scheduled to leave his post in Caracas, the pregnant wife of a pro-vincial governor was kidnapped and the dance began. There was great concern for the child, despite assur-ances from the terrorists, because of the isolation and conditions in which the victim was held. John Wins-low, a distinguished diplomat beginning to consider politics, offered himself as a substitute, an offer that was quickly accepted. Attention from the United States was the Holy Grail for these groups.

The publicity machine at the *Georgetown Star* leaped into action. Reporters and photographers were dispatched to the Venezuelan jungle to get the story. Rather than sneer at the "running dogs" of the most bourgeois nation in the history of the world, the National Liberation Army cooperated completely. It was like a documentary about boot camp. Winslow, always accompanied by one of his minders, was de-picted rising, eating, exercising, reading, eating, working, eating, sleeping. The photographs posed him and his smiling captors debating the fine points of their opposing ideologies and, not surprisingly, the terrorists' creed received the lion's share of the newsprint. After six weeks, the government paid a modest ransom and Winslow was freed. Everyone was happy. The terrorists gained legitimacy, Winslow was a hero, and the *Star* had burnished its broad-minded bona fides. There was no mention of Roberto Gomez.

The arrows on Martin's map extended from the eastern tip of Cuba – where the Mammoth Land Trust and the Cuban Defense Ministry owned five hundred acres – to Columbia, Venezuela and Peru, the three other countries where John Winslow had done his diplomatic service. According to Charly, Winslow returned to Columbia and Venezuela every year to see old friends. Who were they? I tried to remember the acronyms that accompanied Martin's arrows, and failed. And then I recalled something else: Eli Withers had accompanied Winslow on his most recent trip.

I stuffed my notes into a briefcase, turned off the machine and returned the box of film to its cabinet. Outside, rain was coming down in buckets. I met Mark on the steps. "Looking for me?" he said.

"Uh – yes."

He pushed through the door and I followed. His "office" was a large cubicle in the corner of a big room not unlike the Managing Editor's space at the *Richmond Times*. He dropped into a chair behind the desk while I remained in the doorway, leaning against the frame. "What's up?" he said.

Until now, it had not occurred to me that Mark might be involved in whatever was going on in Cuba. I had assigned him to the stock swindle and maybe Regan's kidnapping. I decided to test him. "I think it's possible that Withers and Winslow are involved with terrorists."

"Really? Why?"

His surprise seemed genuine. "There was a map in Martin's notebook. It connects something in Cuba to Latin American terrorists. Winslow used to know some of those groups. Charly told me he goes down there several times a year."

"Charly?"

"Mrs. Winslow."

"Oh." He grinned. "That's all pretty circumstantial. Do you have anything else?"

"No. I thought you might have heard something."

He shook his head. "If you're right, it'll probably come out when they find them. Withers is a dead man, and so is Winslow, politically. The bodies will be very closely examined."

THE ENLARGED photographs didn't help very much, although the identity of the two men was pretty certain. The one facing the camera, Withers' "man," was undoubtedly George Ames. The man with his back turned had to be Gomez. Whatever was being exchanged each time could not be seen despite the aid of a magnifying glass, but it was flat, almost certainly one of the discs that Gomez needed. Charles Martin obviously had irons in the fire other than the stock deal. He was trying to horn in on the Cuba project, too. Why was Ames involved? It was easy to believe that he was planning to cash some Mammoth stock. He was a cheerleader for the nuclear power industry and he'd signed off on the RCA Report, just like Winslow, but this was something else entirely.

Rather than return to the carriage house, I walked to the bottom of 31st Street and approached Regan's apartment building. The sound of automobiles on the freeway above K Street was magnified by the silence of the abandoned storefronts and warehouses not yet reclaimed. The Potomac River was less than a hundred yards away, and the glowing façade of Arlington, Virginia, hovered over the brooding darkness of Mason's Island. A boat moved up the river – its wake slapped the dock and bulkhead. The new apartment building at the bottom of the street, its concrete and windowalls a jarring contrast to the historical "preservation" next door, loomed over its neighbors like a tsunami poised to consume them. I took the elevator to the sixteenth floor.

There was now a notice on the door denying entry to "all unauthorized persons," but I unlocked it and crossed the threshold anyway. The mess was serious, but manageable – unlike the Martins' house, the disarray was selective. The contents of the drawers in the kitchen and living room had been dumped on the floor, chairs tipped over and cushions rearranged, but complete chaos had been avoided. The bedrooms and baths were barely touched. It looked like a half-hearted effort to replicate the disorder on Prospect Street. Something about that troubled me, but I didn't know what. The view was almost identical to Amanda's.

I wandered through the rooms without purpose. The motive behind this gentle wreckage had to be the notebook, and it was gone. I looked in the closets and vanities, vaguely embarrassed at the breach of Regan's privacy, and finally sat down at a café table in the kitchen. The pages of a desk calendar, opened to the day she disappeared, had escaped the attention of the kidnappers. I turned them backward idly, my mind on the futility of everything I had done. My hand grenade on Capitol Hill had shed a little light on the corruption, but everything else – everything that mattered – was darkness. There was a notation on Friday's page – the last day I spoke to her, the day she sent me the notebook: "Dinner at Mr. Smith's – 7:00 P.M." Presumably that was the "engagement" she had mentioned when I, ignorant of who she was, suggested a drink after work. It was an odd way to describe a date. Who was Mr. Smith? Regan had not been missed until the following Monday, but maybe he could provide a clue. Maybe Charly would know.

Outside again, I crossed a grassy median to the boardwalk, sat down at one of the tables and ordered coffee. I had assumed that Regan was abducted to prevent the disclosure of the awful impact of a nuclear meltdown, as well as the Mammoth stock deal. What if that were wrong? What if she had followed up on the deed and discovered something even more serious? If that were the case, the threat to her might be more urgent, too. There had been no word for eight days. I rose and turned for home, and refused to consider the possibilities.

"HELLO."

"Tommy?" It was Mark. "We've had a message from the kidnappers. They want $10 million." I bowed my head for a moment – Regan was still alive. "Tommy?"

"Wow. Does she really have that kind of money?"

"Yes. The bag man's supposed to go to Arlington tomorrow at noon and look for further instructions."

"Have you got somebody to do it?"

"We don't have a choice."

"What do you mean?"

"The kidnappers have already picked him."

"Who is it?"

"You." I nodded. It was Withers – it had to be. Nobody else would have specified me for the job. I had deprived him of his Mammoth profit, and now he would take it from Charly. "All right. Is the money ready?"

"It'll be delivered to my office tomorrow morning. The police are staying away."

"I have to see her before I do this, Mark."

"I'll check with the hospital. Stand by."

He called back a few minutes later. "Go to the hospital at five o'clock today. You have fifteen minutes." He paused. "She doesn't know about this yet. She told her lawyer what to do about the money last week."

"Okay. Thanks." I put the phone down. It rang again before the receiver had settled onto its cradle. "Hello."

"Tommy, it's Gordon Bell. I just got off the phone with Winslow."

"Where is he?"

"He's at his old plantation house on the coast. The Orchard."

"Is Withers with him?"

"He says not. He was, but not now. Winslow says he's afraid."

"Of what?"

"Withers. He told me that Withers is crazy. He's threatening – and these were Winslow's words – to make Chernobyl look like the Fourth of July."

I closed my eyes. "Is that possible?"

"Certainly. Our plants are designed to stop trouble from the outside. Someone *inside*, someone who's trusted, can wreak havoc."

"Did Winslow mention Regan?"

"His daughter?"

"Yes."

"No."

He wouldn't, of course. It might implicate him in her kidnapping. "What are you going to do?" I said.

"I'm waiting to make sure that my guess is correct. Then I'm going down there." He stopped. "I could use some help."

I hesitated. "I can't. There's something very important that I have to do tomorrow morning."

He was silent. "Well, I guess I could call the police, but –"

"Don't do that." Withers would kill Regan at the first sign of the law. "Gordon, listen. We had a note from Regan's kidnappers today. I'm delivering the ransom tomorrow."

"What's that have –?"

"I believe that Withers and Winslow are the kidnappers. If I'm right, she's going to be in the middle of this."

There was a long pause. "So," he said at last, "I might see you there after all."

"Yes. And I don't want anything to happen to her."

"Tommy." He paused again. "A serious incident at the plant I'm thinking of would kill more than 45,000 people very quickly, and many, many more over the next several months. People hundreds of miles away would be sickened. This is about more than a single girl."

I knew that, of course, but all those people were strangers. Regan was *mine*. We talked logistics for a few minutes in case we ended up in the same place, and hung up.

CHARLY WAS asleep. The room's clinical décor and offensive smell, justified by specious claims of hygiene, did not make her feel better, and – according to the nurse – she had insisted that they let her go home. Her doctor – undoubtedly assuming the mien of Solomon that he had studied in medical school and honed for years – had apparently ignored her at first, then responded with patronizing bromides. Finally, grudgingly, he considered her request. It wouldn't do, of course, for the patient to dictate to the doctor – the medical industry might not survive – but Charlotte Winslow was rich and powerful, and it wouldn't do to offend her either. As a consequence, she was going home tomorrow, still cosseted in the cocoon of all the people and paraphernalia that the best science could devise, but half a loaf was better than none.

She opened her eyes and touched me. "Tom."

I took her hand. "I hear you're going home tomorrow." She nodded. "That's great. I have more good news. So is Regan."

She listened as I explained the coming adventure. I hoped that the lighthearted tone would reassure her. It recalled other times when we had been truly carefree. We had lived our lives a day at a time then, but the future, for me, was assured. I knew now that she had not shared my certainty. In her innocence, she had welcomed the prospect of a child – she would marry the father and live happily ever after – but her pregnancy had been used as a weapon to bring her to heel.

The nurse leaned in the door. I kissed her on the forehead and said, "I'll see you in a day or two." The child she had denied me for twenty years needed help. I was going to rescue our baby, and all of our lives depended on it.

"Tom, wait. The notebook –"

"The notebook doesn't matter anymore. Don't worry about it."

Her forehead wrinkled. "But – did you know that John took it?"

"What?"

"I'm sure he did. I left it on my dressing table. When I went back for it, it was gone."

I CLIMBED the hill past O Street and turned into the driveway. No one answered the bell but the lights were on so I tried again. I thought I heard voices – or whispers, or giggles – inside, and sounds of movement, but when Mark opened the door he was alone. I had come to apologize for my suspicions – silently, since he knew nothing about them. I was relieved to have my friend back. "I'm feeling a little nervous," I said. "I know you have something that'll help."

He grinned. "I have a very old bottle of scotch – make that a bottle of very old scotch – I've been saving for a special occasion."

"Great." I followed him into the study, smiling at the perfume that lingered in the air and the red muffler draped over the chair. "I believe that from now on I'll call before barging in on you." He produced the scotch and went to the kitchen for ice. I shifted a load of dry cleaning in its plastic sheath from the sofa to the chair and sat down. "Do you know George Ames?"

He handed me a glass. "All I know is that he's Anne's boss. Why?"

"There were some negatives in Martin's notebook. I took them to be developed. The only person I recognized for sure was Ames."

"What was he doing?"

"The pictures are almost identical. They were taken at Oak Hill in front of the chapel. Ames is giving something or taking something from another man in every one of them."

"You didn't know the other man?"

I maintained a little caution. There was no need to mention Gomez now. "I'm not sure. He always has his back turned."

"Do you have them with you?"

I shook my head. "I think Ames might have been in on the deal with Winslow and Withers."

He rose and looked out the window. "What deal?"

"You know – the Mammoth stock deal. He was certainly in a position to know about the two reports. And the problems at Hanford." I paused. "The next time you see Anne –" I smiled again "– ask her about it, will you?"

He turned away from the window. "Sure."

"What time does the money arrive tomorrow?"

"Ten o'clock."

CHAPTER FIVE

I OPENED my eyes and looked at the clock – 3:00 A.M. Sleep was another narcotic, and it was years since I interrupted it to consider what came next. I went to the kitchen and started some coffee. A full moon threw the shadow of the open shades onto the table, creating a distorted grid that might really be a puzzle or a labyrinth. I looked out the window. It was snowing – the ground was covered, the shrubs bent, the bare black and white branches etched into the lighted sky. I hoped it would stop soon. Despite the sophisticated veneer, Washington was still a Southern town unable to cope with the whims of the weather. Snow meant gridlock or abdication. The streets would be full of cars going nowhere, or there would be no cars at all. In the latter case, the government stayed home and the country was safe for another day. I prayed that it would not impede my quest.

My hand shook as I stirred sugar into the coffee. I was under no illusions about the coming ordeal. It would not be a simple exchange of money for girl. Withers hated me, and would kill me if he had the chance. My only shield was the money. Assuming he really wanted it, he would let me close enough to save her if I could. I shook my head at the folly of imputing logic to Eli Withers. A man who could threaten nuclear carnage would do anything.

The documents from Amanda's briefcase were still on the kitchen table. I piled them up and opened the case. Two binders that I had overlooked before – one blue, the other white – were still inside. The blue one contained the prepared statement that she had read to the House committee three days earlier. The white binder was larger. The first document was a report entitled "Calculation of Reactor Consequences Analysis" – CRAC. It provided the same details as Martin's summary – deaths, injuries and property damage – for every nuclear plant in the country. The summary for Pennsylvania – Senator Bright's home state – was right on top: "Four plants, eight reactors. Fatalities – 464,000. Injuries – 1,616,000. Cancer – 250,000. Property damage – over $1 trillion." The potential "death and destruction" was staggering, and I made a mental note to forward it to the Congress-woman from Kentucky.

The rest of the white binder was less straightfor-ward. There were copies of inspection reports like those I had already seen plus six nearly identical let-ters, on NEA stationery, from Gordon Bell. They were addressed to men in various parts of the country called "Regional Operations Managers." Each letter was four pages, single-spaced, and only the para-graphs referring to separate reactors and plants dif-fered. Otherwise, they all referenced NEA regula-tions – the same as those cited in Martin's notebook – and the "chronic failure" of the equipment – reactors,

turbines, generators – to comply with those regulations. The final paragraph, a single sentence in capital letters, was also the same: "ALL PREVIOUS
WAIVERS GRANTED BY THE CHAIRMAN OR
HIS DESIGNEE WITH RESPECT TO THE
ABOVE-REFERENCED EQUIPMENT ARE
HEREBY RESCINDED." Gordon's name was typed
on the last page but there was no signature, and none
of them were dated. As far as I could tell, the letters
covered every commercial nuclear plant in the country.

I ordered my thoughts. Had they been signed
and sent and, if so, what was their import? Was the
NEA cracking down at last? Had Gordon contemplated a coup? I shook my head. Tomorrow was all
that mattered. The Nuclear Energy Authority, and
the mischief it condoned, was no longer my concern.

About to lay it all aside, I noticed a sort of chart
drawn in a feminine hand on the inside cover of the
white binder. At the top were the words, "Fail-Safe –
Tuesday, October 28, 2014 – 5:00 P.M., Eastern Daylight Saving Time." The rest was a complicated series of arrows and dates that began on October 28 –
the day that Amanda and I testified on Capitol Hill –
and culminated on Sunday, November 2. The third
day, Friday, was circled in red.

I was unsure of the meaning of "fail-safe," so I
rose and found a dictionary in the bookcase. The first
definition had something to do with machinery, but
the second one looked more promising: "An act to
refrain from, or discontinue, a plan of attack, usually

military, upon the occurrence of certain predetermined conditions." I looked at my watch. It was still very early in the morning on Thursday, October 30, 2014. The time for fail-safe, whatever it was, was long past. What was coming?

I LEFT the car near the old mansion and started down a steep hill made treacherous by the snow. The black leather bag slapped against my leg, and the revolver in my coat pocket created a slight tilt in my gait. I had protested the gun – I'd never fired a hand-gun, and the .22 I once used to shoot rabbits at the farm was lost to time – but Mark insisted. "Withers will have a gun," he said. "You have to defend yourself." The snow had stopped, but the deserted streets were wide open all the way to Arlington. It looked like a graveyard now instead of a garden. The ground was covered in a shroud of white pierced by markers, visible only because of their shadows, as far as the eye could see.

I had collected the money at Mark's office earlier that morning. The black case was sitting on his desk when I arrived. He raised the flap. "Would you like to see what $10 million looks like?" I glanced at the thick green bundles piled to the top of the bag, a distillation of the wealth that might stand between me and the new life that was within my grasp. While I was certainly unhappy about Regan's abduction, the truth was that I would be glad to spend the money.

The anonymity imposed by the frozen winding sheet would have made my destination hard to find but for the small bright flame that rose from the gravesite. The snow had been brushed away from a blue-gray stone almost level with the ground. A brown envelope held in place by a rock rested on top of the marker. I stepped over the chain that surrounded the burial plot and picked it up. The directions inside were terse: "The Orchard."

I walked back to the car. I was right, and so was Bell. He had awakened me with his call and said he was on his way to The Orchard, where he hoped to find Winslow and news of Withers. He had narrowed his list of targets to one. "Mammoth operates three of the largest commercial plants in the country," he said. "Two in Virginia and one in Maryland. The biggest one is Deep Creek, on Virginia's Eastern Shore. It's directly across the bay from The Orchard. It has three reactors. If Withers is going to monkey around with one of his plants, it'll be Deep Creek."

"Why?"

"The reactors at the other two plants are undergoing inspection and maintenance. And Deep Creek has just installed brand-new fuel assemblies."

"Are the other plants shut down?"

"No. They're just operating at reduced capacity."

"Both of them?"

"Yes."

"Isn't that unusual?"

"Not necessarily. The operators will take what they need from the grid until their reactors are back up."

I recalled Baldwin's report. "Doesn't that overload the system?"

He laughed. "Since when are you an expert on power plants?"

"Have you told them about Withers?"

"I called a few minutes ago." He paused. "Everything's normal right now. They haven't seen Withers." I wanted to ask him about the police, but decided not to. He told me anyway. "I haven't called the authorities. Withers might be bluffing, or I might be wrong, and any unnecessary interference with the plant's operations would cost millions of dollars."

I pondered that for a moment. "Too expensive?"

I could feel the smile. "Yes. And the reactors are undergoing procedures that I don't want to stop."

SOMEONE WAS sitting on the bench beside Arthur Mottrom's grave. As I drew nearer, I saw that it was his brother. His head was bowed and he had a black book in his hands. As I slowed my pace, he looked up and closed the book. He rose when I reached him. "I'm looking for a man named Gordon Bell," I said. "He's supposed to meet me here."

He nodded. "He asked me to tell you that he's gone ahead. He'll see you at The Orchard."

"Thanks."

He resumed his place on the bench. I turned away. "Mr. Sawyer?"

I looked back. "Yes?"

"Gordon came here to say goodbye."

"Why?"

"He didn't say. Most of his people are buried here." He pointed to one of the markers next to Arthur Mottrom. "Mary was his sister."

We were quiet for a moment. "What happened to Jimmy Mottrom?" I said.

He didn't answer. I turned again to leave. "That *man* –" he barely got the word out "– made him his – his plaything. He used him like a girl and when he was finished he cast him aside like a piece of garbage."

"Is that why he hanged himself?"

He shook his head again. "Jimmy *died* because everybody knew, and he was ashamed and – and we were ashamed. Nobody condemned the monster who preyed on him, not in public. We knew who John Winslow was. We blamed Jimmy instead." He paused. "It was easier."

I gestured toward a tombstone. "And his father?"

"Arthur was the worst. Part of him wanted to kill Winslow, but part of him believed that Jimmy brought it on himself. He turned his back on the boy and said terrible things."

"Gordon Bell was Jimmy's – uncle?"

"Yes."

I hesitated. "Is there a telephone I can use?"

He pointed toward the house. "In the kitchen." He was still sitting on the bench when I left a few minutes later. As I settled behind the wheel, I considered Gordon Bell. Had he come to Wicomico Church to stop a maniac from murdering thousands of people, or to settle an old score? Or both? And why did he have to say goodbye?

THE OLD house perched against the sky like a raptor scanning the horizon for rotting flesh. I parked next to Winslow's car and sat for a moment, pondering the conundrum. I had invited death for years though I was too cowardly to actually embrace it, and now I didn't want to die. I reached for the bag and decided to leave it. I could always come back for it if that's what Withers really wanted. I felt for the gun in my pocket, glad that Mark had made me take it, and left the car.

The front door was ajar. I heard voices raised and, rather than blunder inside, I walked around the side of the house and peered through a window. There was nobody there, so I moved on to the next one and looked into a central foyer lighted by a massive crystal chandelier. The only furniture was a high round table in the middle of the room. The floor was several steps up from the ground which required that I tilt my head to see.

Three men stood around the table. Bell and Withers were shouting at each other. Winslow, next to Withers, clearly wished he were somewhere else.

Suddenly, Withers stepped behind Winslow and threw an arm around his neck. At the same time, he raised his right hand above the level of the table, revealing a long-barreled revolver. He pointed it at Bell and fired. Bell slumped against the table and produced a weapon of his own. Two more shots rang out in quick succession, and Winslow dropped to the floor. Withers turned toward the back of the house.

I hesitated, then made for the rear portico, drawing the gun from my pocket. Withers burst through the back door and raced toward the edge of the cliff. I raised the pistol and pulled the trigger. Nothing happened. I tried again – still nothing. By the time I switched the safety off, he had vanished. I peered gingerly over the edge. Withers was near the bottom of a flight of wooden steps that ended at a narrow dock stretching into the bay. Two boats floated beside it. He tossed a rope onto the deck of the larger one and leaped on board. I finally squeezed off a shot that he ignored and, seconds later, the boat backed away from the dock and turned east.

I looked back at the house. Nothing stirred. Steeling myself, I climbed the steps and passed through the open door. I looked at Bell first. He was bleeding heavily from a wound to the side of his head. I took a piece of linen from the table and pressed it to the shallow groove that the bullet had created. After a minute or two, he opened his eyes. "What –?"

"Hold this to your head, Gordon. He almost missed." I rolled Winslow over and felt for a pulse.

There was none. Something inside me cheered. One of the obstacles I had worried over had been removed, and one of the lower forms of the species had been eliminated. I looked back at Bell. "Where's Regan?"

"He said she's at Deep Creek."

Another figure appeared in the doorway. I turned the gun in that direction. "Please don't shoot me, Tommy." Alice Poole stepped into the room.

I gestured toward Bell. "See if you can stop the bleeding, Alice. I'll be back." I searched the house just in case. Regan wasn't there and there was no sign that she had been. I would go on to Deep Creek.

IT WAS a good thing that Gordon Bell kept a boat on the water near his old home town – the drive, south to Norfolk and across the Chesapeake Bay Bridge, was almost two hundred miles. By water, Deep Creek was only thirty miles away. We stepped down to the dock carefully. Bell clung to the rope railing. Alice had bandaged his head, but he was still shaky and the white hair retained sticky patches of red.

I looked back as we stepped onto the boat. Alice waved. I had promised her a story and now she was part of it. Bell had refused to let her come with us. We were leaving her behind to deal with Winslow's death and get word to the people on the Eastern Shore that calamity was headed their way. He had tried to call from the house, but the line was dead and there was no cell service. "Wait," I said. I climbed the stairs and ran to the car. As I reached for the bag, I noticed something in the front seat of Winslow's car – the attaché case he'd held in his lap at the hearings on Capitol Hill. I tossed it into my trunk. Seconds later, I returned to the boat with the black leather bag.

I watched him as we got underway. The little professor I had laughed at a few weeks earlier had proved a different fellow altogether. "Were you trying to shoot Withers or Winslow?" I said.

He looked around. "It didn't matter. But I wish it was Withers."

"So he couldn't sabotage the plant?"

"Because he killed Amanda. He's already sabotaged the plant."

"He's already been there?"

"Yes."

"What's he done?"

He fiddled with a switch and a couple of knobs and joined me at the back of the boat. "It'll take us an hour to get there." He lifted the top of a bench, produced a bottle of bourbon and handed it to me. I twisted the cap off and took a pull, then gave it back. He turned it up, swallowed a couple of times and stowed the bottle away. We settled back as the boat cut through the dark water. The air was damp, and the scent of the sea grappled with the fumes from the engine. "There are dozens of safeguards built into our plants, but the ultimate protection against accident or – or sabotage is the people who work there. People back up the machinery everywhere." He paused. "It's easy for an insider to create trouble, but he has to do something with the people first."

"How could he do that? He can kill one or two, but –"

"Ordinarily he couldn't, but we've done it for him."

"What do you mean?"

"We've always had evacuation drills, but they were limited as to time and distance. The plant's workers didn't go very far or stay away very long, and key people remained behind. You'll recall that the RCA Report recommends a new drill. In our obsession with the appearance of safety, it requires that *all* plant personnel be removed at least ten miles, and be kept at a protected location for twelve hours. One of Winslow's public relations moves was to override the usual vetting and immediately add it to the protocols for our plants."

"And Withers has started the drill at Deep Creek."

"Yes."

"Everybody's gone?"

He shook his head. "The guards on the outer perimeter are still there, but they have no idea what's going on inside the plant. We'll have to be careful. They're trained to shoot first and ask questions later." He paused. "All that's left are the mechanical safeguards."

I hesitated. "Is Withers crazy?"

"Probably. But he has a plan."

"What is it?"

"I don't know the details, but Charles Martin told Amanda that he thought Withers was going into the bomb business."

I nodded. "Why would he create a Chernobyl at Deep Creek?"

"You mean besides the fact that he's crazy?"

"Yes."

"It would throw the world into turmoil. The NEA would be gutted by the politicians." He grimaced. "It's far from perfect, but it's better than no regulation at all. If that oversight was removed, there would be a vacuum for a while, and traffic in things necessary to build a bomb would be much easier."

"So what's he done?"

"I'm not entirely sure. He might have disabled the power supply inside the plant, or the reactor pumps, but a boil-off would take too long. I think he's probably reset the valves on the reactor's water piping."

"What will that do?"

"It'll remove water from the reactor vessel, and keep fresh water from going in. It's the quickest way to drain the reactor."

"Which will cause the fuel to overheat and melt."

"Yes. And it's very hot fuel." He paused. "There are automatic interlocks inside the fast-drain paths from the reactor that cannot be overridden when it's in operation. They close the drains when the water level is still four feet above the top of the fuel." He checked his watch. "From what he said that probably happened about three hours ago."

"But that's not the end of it?"

"No. The slow-drain paths have no interlocks. It's just a question of how quickly they drain. When the top of the fuel assemblies are uncovered, the increased heat will initiate a boil-off and quicken the loss of water."

"Is he on his way back there?"

"I think so. Probably because of the girl."

"Can we stop it if we get past Withers?"

He stared at me, a strange expression on his face. "Yes. I can stop it."

"What are you going to do?"

"I'll reset the valves so that the vessel holds water again, and shut down the reactor."

"How long will that take?"

"A few minutes for the valves, a few seconds for the shutdown."

"A few seconds? I thought it took days to shut down a reactor."

"In the normal course of things, it does, but this is an emergency." He paused. "All I have to do is push the SCRAM button."

"SCRAM?"

"Yes."

"What does that do?"

"It cuts the power to the control rods and drops them into the reactor."

"So it's just a quicker way to turn the reactor off?"

"Yes, but it's only used in emergencies. It takes months to restart a reactor after an emergency shutdown." He paused. "It's very – involved."

We sat without speaking. Night had already fallen, and the sky was indistinguishable from the sea. It was a prelude, one fixed by the speed of the boat, and we had time on our hands. "Do you remember when we talked about enriching uranium?" I said.

"Yes."

"What's so secret about it?"

"Why do you want to know?"

"I think Withers is up to something, too."

He nodded. "We enrich uranium in machines called centrifuges. They separate the isotopes in raw uranium and isolate those we need for the reactors. The secret is the design of the machine and the mix of uranium and gas that produces the enriched product."

"What do they look like?"

"A centrifuge is a hollow cylinder that rotates very quickly. Thousands of them are tied together, and the gas flows from one to another, becoming richer with the necessary isotope as it goes."

"Is that called a cascade?"

"Yes."

"Who has the secret?"

"Well – the enrichment plant, of course, but it's like everything else. The NEA is ultimately responsible."

"Does somebody want it?"

"Every rogue regime on the planet."

"And Withers?"

He nodded. "Yes. You can't make nuclear bombs without highly enriched uranium."

I hesitated. "I came across some letters from you this morning. They seemed to be telling the plant operators that the waivers for their old equipment were revoked. Is that right?"

"Where did you find them?"

"In Amanda's briefcase."

He nodded. I waited for an answer to my question. When it didn't come, I said, "Has some new program started? Is something happening tomorrow?"

He smiled. "Yes."

"What is it?"

"You'll find out tomorrow."

We were quiet again. "I talked to Reverend Mottrom this afternoon," I said. "He told me about Jimmy." He made no answer. "Is that why you didn't mind shooting Winslow?"

"It's one of the reasons." He stopped. "Some eighteen-year olds are men – not Jimmy." He looked away. "I was surprised at his courage, if that's what it was."

"I guess his father didn't –"

"Arthur Mottrom was a decent man who knew nothing beyond his church and a narrow little community of five hundred God-fearing souls. Anything other than that was alien and – and evil." The bitterness in his voice was palpable. "Jimmy was different, so he had to go. He just took the wrong way out." He frowned. "The fact is that Winslow died too easy. I wish he'd lived, for a few more days at least."

He returned to the bow of the boat and adjusted the wheel. We were quiet as a strip of lights up and down the Eastern Shore began to materialize. "Gordon?"

His voice came from the dark. "Yes?"

"Is it worth it?"

"What?"

"The nuclear genie."

"I believe it is. If people would just get out of the way we could have a nearly infinite supply of cheap, clean energy."

"People?"

"Politicians. Agitators." He laughed. "Capitalists."

"Isn't that how it started? You and your friends knew better?"

He laughed again. "You're a hard man, Tommy Sawyer." He paused. "I know this. The business as usual at our commercial plants is a much greater threat than Deep Creek. We could make it far more efficient than it is now, and find a place to store the spent fuel until we can figure out how to dispose of it. We already know how to reduce the radioactivity of the waste, and some day we'll build reactors that don't produce any. It's just too – expensive right now." He stopped again. "But they won't let us. It'll take a catastrophe for them to understand."

"Are you expecting one?"

He didn't answer. Instead, he pointed to a cluster of light three hundred yards ahead of us. "That's Deep Creek." He throttled the engine down. "We'll go in quietly. There may be a guard." He handed me a plastic bottle. "Take as many of these as you can stand."

"What are they?"

"Potassium iodide. For the radiation."

I swallowed half a dozen pills. "Aren't you going to take any?" He paused, then shook his head. "Why not?" He didn't reply.

It was just past five o'clock when Bell cut the engine entirely. We floated silently to the dock and tied up next to Withers' boat. The landscape looked like the set of an old science fiction movie – domes and towers and tall square buildings reflecting light with a greenish tinge, all surrounded by layers of fencing topped by razor wire. Suddenly, I felt the cold. "Ready?" he said. I nodded. "What about that?"

"That" was a black leather case containing $10 million that I'd been dragging around like a bag full of dirty laundry. It represented a substantial portion of Charly's wealth, and yet she had handed it over without a word, and I had almost forgotten about it twice. In a world where gold was everything, this particular chunk seemed to have lost its glitter. Still, it was barter for my child. I picked up the bag and stepped onto the dock.

I nearly fell over the guard. He was laying face down, dead. We left the dock and ran for an open gate. "Oh, God," said Bell, pointing to one of the three reactor buildings. Great clouds of steam, littered with glowing red and yellow particles, rose from its dome into the sky. "The discharge has already started. Hurry!" We ran toward it. There was a muffled sound, like a klaxon, coming from inside. I reached for the door handle. Bell knocked my hand away. "No!" he shouted. Startled, I drew back. "I'll take care of the reactor. You find the girl." I turned away, scanning the area for likely hiding places. When I looked back, he was still standing by the door, watching me. I moved aimlessly down a paved road between the reactor buildings and two smaller structures that probably contained the turbines, generators and condensers. Huge concrete cooling towers rose straight ahead. I heard a new sound. It, too, sounded like an alarm, but with a different tone. I turned toward the far side of the reactors and approached another building, a tall, wide structure with a façade of corrugated steel. As I drew nearer, the sound grew louder and light showed through a few windows. I hesitated, then opened the door.

Three massive concrete tubs loomed over me. There was a set of metal steps leading to the top, and amber lights flashed over two of the tubs. As I watched, the noise increased and the light over the third one switched from green to yellow. I climbed the stairs and looked across Deep Creek's waste pools, eerie ponds of glowing green water that promised death if you came too close. I could see the racks that held the fuel rods, but the rods themselves were invisible beneath the layer of poison water.

I crept carefully around the perimeter, gripping the bag of money tightly in my left hand – my right was closed over the butt of the gun in my coat pocket. "Withers!" I raised the bag. "I have the money!" The only answer was the echo of my own voice. "Withers!" I moved a little further. The water level in the pools was different, and all three were below a yellow line painted on the sides fifteen feet from the top. As I looked, the water in the first pool dropped below a red line and the flashing light turned red as well. A mist began to rise from it. I edged away.

Something hard poked me in the back. "Stand still," said Eli Withers. He put a hand inside my pocket, withdrew the pistol and tossed it aside. "Drop the bag." I complied. "Move away from it." He lifted the bag and stood facing me, his back to the pool. He wore a white jumpsuit that covered his entire body, and gloves, and a hood over his head.

"Where's Regan?"

He shook his head. "I have no idea."

"Look, Withers, there's no reason not to let her go. You have the money. What else do you want?"

"I want you dead." He gestured toward the pool. "You're going for a swim." I tried to concentrate. The waste pool was certain death. The sides were sheer, and once in there was no way out. Even if I escaped, immersion in the contaminated water would kill me. He tapped my chest with the barrel of his gun. "Move."

"Withers!" Bell was standing near the top of the stairs, gun pointed at us. Withers turned his head, and I lowered my shoulder and drove him to the floor. As we fell, the hood fell off and he let go of the bag. Wrenching himself from my grasp he dove for it, still clutching the gun. The bag teetered on the edge of the pool for a second, then disappeared. He turned back to me as I rose, his sallow face once more twisted in rage. He raised the gun and climbed to his feet.

A shot rang out, then another. Withers stumbled backwards, still trying to level the pistol at me. Bell fired again. Withers pulled the trigger, loosing a bullet that lodged in the wall behind me, and the recoil of the gun seemed to add to his momentum. His foot stepped over the edge. He wavered for an instant, a doomed scarecrow clawing frantically at the air, and vanished. I barely heard the splash and there was no struggle. His protective gear was no use in the poison pool – Withers was dead one way or the other. The black bag rested on top of the racks under ten feet of toxic green water.

"Tommy!" Bell was almost to the bottom of the steps. "I have to reverse these valves. We need to get out of here. Find the girl!" As he reached the floor he stumbled and caught himself. "I'll meet you at the boat. Hurry!"

I retrieved my gun and left the building. Twenty minutes later, I returned to the dock. There were few hiding places at Deep Creek and I had searched them all, to no avail. I would return to Charly with neither her daughter nor her money.

Bell was standing on the dock. As I approached, he backed away. "Don't get too close," he said.

"What?"

"My skin and clothes are contaminated. Don't touch me."

Surprised, I spread my arms and looked down at my body. "What about me?"

"You should have avoided the worst of it. Where's Regan?" I shook my head. He began to shake uncontrollably. I reached for him but he waved me away and turned abruptly to vomit into the water, heaving violently long after the bloody contents of his stomach had stopped erupting from his mouth. He stood there, bent, for minutes that seemed like hours. When he finally straightened and looked back, his face was white and beaded with sweat, and his eyes – cavities without light or color – seemed to recede into his head. He gestured toward the boat. "Go due west," he croaked. "You'll find a place to land."

"Why didn't you take the pills?"

"They couldn't help. Too much radiation."

"But –"

"Go on, Tommy. I'd be dead before we arrived."

"Gordon –"

He shook his head. "It's too late. It was too late before we started." He drew the gun from his pocket and smiled. "But don't worry. You'll be hearing from me." Before I could move, he slid the barrel into his mouth and pulled the trigger.

THE NEWSPAPERS got it mostly right, thanks to Alice Poole. Her story was picked up by papers and wire services all over the world. Eli Withers was crazy – Gordon Bell had killed him and averted a nuclear disaster. John Winslow had been in the wrong place at the wrong time. My name wasn't mentioned. Neither was the money.

The ease with which Withers had almost succeeded was the elephant in the room. Cries for an immediate investigation of Withers and, by extension, everyone else in the nuclear power industry, came from all sides – editorial pages, legislatures, the Chamber of Commerce – but the false promise of "safe" nuclear energy was still unquestioned. A few "agitators" brought it up, and they were ignored. The same people suggested that the discharge of contaminants at Deep Creek before Bell intervened would kill lots of people eventually. Government and industry scoffed but quietly set aside funds, and made plans for facilities to deal with the inevitable sickness and death.

Purely by chance, I landed at the pier below the bluffs at The Orchard. Whatever activity had occurred at the house was over. I walked into town and reclaimed my car from Alice. Refusing her offer of food, I turned onto Highway 3 and headed west. Questions had been answered, and questions remained.

CHAPTER SIX

I SLEPT for a few hours despite the turmoil in my brain. When I woke, it bubbled over. Winslow and Withers were dead. Could anyone else tell me where Regan was? Withers claimed that he had "no idea." If he wasn't the kidnapper, who was? The idea that she had discovered another, more pressing, plot now seemed more likely, as did the possibility that she was already dead. The prospect sickened me. To find the child that I had lost, and lose her again, would be unbearable.

Winslow's attaché case, locked, stood next to the front door where I'd left it the night before. It was tan leather, and could only be opened if the correct series of numbers was dialed up on the brass catches. I considered forcing the clasps with a screwdriver, then decided to find out if Charly had the combination first. It was still too early to see her, so I climbed the hill to Mark's house instead. I had reported my failure before leaving Wicomico Church the night before. He had agreed that we *would* find Regan. We still had the $10 million, and there had to be somebody left who wanted it. "There is no $10 million," I said.

There was a long silence. "What do you mean?" I recounted the fate of the black leather bag. "It's still in the pool?" he said.

"Yes."

"Can it be salvaged?"

"I doubt it. Between the water and the radiation it's probably just a soggy pile of poison paper by now, and it'll be months before anyone can get near it."

I climbed the steps. No one answered the bell and the door was locked. As I turned away, Anne Clark came round the corner of the house and started up to the porch. Head down, she didn't see me. "Anne." Startled, she lost her balance. I had to grab her arm to stop her from tumbling backwards. She looked frightened for an instant, then angry, almost savage.

"Tommy! Don't sneak up on me like that."

"I'm sorry." She crossed the porch to the door. "Where's Mark?"

"The President's in New York. Mark went up there last night." She paused. "He asked me to feed Bo." She unlocked the door and entered the house. I followed.

"When's he coming back?"

"I'm not sure."

I felt abandoned. I knew Mark still had a job to do, but he'd said nothing to me about leaving town. For a moment, Regan's disappearance and the sudden death of four people I had known so briefly seemed like a dream, or a sort of play. Any minute now Regan would appear at stage right, a bundle of roses in her arms, and the dead people would rise from the floor to accept the plaudits of the crowd. I had seen each of them die but, just then, I wasn't sure. "Did he tell you about Gordon? And Withers?"

"Yes."

I watched as she searched the cabinets for Bo's food, opened a can and emptied it into his bowl. She moved slowly, like the last time she'd been at my place, as if she had a part in the play but wasn't yet comfortable with her role. She began to remove dishes from the dishwasher, looking over her shoulder, obviously waiting for me to leave. "I'll see you." She didn't respond.

I left the house and turned toward 28th Street. Her coldness puzzled me, but it confirmed the idea that our evening together was meaningless. She and Mark were obviously a couple again. Was she afraid I would mention it to him? Her lack of curiosity about Deep Creek seemed strange, too. Maybe he'd left me out of the story.

There was a police car parked in the cobblestone courtyard. The gold badge painted on the door announced the man who rode inside it: "Chief." A policeman sat behind the wheel. I was admitted to the house by a woman wearing a nurse's uniform, and directed to a sitting-room just off the foyer. "Mrs. Winslow has someone with her right now," she said as she started from the room.

I hung around the door. When I heard his footsteps on the stairs, I stepped into the foyer. "Chief?"

"Yes?" He looked down at me, a massive Othello who bore the accouterments of his profession – uniform, badge, gun – with an easy élan. They looked like toys against his bulk. His eyes drilled into mine and, detecting nothing of interest, returned to the surface.

"My name's Tommy Sawyer. I'm a friend of Mrs. Winslow's."

"Yes?"

"Has she been told about her –?"

"Yes, Mr. Sawyer. That's why I'm here."

He started for the door. "Is there anything new about her daughter?" I called.

He stopped and looked back, the eyes searching again. "No."

"Mr. Sawyer?" The nurse was perched on the landing. "You can go up now. It's the last room on the right."

"Thanks." I climbed the staircase. The Chief didn't know who I was. Bag man and one-time custodian of Martin's notebook, I had imagined that I was on the periphery, at least, of official notice. Apparently that was not the case.

The widow was radiant. Resting against pillows in blue silken slips, she sat upright in a large bed with an intricate woven headboard shot through with gold and silver threads. A pitcher full of drooping yellow roses sat on the bedside table. I hardly knew what to say – my emotions pulled me in all directions. Her odious husband was gone but our child was still missing, and a significant part of her fortune was lost. She kept trying not to smile and finally burst out laughing. "You should see your –" she began.

"Charly. I didn't find Regan."

"Oh. Oh, no." The smile disappeared and she opened her arms. I sat down on the edge of the bed and embraced her carefully. She murmured into my neck. "You don't know how miserable I've been. He was a vile, hateful man." She trembled. "When Regan was born, I swore that he would have nothing to do with her. And it took everything I had to pretend that we were a family."

"Why didn't you leave him?"

"I couldn't do that to Regan. I was afraid the whole thing would come out."

"You mean the Mottrom boy and –"

"Yes. And all his other little friends, too."

"How did you find out about Jimmy Mottrom?"

"Mother told me. *After* we were married." She threw her arms around my neck again. I held her without speaking. Finally, she leaned back and said, "What can we do?"

"I think we should turn it over to the police. I have no idea where she is now."

"But they said not to."

"I know, but it's been almost two weeks. I'm afraid she may be somewhere alone. Without help."

"All right." She reached for the telephone. After a short conversation, she laid the receiver down. "Someone will be here in a few minutes." She smiled. "Now tell me about your adventure." I gave her the short version but it still took a while because of her eager questions, and then we drifted seamlessly into the world we had created twenty years before. It was like our very first conversation, on the benches in front of the red granite vault. I held nothing back, and this time neither did she. We were "Tom" and "Charly" again, at least for the moment.

The nurse knocked and leaned in the door. "You really should rest now, Mrs. Winslow."

"Just a few more minutes. Thank you." She waited until the woman closed the door. "So I'm out $10 million."

It was like she was talking about Monopoly money. "I'm afraid so."

"What are you going to do?"

"There are some odds and ends that don't make sense. They probably don't have anything to do with Regan, but –" I stopped. There *was* something. "When Regan gave you the envelope, did she say anything about a project in Cuba?"

"No. She just said that Eli had a bank account there."

"There was a deed in the envelope. Did she mention it?"

"No."

"Did you talk to the Chief about my trip yesterday?"

"I started to ask him about it but after a few words it was clear he didn't know what I was talking about. I thought maybe the police weren't supposed to know, so I shut up."

I rose. "Tell them I'm available whenever they want me." I reached the door and looked back. "Winslow carried a brown leather attaché case. Do you know the combination, by any chance?"

"No."

"Okay. I'll see you later."

"Tom?"

"Yes?"

"Please be careful. I don't want to lose you again."

I hesitated outside the gate. Oak Hill called me – I wanted to celebrate, to leave her a note and open the gate at last, but joy was before time while Regan was missing. Something else *was* going on, something more serious than Winslow's stock scheme. Eli Withers and Roberto Gomez were undoubtedly building centrifuges – cascades – in Cuba, and nuclear bombs would certainly follow if they weren't stopped. Martin knew something about it. Gomez's telephone number was in his notebook, as was a map of Cuba marked with potential sites, one of which had been purchased by the Mammoth Land Trust. Ames was providing the necessary information – the "disc" that Gomez needed – and Gomez's "clients" were probably South American terrorists with ties to John Winslow. But Withers and Winslow were dead now, and Gomez presumably still needed the money and maybe the disc. Was it over, or would Gomez and Ames press on? And then there was Mark. The old, painful suspicions had returned. Back at the carriage house, I found the frayed list of telephone numbers and looked at it once more – the *Georgetown Star*, unknown, Anne, Winslow, Anderson, Gomez. I *knew* the unknown number, I just couldn't remember. I picked up the phone. Anne answered on the first ring: "Hello. Mark?" I hung up. "Anderson" was still a puzzle. Something in the back of my mind told me I should know, but it evaded me.

As I started to rise, the telephone rang. I hesitated before answering it. "Hello."

A slow, Southern voice, an unhurried series of syllables that was almost extinct, responded: "Is this Tommy Sawyer?"

"Yes."

"Zack Collins, Mr. Sawyer."

The Managing Editor at the *Richmond Times.* "Thanks for calling me back."

"You wanted to talk about that boy's suicide – Jimmy Mottrom?"

"Yes, sir."

"Mind telling me why you're interested?"

It was a good question. Despite a total lack of evidence, I was sure that the death of Jimmy Mottrom twenty years earlier would shed light on the only question I cared about. "My daughter's been kidnapped, Mr. Collins. I believe it might be related to Jimmy's death."

He hesitated. "Well – what can I tell you?"

"In your story about the inquest, you mentioned a doctor who wanted to testify, but the coroner wouldn't call him. What do you remember about that?"

There was a long silence. "Do you believe in ghosts, Mr. Sawyer? The kind that haunt you?"

"Uh, well –"

"That kid's ghost has been sitting on my shoulder for twenty years. He's never done anything before. He usually just sits there, but he's screaming in my ear right now."

"What's he saying?"

"He's saying, 'Tell this man the truth.'" I waited. "Jimmy Mottrom was murdered, Mr. Sawyer. Strangled."

"How do you know?"

"The doctor told me. Palmer, I believe his name was."

"Was?"

"He's been dead for years."

"What did he tell you?"

"The marks on the boy's neck were caused by a pair of hands, not a rope. He'd been dead way longer than they said, too. Somebody –" he paused again "– strung him up after they killed him. Palmer was going to make it public, but they shut him up somehow."

"But – surely the coroner or – or his medical guy knew that."

"Yes, sir. I believe they did."

"But –"

"The Winslows ran that county for over a hundred years. John's daddy was still alive then and – and Jimmy Mottrom was a queer." He stopped. "John Winslow was, too, but that didn't matter. He was a Winslow."

"So you –"

"I told myself I didn't *really* know. That's what my editors said, too. They didn't want anything to do with it."

"Why speak now?"

"I saw this morning that Winslow was dead. The boy started whispering in my ear. When I got your note, he started screaming." He paused. "I'm out of excuses."

"Does anyone else know about this?"

"I don't know. Nobody else reported it."

"Do you know a man named Charles Martin?"

"I believe that's the fellow who called me a couple of months ago. The ghost was still quiet then."

"Was there anything more? An autopsy report?"

"There was no autopsy."

I considered again. "One of the stories referred to a 'spokesman' for the Winslow campaign. Do you recall his name?"

"No, I don't. I'm sorry."

"Do something for me. Go down to the morgue—"

"I'm there now."

"Look at the story on October 27, 1994. It's Winslow announcing his withdrawal from the House race."

"Hold on." He was back a few seconds later. "Okay, I have it."

"Do you see the picture?"

"Yes."

"Look at the man on Winslow's left. Is that –?"

"Yep. That's him. And I remember his name now – Ames."

I nodded. "Did Winslow attend the inquest?"

"No. Ames was the only one from the campaign who testified."

"I've read your story. Did he say anything else? Anything that wasn't reported?"

"He told one big whopper. Nobody called him on it."

"What?"

"He testified that everybody, except for Jimmy, went back to Washington right after the interview with the *Star*. I talked to the boy's mother. She said she never saw him."

"Where was he?"

"At The Orchard. With Winslow."

DETECTIVE RALPH Blake frowned. "Didn't I see you with Singer the other day? When Mrs. Winslow was attacked?"

"Yes."

His eyes narrowed. "And you just happened to receive the ransom note?"

"Not me. Mark."

"Mr. Sawyer's not a suspect, Detective Blake," said Charly. "He's a very dear friend."

I could tell that he wasn't convinced. "So somebody finally received a ransom demand?" I nodded.

"And you bungled it." I didn't respond. I agreed with him, but it seemed unfair to put it into words.

Charly defended me. "What would you have done, Detective?"

The hard eyes softened and looked at her. "I'm not saying we would have done anything different, Mrs. Winslow. It's just that we might be further along now." He turned back to me. "Didn't it occur to you to at least tell us about it?"

"Mark said that he was the point man. I assumed that he told you."

"Where's the note?"

"I don't know. I guess he has it."

He frowned again, and sighed, an unexpected – and incongruous – sign of impotence. "I've tried to call Singer. He's not at home or his office. Any idea where I can find him?"

"He may be in New York. With the President."

He rose. "Is there anything else?"

I put my hand in my coat pocket. "I have a couple of things I took from the book. There's something –"

"What book?" I removed the hand from my coat, empty, as the new foreboding – one that had been building all day – gained purchase. "What book?"

Charly felt it again. "Is something wrong, Tom?"

"No." I raised my eyes, and forced myself to meet his gaze. "It's – the book I used up on the Hill the other day. With the Energy Committee."

"What does it have to do with the kidnapping?"

"Well, I – I don't know."

He shook his head and walked to the door. "We'll pick up where we left off, Mrs. Winslow. I'll keep you posted."

"Thank you, Detective."

He looked at me. "Don't go anywhere. We'll want to talk to you again." I nodded. He closed the door behind him.

I stood up. "I'll let you rest, Charly. I –"

"What's the matter?"

"Nothing's the matter."

She smiled. "That's a lie, Tom. I believe it's the first one you've ever told me."

I sat back down. "Tell me about the day you received the CD from Regan."

She paused. "It was about three in the afternoon. Mark called and said they had a recording from Regan."

"Didn't it seem strange that it went to him instead of you?"

"Well – I don't know. There was so much going on. I'm not sure I thought about it."

"What did you do?"

"John and I walked over there and listened to it."

"Was the Chief there?"

"Yes, and several other policemen. And someone from the FBI."

"Why did Mark keep it? Why didn't the police take it?"

"The CD?"

"Yes."

She hesitated again. "There was some discussion about that. All I remember is Mark finally putting it in his desk drawer."

I nodded. "How did Mark become the point man?"

"He volunteered. I thought it was a good idea. The kidnappers had sent the CD to him, and he'd already decided to handle everything from the *Star's* end." She cocked her head. "What are you getting at?"

"I don't know." I paused. "How did you arrange the money?"

"We didn't know how much they would demand, so I told my lawyer to sit down with the brokers and liquidate everything except the house."

Despite my dismay over her money, I felt a little sick. "Is that the $10 million?"

She laughed. "It came to a bit more than that. I think we have a few million left."

"How did you leave it with your lawyer?"

"He was at that first meeting. I told him to be ready to deliver cash if we received a ransom demand."

"How long have you known him?"

She raised her brows. "All my life. He was Mother's attorney."

"Have you talked to him since you got out of the hospital?"

She nodded. "He called this morning."

"Did you talk about the ransom demand?" She shook her head. "Would you call him and ask him what happened?"

"Yes. Do you think my lawyer has something to do with Regan's kidnapping?"

"No. Just ask him."

"All right." I stood up again. "What are you thinking?"

"I'm not sure. There are things that don't add up." I bent to kiss her. "The CIA Director's a friend of yours, isn't he?"

"Yes."

"I'd like to speak to him about something. Can you arrange it?"

She nodded. "Is it about Regan?"

"Maybe."

"When?"

"As soon as you can."

I turned for the door. "Tom?" I looked back. "I meant what I said this morning. Please be careful."

Outside, I stood at the top of the hill and looked down at Georgetown again. I didn't really belong here and I didn't like it, and I never intended that it be part of our world. I was pretty sure that she didn't either, back then, but it was her town now. I shook my head. Despite the ease of our reunion, and her nonchalance about the money, the intervening years couldn't be wished away. I despised the doubt that time had enabled, and cursed the reality that now demanded our attention. People change – everyone said so. It could never be the same. But what if they were wrong? Or what if we had changed together? Who would we be now if the world had never interfered?

A light rain began to fall, adding to the slop of dirty, melting snow. It was time to confront George Ames. I hailed a passing cab.

THERE WAS an ambulance outside the building, and a little crowd of people hovered around the steps. Several of the women were weeping. "Jane?" She turned her head. "What's happened?"

"It's George. He's shot himself."

"Dead?" She nodded. "Was there a note or – or something?"

"I don't know."

We moved aside as an elevated table with wheels, attended by two men in green smocks, was carried down the steps. The body was covered by a thin plastic sheet. Several uniformed police officers brought up the rear. I was surprised to see the Chief among them, and tried to avoid his gaze, unsuccessfully. He looked unhappy. "What are you doing here, Sawyer?"

"I work here, Chief." He pursed his lips and started to say something else, then thought better of it. "Did he leave a note?" He shook his head and continued down the steps.

I walked past the elevator and took the stairs to the fourth floor. Inside my office, I sat back in the chair to wait. Jane appeared in the doorway. "We didn't think you were coming back."

"I wasn't, but I wanted to talk to George. Did he say anything before he did this?"

"Not to me."

"Is Anne here?"

"She's on vacation this week."

"What – what was her connection to Withers?"

She arched her brows. "I believe it was the usual thing. His wife found out about it and left him. At great expense, I'm told."

"When did the affair with Martin end?"

"When he died." She paused. "Do you need anything before I leave?"

"No." I checked my watch – it was just past five. "I'll be going myself in a few minutes." I had accepted the view of George Ames as a career bureaucrat back-stroking his way toward retirement. I still believed that was true but, like Gordon Bell, there was more. Unlike Bell, the other facets of his life didn't seem so attractive. He was involved in Jimmy Mottrom's death, and he was passing nuclear secrets to Roberto Gomez. I had come to inquire whether those things were connected, and to discover what he knew about my daughter. He could no longer be interrogated, but perhaps he had left something behind.

A warning identical to the one at Regan's apartment was posted on the door to his office, and I ignored it, too. The room still smelled like his cologne. I pushed the chair out of the way – it bore the residue of his suicide – and searched the desk, then the credenza. There was nothing of interest in either one.

Indeed, the accumulation of the usual detritus of a career defined by four walls and infinite commands – memos, directives, binders to keep them all straight – was surprisingly small, a hint that Ames was not quite as obedient as he seemed. A low wooden cabinet beside the door was empty except for a full bottle of scotch and a couple of glasses. I poured some scotch and walked back down the hall.

Behind my desk again, I sipped the whisky and considered the options. There didn't seem to be any – all my suspects were dead. Beginning with Charles Martin, seven people associated one way or another with the Nuclear Energy Authority had died, eight if you counted Jerry Wallace. In a sense, I had accomplished what I set out to do. It would be years before the NEA returned to business as usual. I entertained the possibility that it might actually be reformed, or abolished, but too many people had too much at stake in the status quo. After the furor over Hanford and the CRAC Report – and Withers' aborted disaster at Deep Creek – died down, the pig would get some lipstick and things would continue as before. The people would read new headlines, and the people's representatives would return to the trough.

In the meantime, I had Charly and Regan to consider. I wanted to start over and I thought Charly did, too, but Regan's fate was paramount. The Chief had the case now, but I wasn't finished.

CHAPTER SEVEN

THE GREAT house was brilliantly lighted, as if in celebration. The patient, back in her own baili-wick and more certain of her survival with each pass-ing moment, had demanded a change of venue. I was ushered into her drawing room, a bright, cheerful place with two huge windows draped in pink and blue fabric. The walls were covered with yellow pa-per and the furniture – Chippendale tables and chairs and an overstuffed sofa – was pastel. A small, ele-gant chandelier hung from the middle of the ceiling. It was only one of a dozen such rooms in the house – libraries, studies, conservatories – and it reminded me again who she had always been.

A portrait of Alison Blaine hung over the fire-place. Surprised, I paused to inspect it. Why would she display the image of a woman who had done her so much harm? I shook my head. Maybe it was a matter of caste, like the Borgias or the English aris-tocracy – acknowledgement of ancestors was com-pulsory, no matter their crimes.

Charly was propped up on the pink sofa, wrapped in a heavy silk comforter. She pointed to a bar built into one of the bookcases. "I waited for you to have my first drink. Would you make me a marti-ni?"

"They're letting you have booze now?"

"He said I could have *one*. Be generous." I smiled and fixed her drink. "Aren't you having something?"

"Maybe later." I sat down in one of the fragile chairs. "George Ames is dead. Suicide." She nodded. "You don't seem surprised."

"I guess I'm not."

"Why not?"

"He was always tied to John somehow. I could go for years without seeing him, and he would suddenly pop up for a day or two and disappear again. He's been a constant since John went to the NEA."

"What's the connection?"

"They were in college together. When we were first married he was around all the time."

"Did you know that he worked on the congressional campaign?" She nodded again. "You were with Winslow and Mark when they talked about me, weren't you?"

"Yes."

"What did they say?"

"The job was open and Mark said he had a friend who was perfect. He was very complimentary."

"Did they talk about my – experience?"

She nodded. "John said he was looking for someone new, someone who wasn't from the Washington culture."

"Someone who knew nothing about the NEA?"

"Well – yes. That's when Mark brought up your name."

I crossed the room and stared into the fire. "Did Winslow have a place here where he kept his personal things?"

She nodded again. "His study's right across the hall. Why?"

"I'd like to go through it. There may be something that would help with Regan."

"Do you think John kidnapped her?"

"I honestly don't know. I used to believe that he and Withers were responsible, but now I'm not sure." I returned to my chair.

"You can look in his desk any time." She paused. "He keeps – kept – it locked. A long time ago, I wanted to know what was in it. Then I decided that I didn't." She stopped again. "Somebody around here can unlock it."

The man who tended the front door leaned in the room. "Mr. Anderson is here, Mrs. Winslow." He stood aside, and the Director of the Central Intelligence Agency – a short, bald man wearing a pin-striped suit and a red and blue repp tie – crossed the threshold. I rose. He ignored me and approached the sofa.

"Andy," Charly said. "Thank you for coming."

She extended her hand and he took it. "You look great, Charlotte. How are you feeling?"

"I'm fine."

"I was – sorry to hear about John."

"Please, Andy. You of all people should know better."

He looked uncomfortable. "Sit down." She gestured toward me. "You've met my friend, Tommy Sawyer. He wants to speak to you."

He watched as I resumed my seat. We had met a few weeks earlier during my first visit to this house. I'd forgotten that his name was Anderson. "Mr. Anderson, I work at the –"

"I know who you are, Mr. Sawyer. Everyone in town knows who you are. That was quite a turn on the Hill the other day."

I couldn't tell if he was praising or condemning me, but it didn't matter. I could do nothing about the bomb factory in Cuba and he could. If that was the real reason that Regan had been taken, he might help us find her. I drew the deed from my coat pocket and handed it to him. "I think Winslow and Withers were planning to sell nuclear weapons to terrorists." I pointed. "Regan turned that up when she was looking into something else."

He placed a pair of gold-rimmed spectacles on his nose. A moment later, he looked up and said, "If this is genuine, it proves that the Mammoth Land Trust was doing some kind of deal with the Cuban Defense Ministry. That's illegal, but not nuclear terrorism."

I told him about the map in Martin's notebook, the reference to the National Liberation Army and Winslow's periodic trips to South America. "I spoke to a man at the Cuban Consulate. He thought I was Withers. He said that he and his clients were anxious to complete the cascades."

"What was his name?"

"Gomez."

He looked at Charly. "Roberto Gomez?"

"Yes."

"I know Roberto Gomez," she said. "We all do. He's been here for ages."

Anderson leaned back in his chair and stared at me, considering. He already trusted Charly. "This isn't the first time I've heard this story, Mr. Sawyer. Your predecessor told me about it, and showed me some pictures he'd taken."

"Two men standing in front of the chapel at Oak Hill?"

"Yes. He didn't know it was Gomez then. We were beginning an investigation when Martin died. A lot of it was still in his head." He paused. "What I'm about to tell you is classified. It goes no further than this room. All right?" I nodded. "We do satellite surveillance of Cuba around the clock, but that end of the island is covered with a canopy of vegetation. Our clearest pictures come from the harbor at Santiago. Large containers are off-loaded there and disappear into the mountains. They've been very careful, and whatever they're building is invisible to the satellites." He paused. "If you're right about this, we want to deal with it quietly. That probably means a raid from our base at Guantanamo." He tapped the map. "But this is not definitive. None of it is. It would be a propaganda nightmare if we're wrong. We need something more before we launch any kind of attack."

"Like what?"

"We need to catch Gomez red-handed."

"With what?"

"With whatever he needs to finish the cascades. The last compact disc." He paused. "Did he mention anything about a time or place?"

"Sort of. He said that Withers should have his man at the usual place this week."

"His man?"

"I believe he was talking about George Ames. The guy in the pictures. He's General Counsel at the NEA."

"Okay. We'll make sure that Ames shows up with the disc."

"We can't. Ames is dead." He frowned. "He blew his brains out this afternoon."

We sat in silence. "I guess the usual place is Oak Hill?" he said.

I nodded. "When the tour starts. Four o'clock tomorrow afternoon."

He stood up. "We need to find the actual disc to prove that Gomez is stealing sensitive information. I don't suppose you know where it is?" I shook my head. "I'll put my people on it immediately. We need to be ready to move tomorrow afternoon." He paused. "And I'll try to keep Ames' death quiet." He drew a card from his wallet and handed it to me. "That's a direct line. Call me if you hear anything."

The number was familiar. "Did Martin have this?"

"Yes."

I hesitated. "There's something else."

"What?"

"Regan may have been taken because of this. We have to be careful."

"Of course."

After he was gone, I stood and looked around the room. "Charly?"

"Yes?"

"You were right about all this." I gestured with my hand. "Maybe not the way you thought. I'm glad I didn't know." She started to speak, but I stopped her. "Everything would've been different. It would be about the money even if it wasn't." I looked away. "We would never have had those days twenty years ago."

We sat again without speaking. "And?" she said.

"I don't want to lose them now." I walked to the door. "Did Regan know someone named Smith? Someone who might have asked her to dinner?"

"Not that I know of."

"Didn't you say that you found the receipt for the notebook in Regan's laundry?"

"Yes. They delivered it while I was there."

"What did you do with the laundry?"

"I hung it in her bedroom closet."

"Still in the bag?"

"Yes. Why?"

"Just wondering."

WINSLOW'S CASE was tougher than it looked. The dinner knife I tried first bent and broke, as did the screwdriver I used next. I finally pried both of the locks from the top of the case with the claw end of a hammer and levered it open with a chisel. The contents were disappointing – a copy of the RCA Report, a passport, a recent brokerage statement showing his holdings in Mammoth Power and Light, and Martin's notebook. I stared at it for a minute, recalling all the death that it represented, then laid it aside. Winslow had taken it, just as Charly said, and she had been attacked for her money and jewelry after all. Its secrets known, the book was no use to me now. I had assumed that blackmail was the point, but there was no evidence at all that Martin actually tried to extort anyone. If that were so, why was he dead? Anderson's revelations had cast him in a new light. Whatever else he was doing, he wasn't trying to cash in on the bomb factory.

I turned back to the attaché case. The flexible filing compartments were empty. I noticed that the leather lining in the top was frayed where it met the sides of the case, so I used another knife to slice it away – still nothing.

I closed the case and stared at it. After a moment, I opened it again. The interior was smaller, shallower, than the exterior. The bottom and sides were lined with a stiff fabric rather than leather. I pulled at it with my fingers and the entire thing separated from the shell like a tray, revealing the true bottom of the case and a large, unsealed envelope addressed to Winslow. It contained a photograph of the head and torso of a naked Jimmy Mottrom with a ring of dark bruises around his neck, and another of Winslow and Ames twenty years earlier. A smiling Jimmy Mottrom stood between them. There were also three small containers of microfilm pilfered from the morgue at the *Georgetown Star*.

Another statement from Winslow's brokers, this one dated several months earlier, was last. Handwritten calculations similar to the ones I'd made a few days before appeared in the margins, and there was a terse note at the bottom:

> *John – You're a rich man now. All I require is your silence.*
> *E*

That didn't sound like a partnership to me. Withers had what he wanted from Winslow – introductions to Gomez and his friends in South America – and he and Gomez would take it from there.

THE TELEPHONE woke me up. Bone tired, and unaccustomed to so much activity, I had fallen asleep on the couch after wolfing down a can of chili and some crackers. According to the clock on the mantel, it was almost midnight. "Hello."

"Sawyer?"

"Yes."

"Jim Baldwin. Do you have your TV set on?"

"No."

"There's something interesting going on up here. Why don't you turn it on? Don't hang up. We'll talk while we watch."

"What channel?"

"I think it's on all the networks. I'm watching CBS." I flipped on the television and sat back on the couch. A man with a microphone, the raven of our modern-day mythology, gestured to the blackness over his shoulder. "He's standing on a hill outside Syracuse," said Baldwin. "That's the city behind him."

"Without lights."

"Without power of any kind, apparently. Syracuse gets all its power from the Nine Mile Point Nuclear Station. The info has been a little garbled, but it seems that both reactors there have been shut down."

"Why would they shut down both reactors at the same time?"

"Some kind of emergency, they say."

"According to your report, Syracuse should be getting power from someplace else."

"I know."

"Well?"

"I don't – Wait. What did he say?"

"I missed it."

Baldwin was quiet for a few seconds. I decided to listen to him instead of the man with the microphone, and turned the sound down. "One of the reactors at Indian Point is out, too," he said. "New York City gets some of its power from Indian Point which explains the problem in Syracuse – the grid is responding to New York. There's not enough juice for both of them."

"Is Indian Point an emergency, too?"

"I don't know."

We spoke for a few more minutes before hanging up. I thought about Eli Withers. Had he somehow set another cataclysm in motion before falling into the pool at Deep Creek? Or was it something else? Bell had promised that we would hear from him, and today was Friday, October 31, 2014. Halloween. The date circled in red in Amanda's white binder.

THE TELEPHONE was ringing again. I struggled up from sleep and staggered into the living room. The receiver dropped to the floor. I could hear Baldwin's voice. "Sawyer? Sawyer? Are you there?"

I found the phone and fell onto the couch. "Yes, Jim, I'm here. What time is it?"

"Nine o'clock. Have you heard what's going on?"

"No."

"We're having major power outages all over the country. Reactors in Minnesota, Wisconsin and Texas have shut down. People are going nuts."

"Is anything exploding or – or burning?"

"No. Everything seems to be quite orderly. They're just not generating any power."

"What do the operators say?"

"They're not talking."

"What do you mean?"

"None of them have come forward."

"Maybe they don't know."

"Maybe. The politicians are demanding answers. You fellows down there are going to be on the hot seat." He hung up.

I fixed a pot of coffee. As I watched the liquid drip through the filter and fall into the carafe, I pondered the possibility that it might not happen tomorrow. There were already lots of people whose coffee pots weren't operating. I poured a cup and turned on the television set, another essential that might go at any time.

The power outages were serious but isolated, and unaffected operators were scrambling to reach maximum capacity in an effort to provide electricity to the areas in question. The power in Syracuse had already been restored, though it was not yet reliable – different parts of the city did better than others. The problem was that no sooner had the lights in one sector come on, those in another went out. Power plants, always *nuclear* power plants, were going off-line at the rate of one per hour, and the frequency seemed to be accelerating. As of 10:00 A.M., a quarter of the country's 104 reactors were shut down.

I removed everything from Amanda's briefcase and spread it on the table. Eli Withers wasn't the problem – it was Amanda and Gordon Bell. I ordered her "Reactors" sheets by the durations noted at the end of each one. Without exception, the reactors that had already shut down had durations of three days. Those with estimates of four days would undoubtedly be next, and those requiring five days to shut down would go off-line on Sunday. I dialed Baldwin's number.

He picked it up on the first ring. "Hello?"

"Tommy Sawyer, Jim. I believe I know what's happening." I explained the contents of Amanda's briefcase. "I think the plan is to stop generating power. Period."

"But why? That would be incredibly destructive, not to mention criminal."

"I'm not so sure about the criminal part. Those plants are deteriorating badly. Every one of them is operating on time borrowed from the NEA. I suspect that the regulations have been followed scrupulously. That's what the inspection reports and letters were for." I paused. "As to why, the man responsible for it was a true believer. Nuclear power was the answer to all our energy problems if everyone would just get out of the way." I stopped again. "I guess he got tired of waiting." There was another reason. The wormwood sown by John Winslow twenty years earlier had ripened and dropped its bitter gall two days after Winslow's death, but there was no need to mention that now.

"What are you going to do?" said Baldwin.

"Me?"

"Yes. You work at the NEA, don't you?" I didn't answer. "Listen, Tommy, the scenario in my report is nothing compared to this. Multiply it a hundred times. The damage already done is incalculable. If all of them shut down, the country will never recover. You've – hold on." There was a pause. "The power's out in Boston and Philadelphia. You have to do something."

It was Saturday, but I suspected that the Nuclear Energy Authority would be open for business. I threw everything back into Amanda's briefcase and jogged down the hill. At M Street, I waved down a cab and settled back for the ride. This was a death knell for the NEA – it couldn't survive the coming chaos. Gordon Bell had called everyone's bluff. Those who profited from nuclear energy without really paying for it, and those who decried its use while impeding the search for solutions, would now have to get along without it, as would the bulk of the population who had ignored it altogether. The overarching misery about to be delivered would demonstrate our need, and the neglect that had allowed it to occur would be remedied.

It was an elegant plan, but it suffered from the same fundamental flaw as nuclear energy itself. The bomb, and all that came after it, was a product of crisis. Shortcuts were taken, critical decisions deferred. Bell had created a new crisis, and the rational response that he seemed to expect – entirely absent before – would probably be in short supply again. The more likely scenario was a circular firing squad – maybe several – followed by a monumental burst of activity that would undoubtedly create as many problems as it solved.

I climbed down from the cab a block shy of the building and approached it on foot. On the day their demands had finally been met, the usual demonstrators were nowhere to be found. A crowd of reporters with microphones and cameras preceded me through the door. I showed my identification, and again took the stairs. Ames' office was directly across from the stairwell. I slipped inside and placed the briefcase in the cabinet by the door. I didn't have time to be involved in this crisis, but I could make sure that someone else figured it out.

Jane was dealing with the press. "Come to help in our hour of need?" she said, after dispatching the last reporter to someone else in the building.

"Maybe. Where does it stand?"

"Thirty-two reactors shutdown. Power out in parts of twenty states."

"Can't they be re-started?"

"Not for weeks or months."

I hesitated. "A few days ago Gordon told me that he had wind of a problem like this. He went to Ames with it. There might be something in George's office that could help." She was lifting the telephone as I backed out of the office.

It was a beautiful morning. The bright sun warmed me as I climbed the hill to Pennsylvania Avenue, and all the snow was gone. There was no hint of the impending doom in other parts of the country. Weekend shoppers crowded the sidewalks, young matrons pushed their prams through the parks, and taxicabs and buses angled for position in the streets. Washington was smug. Whatever afflicted everyone else would never be permitted here.

I CLOSED the last drawer of Winslow's desk and leaned back in his chair. Whatever Charly had been afraid to see, it was no longer there – every drawer was empty. Either Winslow never kept anything in the desk, or he had purged it recently, perhaps anticipating a lifestyle change. I looked around the room. The furnishings – the dark leather and wood, bookcases full of old law books, gun cases with every variety of rifle and shotgun – reminded me of his office. Oil portraits of his mother and father glared down at me. Nothing in the room indicated that he was married to Charlotte Winslow.

Someone behind me cleared his throat. The man who had unlocked the desk a few minutes before stood in the doorway. "Excuse me, sir," he said, holding up a fistful of envelopes. "Today's mail." He advanced and laid it on the desk. John Winslow had a new address, one where mail was neither sent nor received, but life at the palace went on. I pushed the envelopes around without curiosity. The large one on the bottom had a familiar return address: "Nuclear Energy Authority, Washington, D.C." The name typed over it was "George K. Ames." I opened it.

There was a newspaper clipping, two black-and-white photographs and a hand-written note inside the envelope. The news piece was the Collins story about Jimmy Mottrom's inquest, accompanied this time by a picture of Ames standing on the steps of the Northumberland County Courthouse. Several lines in the article were highlighted in yellow, including the coroner's refusal to allow Doctor Palmer to testify and Ames' "whopper" about the day the campaign left town. There was a name, tiny and vertical, in the margin of the news photo that was also marked – I couldn't make it out. The small picture was of Jimmy Mottrom, the same as the one in Winslow's case. The larger photo was almost a duplicate of the one published in the *Richmond Times* and the *Norfolk Tribune* showing Jimmy hanging from the tree at The Orchard. The only difference was that George Ames was also in the photograph, clutching the other end of the rope that looped around Jimmy's neck. Both pictures were dated October 18, 1994. The date of Jimmy's death, as determined by the coroner's jury, was October 20.

The note had been written on Wednesday past, the day between my appearance on the Hill and the day that Winslow died.

> *Dear John,*
> *It will all come out now. I can't bear*
> *it. What can I do? The CD is up to you.*
> *George*

Was he right? You could survive a storm in Washington if you had powerful friends and a pliable press, and Winslow – and Ames – had weathered one twenty years earlier. But the sins were never forgiven or forgotten. They were simply filed away in the collective memory of the Leviathan, ready to be resurrected if you stumbled again. The fury at Winslow over the CRAC Report would undoubtedly lead to the murder and other things at Wicomico Church. He was now beyond their import, and Ames had chosen to join him. Why?

Ames had lied at the inquest, and tried to cover up Jimmy's murder in a particularly gruesome way. Was the potential exposure of those secrets sufficient to cause him to give away the centrifuge design? It was Ames, after all, who met Gomez at Oak Hill every Saturday. I had assumed that Winslow killed the boy, but the note and other things in the envelope might be evidence that it was Ames.

And what about the bomb factory? The implication was that Winslow knew about it, but wasn't part of the plot. That was consistent with the things in his attaché case. Or maybe not. Maybe, in the end, Ames was just an errand boy. We might never know. The three men were dead, and something much more important was still unresolved.

The last thing in the envelope was an ordinary compact disc in an ordinary plastic case. There was a sticker attached to the jewel case:

PROPERTY OF THE UNITED STATES GOVERNMENT

Unauthorized possession or use of this disc or the information contained therein will result in fines or imprisonment or both.

There was a lot more, but I didn't need to read it. I picked up the telephone.

IT WAS unusually warm for the first day of November and some of the trees – the sourwoods and poplars, especially – retained their color. The grass, though, was brown, and the flowers were gone and, just like that summer twenty years ago, green – this time the evergreen of holly and yew and spruce and pine – dominated. The stones were all blue in the late afternoon sun that struggled to penetrate the trees. A crowd was gathered in front of the Renwick Chapel. I stood among the people, my eyes searching for Roberto Gomez.

"There's no need for you to do this, Sawyer," Anderson had said. "It might be dangerous. We have people who are paid to take these risks."

"You can't make him speak, can you?"

"What do you mean?"

"He'll have diplomatic immunity and lawyers. All you can do is send him back to Cuba."

"Maybe. The important thing is that he takes the disc in the presence of witnesses."

"That's what's important to you. I have other priorities. He's my next-to-last suspect."

A man wearing a hat and a raincoat with the collar turned up strolled toward me. I recognized him immediately, seemingly unchanged by the years since he'd held John Winslow captive in the Venezuelan jungle. His head revolved slowly as he scanned the crowd. I waited until he was beside me. "Gomez?" He stiffened, but refused to look at me. "I have the CD." I held it up. He turned, smiling, and reached for it. "No. Not yet. Where's Regan Blaine?"

He lowered his hand. "I don't know."

"You and Withers took her, didn't you? Because she knew about this?" I raised the disc again. "Where is she?"

"I don't know what you're talking about."

I stifled the urge to throttle him. It had the ring of truth, and there was nothing more I could do anyway. The disc *was* important, and there was never a chance that I could withhold it until he told me what I wanted to know. The odds were a hundred to one that he would say something useful, and I had lost the bet. I handed him the disc, imagining the click of shutters and the whir of cameras as Anderson's people recorded the exchange. He turned toward the gate. Seconds later, he was surrounded by a phalanx composed of men who, only a moment before, had been part of the weekly tour at Oak Hill Cemetery. I had one suspect left.

Rather than follow them, I made my way past the red granite vault and climbed the iron gate. I paused on the other side. It was nearly dark, and the lawns and gardens and walkways leading up to the house stretched before me. A Georgian "temple" – really a round, open-air pavilion with eight white columns supporting a green copper roof – rose over a shallow pool. As I climbed the hill, the treasures of Charly's garden were revealed in the deepening twilight – cherubs spewing water, a fluted granite fountain in a circular pool, columns and benches and statues artfully draped in foliage. The rear of the house was almost a mirror image of the front. When I reached the steps, I turned and looked down on the city. It was a vantage that would be hard to give up.

Charly was on the sofa. The drapes were closed, and all the lights were on. A cheerful fire burned in the fireplace. I leaned in the door. "Can I talk to you for a minute?"

She smiled. "Of course."

I sat down. "Gomez has been arrested with the CD. The Republic will survive." She smiled. "He said that he knew nothing about Regan."

"Do you think that's true?"

"Probably."

She sighed. "Does anybody know anything about Regan?"

She was right. Nobody knew where Regan was. The primary suspect had always been Eli Withers, with the possible assistance of John Winslow. Winslow was dead. Withers was just about to kill me when he denied knowing where she was, and it would have pleased him then to tell me that he had her, or that she was dead. Gomez was a poor third choice. He would certainly have delegated the dirty work to Withers. Who was left? "Have you talked to your lawyer?"

"Yes. He called this afternoon."

"What did he say?"

"He said that Mark called him, and he delivered the money the next morning."

"Did he read the ransom note?"

"No. Mark had already given it to the police."

I hesitated. "How long have you known Mark?"

"I don't know. A long time."

"The telephone number for the *Georgetown Star* was in Martin's notebook. I assumed that it was Regan he called but the next number was Mark's home phone."

She frowned. "That doesn't make him a kidnapper."

"He said he told the Chief about the notebook. The police never heard of the notebook."

"Still –"

"Regan's CD was supposedly sent to him. He fielded the ransom demand, arranged for the money and sent me on my way." I stopped. "Withers said he didn't know where Regan was, either."

"He's hardly a credible witness."

"I know, but the point is that Mark's in the middle of it. According to your lawyer, he gave the ransom note to the police, but Blake knew nothing about it."

"But – what's the motive? Why would Mark Singer kidnap Regan?"

"It must be the book. Mark was involved in the stock deal or the bomb factory, or both, and Regan figured it out."

She hesitated, then seemed to make up her mind. "Did you know that he was in financial trouble?"

"I know he writes big checks to his ex-wives every month."

She shook her head. "It's more than that. He gambles. Junkets to Las Vegas and Macau. I – loaned him a substantial sum a few months ago." She paused. "It was supposed to be a short-term thing, but he hasn't mentioned it since."

We sat without speaking. "Have you said anything to the police about all this?" she said finally.

"No."

"I think you should. Let them handle it."

"Not yet."

"What are you going to do?"

"There's another thing I have to check. If I'm right –" The lights dimmed, then came back up. "If I'm –" The lights flickered sluggishly, like an old newsreel cast on the screen in a dark theater, and went out. The fire still danced merrily in the fireplace. Our original genie, it provided the only illumination.

CHAPTER EIGHT

WE WOULD abide with God's generation of light for the next few months, whether we believed in God or not. A few insignificant contrivances – candles, torches, things with batteries – might serve to relieve the intensity of the darkness but, when the sun fell below the horizon, we would see as our ancestors saw. The vagaries of the moon were important again, and landscapes meant to be seen always in a luster created by man took on a different aspect altogether.

While the revival of darkness was the most universal effect of the absence of power, the lives of millions were also disrupted repeatedly. Life – eating, drinking, sleeping in closed spaces where the temperature was no longer regulated and the windows were inoperable – was problematic. People who worked in offices struggled mightily to get there only to find themselves helpless once they arrived. Those less in thrall to modernity – farmers, fishermen, priests – had it easier, but they suffered, too. Progress, never-ending and presumably never over, had made life easier and more complex. Its lack would now add burdens and restore the primitive. Days and nights, devoted to toil and sleep, would be longer.

There were exceptions, of course. The marble palaces in the Federal City, long deemed indispensa-

ble by those inside them, came equipped with generators, and the great houses in Georgetown Heights –
including the one on 28th Street – already gleamed in
the darkness. Even former notables were accorded
their share of the precious light. From Charly's back
steps, the monuments to Lincoln, Washington and
Jefferson were plainly visible on the far side of the
creek. The symbolism was troubling.

A fabulous commercial enterprise was coming to
an end. Amanda was right – everything *was* for sale
so long as buyer and seller had the means to reach a
deal. Commerce was religion and the acquisition of
things – Winslow's office décor, for example – the
bulwark of the economy. Much of it was mindless,
like the ridiculous extravagance lavished on Mark's
old mansion in the middle of the river, a circum-
stance that would have astonished the original owner.
Buying and selling would continue, but the buyers
had more basic needs, and Madison Avenue was silent. The flacks who enabled the sales could no
longer communicate, and many of the things they
flogged could no longer operate. The billions of dollars that changed hands every day would stop. Business would look different when the power was restored.

The most astounding thing was how easy it was.
The life of an expanding nation had been tied to a
finite source of power that grew less reliable every
day. When anyone gave it any thought at all, it was
to hinder or oppose an increase in the country's capacity to create electricity. On warm summer days

the grid was stretched to the max, and any suggestion that power be cut back was met with fury and indignation, a rage that was as nothing to what was coming. Life would be mean, and the order of things would revert to an earlier, less sensitive, time.

I walked home in the rain. Inside the carriage house, I lighted one of the decorative candles on the mantel and carried it to the kitchen table. The tiny name was even harder to see in the flickering light. I placed a magnifying glass over each of the newspaper photographs. All the ones I had – those featured with the interview, Ames on the courthouse steps and, most significantly, the image of a boy hanging from a tree – were credited to the same man: "M. Singer." Mark had been part of the *Star* team that covered Winslow's ill-fated campaign for Congress. It seemed certain that he had taken the glossy photos in Ames' envelope as well. He and Withers had used them to extract the centrifuge plans from Ames.

The darkness around me prompted another thought. How much of Bell's plot had Martin discerned? Its success was assured even if the NEA succeeded in stopping the reactor shutdowns, and the certain economic destruction was arguably worse than a rogue bomb factory ninety miles from Miami. Martin had known enough to commission Baldwin's report, but there was nothing to show that he had gone beyond that. It was all a far cry from the petty stock scheme that I once believed was at the center of the mystery.

The candle reduced the room. The carriage house beyond the globe of light was still there, but I could no longer perceive it. I rose and walked in the general direction of the refrigerator. The ice was already starting to melt. I added a few more cubes than usual to an empty glass and poured some scotch. Ice, a product of electricity, was going to be hard to come by, but it was no longer the necessity it had been.

The rain stopped, and the emerging moon provided more light on the other side of the window. I finished the drink, put out the candle, and slipped the gun into my coat pocket. At the corner of Olive and 30th Street I turned north. Some of the houses glowed with candlelight, others were completely dark. Already my sense of smell was more acute – various odors I couldn't identify assailed my nostrils. I met no one on the street. The driveway was a web of shadows, and moonlight bathed the house as if it were one of the great monuments on the Mall. I pushed the door open. "Mark?" I climbed the stairs to the landing. "Mark? Anybody here?" I paused for a moment, allowing my eyes to adjust to the semi-darkness. His bedroom showed signs of recent occupation. The bed was unmade, dresser drawers were open, and newspapers lay scattered about the floor. There was isolated evidence of Anne's presence. A nightgown was draped over the foot of the bed, and lotions and a jar of face cream rested on the vanity in the bathroom. A woman's robe hung from the door.

Downstairs, dirty dishes were stacked in the sink and wine glasses sat atop the coffee table in the study. Two or three CD's – the same high quality brand as the one tucked away in his desk at the *Star* – lay beside them. The absolute silence was disconcerting. "Bo? Where are you, boy? Bo?" The mess on Mark's desk was worse than before. I held up a stack of unopened envelopes to the moonlight. They were all bills, some postmarked more than two months earlier. I searched the drawers. As far as I could tell, there was nothing about Cuba or the bomb factory. Anne's red muffler still hung over the chair.

I looked out the window at the summerhouse. The full moon, now completely uncovered by the clouds, provided an illusion of daylight, but it was all black and white and shades of gray. The little house was enveloped by the shrubbery that surrounded it. Something white lay outstretched beside the door. I closed my eyes for a long moment. Then, afraid of what I would find, I walked down the back steps and approached the summerhouse.

It was Bo. He lay full length, his head resting on an overturned water bowl. A butcher knife had been plunged through his neck, pinning his body to the ground, and other wounds had been inflicted upon his belly and haunches. He was covered with ants and it looked like birds or small animals had already begun to feed. Sickened, I turned away and fell back on the steps.

The summerhouse remained. I considered giving up and calling Blake, but it was somehow absurd at this stage of the game. The door was locked. I tapped on a heavily curtained window, but nothing stirred. I stumbled around the yard until I found a rock, and used it to break one of the panes. Bracing myself, I lifted the sash, pushed aside the curtains and squeezed inside. It was pitch-black – the dark drapery had fallen back into place, cutting off the light from the moon. Suddenly enraged, I ripped the drapes from the window and turned to confront whatever was in the room. When I realized that mine was the only body there, I almost sobbed with relief.

A few tools still hung on the walls, but the summerhouse had been converted into a tiny cell with a low neatly-made cot, a round table and two folding chairs, and a portable television set perched atop a bookcase. The sunglasses that Regan had worn the day I met her lay beside the television. Less prosaic was a chain locked to the grate in the concrete floor. It had a steel cuff at the loose end that limited the prisoner's ambit to only a few feet. Anne's demeanor was explained. She was the jailer in Mark's absence, charged with Regan's care and feeding, and my visits to the house had raised the possibility of discovery. She was a partner in the crime and, judging by the champagne flutes and whispers behind closed doors, a willing one.

Everything else could probably be explained away, but not this. I had been right about the motive and wrong about the kidnapper. Regan had indeed been taken to prevent the disclosure of the secrets in Martin's notebook, but it was Mark – not Winslow or even Withers – who had taken her. He had forced her to record the disc and pretended that it was delivered to the *Star's* office, and volunteered to manage the details in the absence of the police that he had engineered. If there *was* a ransom note, he had written it. He had commandeered the money and given it to me for delivery to his partner in the bomb business. It was unlikely that he and Anne had mourned Withers' death, but the loss of the $10 million was undoubtedly a blow.

I wondered about the room. It wasn't exactly foolproof – a small building with thin walls and glass windows in the heart of a crowded neighborhood – but it had served its purpose. Regan was probably controlled somehow – drugged, gagged or merely threatened – when people were around, forestalling any effort to make her captivity known.

Where was she now? I returned to the house and searched the rooms more carefully, but there was nothing to indicate where they had taken her. I picked up the phone and dialed Charly's number. Despite the darkness, she was still awake – it was only nine o'clock. "Call Blake," I said. "Tell him to check the summerhouse at Mark's. I believe that Regan has been kept there." I paused. "She's not there now."

"Why would Mark –?"

"I think it has to do with the project in Cuba. She must have known something she shouldn't."

"What are you going to do?"

"There's one more thing I have to check and then I'm going home. I'll be there if the police want me."

About to step out onto the porch, I noticed that the keys that usually hung beside the door were gone. The absence of one in particular gave me pause, and suggested an answer to the question I had asked myself a moment before.

I walked down the hill to M Street. There were a few pockets of light – Mark's bistro, where the odyssey began, was one of them. I stood there for a moment, turning a thought over in my head. The conviction, formed only minutes earlier, wobbled.

The places with power were full of people trying to deny the darkness and the solitude that came with it. They spilled onto the sidewalk, drinks in hand, in a sort of celebration, like New Year's Eve or an unexpected day off from school. Most appeared unaware of the true nature of the dark, but there were some – standing apart from the crowd – who seemed to understand. I wondered how things were at other, less privileged, enclaves.

I crossed M and continued down 31st Street. The door to Regan's building had been propped open and several people leaned or squatted beside it, seeking comfort from the moonlight that contrasted so sharply with the near-total blackness of the building. They were silent as I passed through them and walked inside. I found the stairwell and began to climb, grateful for the emergency lighting at each landing. At the sixteenth floor I pushed through the door and walked to the end of the hall.

Regan's apartment, its furniture disarranged and scattered, was a minefield in the dark. After falling over the sofa and banging my shin on an overturned table, I found a wall and followed it with short, sideways steps. I identified Regan's bedroom by the broad window that looked across the Potomac and inched my way to her closet. The darkness inside it was complete, so I scooped out all of the clothing and laid it on the bed.

There was no laundry. Charly had hung it in the closet after Regan was kidnapped, and now it was gone. It wasn't there when I first visited the apartment, either, though the import of its absence evaded me at the time. Someone had removed it. Why? The obvious answer was that Regan wanted a change of clothes, but it seemed odd that Mark would risk exposure to accommodate the sartorial whims of his victim.

I crossed the room carefully and stood looking out the window. I could see the lights of the old mansion glowing in the darkness on Mason's Island. Northern Virginia still had power but, as I watched, the lights blinked in unison and disappeared, turning the other side of the river black. The moon made the cluster of buildings look like a sculpture hacked from the landscape, and the light from a solitary automobile that wound around it recalled a miner's trolley. Three or four boats – their battery-powered lights feeble against the murk of the water – plied the Potomac. Light from still another source drew my attention. Lightning, followed by the low rumble of thunder, flashed in the east.

Rain driven by gusts of wind had forced the people by the door inside and, looking down river, I could see the storm coming toward me. The cafes on the boardwalk were deserted, and a dozen boats rocked in silence at their moorings. The one I was looking for – an old red, white and blue trawler in a prominent slip – was gone. Convinced now that Mark had used his boat to spirit Regan away, I was drawn irresistibly to Mason's Island. It was deserted, and Mark had the keys to the house.

The journey by car was a complicated route involving freeways, exits and a change of jurisdiction. I would have to go back to the house and find directions, and it was almost certain that I would get lost in the dark. Like my recent trip to the Eastern Shore, the quickest way to the island was across the water. I didn't have a boat, but maybe I could borrow one.

I scanned the horizon, looking for a vessel whose silhouette was similar to that which Bell and I had taken to Deep Creek. I wasn't much of a seaman, but my solitary cruise across the Chesapeake had provided a little experience that might help me now. There were three with lights and controls that looked familiar. None came with keys, of course, so I broke into the dockmaster's shed to find one. I picked a boat that was already pointed across the river and got underway. Mason's Island was just more than a half mile. If something happened, I could probably swim.

CHAPTER NINE

ONCE HOME to one of Virginia's most prominent families, Mason's Island – and the stone mansion that rose from its highest point – had been abandoned for more than eighty years. The lawns and
gardens around the house had reverted to nature and
the rest of the island, never disturbed, had flourished
in the dearth of men. That state of grace was threatened now by Mark's restoration, but current circum-
stances would slow, and perhaps halt, his effort to
reclaim it. For most of its history, those without a
boat had traveled to the island by ferry, but there was
now a narrow footbridge from the Virginia side.

A recent addition, visible a hundred feet from
shore, was a small temporary dock anchored to boulders on the northeast corner of the island. It took me
ten minutes to finally align my boat alongside Mark's
and tie up to it. The rain was a deluge and the river,
influenced by storm and tide, a torrent. The moon,
low in the western sky, had not yet been overtaken by
the clouds, and I could see the outline of the house
rising from the trees a few hundred yards away. After taking a moment to examine the cargo in the
trawler, I stepped onto the dock.

The raised river had separated the boulders from the island by a stretch of water three feet deep. I waded ashore and turned in the direction of the house. A path had been hacked from the trees and underbrush, but stumps and holes filling up with water still made the going treacherous. The house stood in an overgrown clearing. Dead wax myrtles and twisted live oaks cast bizarre shadows, and fig wound around the columns on the porch. I climbed the stone steps, careful to avoid the gaps. The rainfall, suffused with the rumble of thunder, was a Niagara, and the flicker of the lightning a kinetoscope of light and dark that made the shadows dance.

I paused just inside the door. A noise on the porch startled me, but when I looked back there was nothing except an overturned rocking chair leaning against the railing. The two-story foyer had no windows, but gradually the rugs and paintings and chandeliers came into view. The rooms on either side were stuffed with furniture, and the table in the dining room was festooned with place settings of silver, china and crystal. The kitchen was still a work in progress. Some of the appliances had been installed while others remained in their cartons. The extension cords were ubiquitous, though artfully concealed beneath rugs and behind counters. An empty champagne bottle sat on the counter.

When I returned to the foyer the front door was open, and a puddle inside the threshold was growing. The wind was a gale now, pounding the old house from all sides. I leaned against the door and closed it.

Curved staircases rose from each side of the foyer to a landing on the second floor. At the top of the steps, doors on both sides led to an exterior gallery that ran around three sides of the house. Directly in front of me was a wide corridor with more doors – two on the left and two on the right – and, on the far side, an elaborate entryway that undoubtedly led to the master bedroom. I hesitated, then stepped out onto the gallery and turned left, looking through the French doors as I passed. The moon, behind me now, revealed rooms in various styles of decoration. Antique furniture, lamps, layers of bed linens – the same excess demonstrated downstairs – covered every available square foot.

The last pair of doors was flanked by tall lancet windows with diamond panes. I watched the people inside – for a minute or an hour – until the storm, abating in fury but still powerful, finally caught the moon and extinguished the light. The shadows were gone, the dark absolute. I retraced my steps and descended the staircase to the foyer. There was a leather-covered bench directly opposite the steps. I crossed the room and sat down to wait.

A few minutes later, Mark stood at the top of the stairs, bearing a lantern that emitted a sickly fluorescent light. He didn't see me. I was hidden in the gloom beyond his lamp. At the bottom of the steps he turned toward the back of the house. "Mark." The lantern rocked slightly, causing the shades that it created to tilt.

He turned toward me and lifted the lamp. "Tommy?"

"Yes."

"What brings you out on a night like this?"

"I was looking for you."

His teeth smiled in the dark. "Well, you've found me." He turned around and placed the light on a tread several risers above the floor, then lowered himself to a step beside it. His head was at the same level as the lantern. Half of his face was revealed, the other half obscured. "What can I do for you?"

"I was just upstairs. This kidnapping looks pretty friendly." He laughed, but didn't respond. "Did you kill Martin?"

"No."

"Who did?" Again there was no answer. "Do you know?"

"I'm – not sure. Maybe Withers."

"Why?"

"Because Martin found out about Hanford. And the report."

"But how did Withers know? Was Martin trying to blackmail him?"

"I don't know."

A voice came from the landing. "Mark? Who are you talking to?"

He turned his head. "Come on down, sweetheart. The jig is up."

Shadows cast by the lantern merged and parted as she descended the stairs. The door to the gallery was open, and the white gown she wore swirled in the breeze. Her shadow, huge against the wall, followed her, while the murk at the top of the staircase seemed to shimmer outside the light. She sat down beside him. Only part of her face was visible, too, and the copper hair was the only color in the room. She peered in my direction. "Tommy? Is that you?"

"Yes."

"Why are you here? Did Mother send you?"

"No."

"I can answer your question. Anne Clark told Withers about Martin."

Mark started to speak. "Regan, don't –"

"It's true. She was sleeping with Martin, and he told her about the CRAC Report and the leaks at Hanford. She went to Withers, and he cut her in on the deal."

"How do you know?"

"She told me."

"Why would she tell you something like that?"

"Because it's part of her grand fantasy about Mark. Her plan to win him back." Her voice dripped with sarcasm. "She sat with me in that little house and told me how it would be. It's all she talked about."

"Regan, stop it."

"Mark's creditors are growing impatient. Anne was going to use her share to bail him out, and they would live happily ever after." She laughed. "Then you went up to the Hill and blew it all sky high."

"Regan, shut up."

She swung her head toward him. "Don't tell me to shut up. You know it's true. You encouraged her." She looked back at me. "He doesn't even like her. When her scheme fell through, he put her to work on ours. She thinks it's real."

"The kidnapping?"

She nodded. "She still believes the fairy tale. Anne and Mark, together again."

We were quiet. "What about Mrs. Martin?" I said.

"Anne did it," Regan said.

"Regan, for God's sake –"

She rounded on him again. "That notebook would've ruined her plans." She paused. "I saw you looking at her car."

He was silent. I almost felt sorry for Anne. "What about her car?" I said. Again, he didn't answer.

"Tell him," Regan said. He shook his head. "The fender was bent. There were brown stains on it."

That was easy to check. I turned to him. "What was your payoff for the project in Cuba?"

He seemed startled. "All I know about Cuba is what you told me."

"You weren't blackmailing Ames? With the pictures of Jimmy Mottrom?"

He was surprised again. "No."

He looked sick, and shrunken, in the harsh light, the outsized ego gone. I had believed him to be a devious criminal stealing the country's nuclear secrets –

someone on a par with, say, Eli Withers – or at least a kidnapper risking serious jail time. In fact, he was just a fraud stealing money from his girlfriend's mother, and the risk, if any, was minimal. Judging by Regan's tone and posture, the bloom was just about off the rose. Was she ready to abandon him? "Tell me about the pictures."

"Withers approached me at a White House dinner. He threatened me at first, but eventually offered money. I needed it. We struck a deal."

"Did he tell you why he wanted them?"

"Not specifically. I mean, he obviously wanted something for leverage over Ames and Winslow."

"What – why did you take them in the first place?"

"That's what photographers do. Everybody knew about Winslow and Ames and their disgusting little games with Jimmy Mottrom. I just happened to be around when Ames was trying to clean up the mess."

"Why not come forward then?"

"I worked for the *Georgetown Star.* Mrs. Blaine understood that Winslow had to drop out of the House race, but she drew the line at calling him a murder suspect." He stopped. "She *made* John Winslow. She wasn't about to throw him to the wolves."

"And yet, knowing who he was, she allowed him to marry her daughter."

"She didn't allow it. She insisted on it. It gave Winslow cover, and sealed the deal to keep everything quiet and not embarrass anybody."

"What are you saying?" said Regan.

It was all so *sleazy*, so unlike her idea of who they were. He turned his head toward her. "It was a good career move for me," he said, pleading now. "And Jimmy was beyond help."

"My mother was forced to marry that – pervert, and you let it happen?"

"Regan, there was nothing I could do."

Charly had been sacrificed to protect a predator and preserve a corrupt status quo. Regan was raised in the aftermath of that noxious arrangement, and the scars showed. "What made you decide to fake a kidnapping?" I said.

He lifted his head. "We had dinner the day Regan sent you the book –"

"At Mr. Smith's?"

"Yes. She told me about the notebook and –" He hesitated. "We both needed money. It was a way to get it from Charlotte and blame Withers."

"Whose idea was it?"

Regan broke in. "I – we – it was both of us. Mother's just being selfish. It's going to be mine sooner or later anyway."

"Why put her through this, then?"

"Because I need the money *now*."

I nodded toward Mark. "Has it ever occurred to you that it's the money he's really after? Did you know that he's already 'borrowed' from your inheritance?"

She turned her head. "Is that true?"

"No. Yes. I – I'm going to pay her back."

"Why didn't you tell me?"

He lapsed into silence again. "What was the plan?" I said. "Mark?" He didn't respond. I looked at her.

She, too, was quiet for a moment, weighing the need to tell me anything more. It was almost certain that the idea was really hers. *She* was the aggressor, and she knew that nothing bad was going to happen to *her*. "It was a little disorganized at first," she said, finally. "We messed up my apartment and made the CD. We were counting on you to turn the notebook over to the cops. After that we would figure out a way to collect a ransom while the police were pinning the kidnapping on John and Withers."

"Because you were about to reveal the CRAC Report."

"Yes. We were at loose ends when you kept the book, so we decided that I would stay out of sight while we waited to see what happened."

"And you stayed in the summerhouse?"

"Part of the time. The summerhouse was mostly for Anne. It had to seem like I was really a hostage." She paused. "We needed help, too. Mark still had a job and things to do, and I had to stay hidden. People drop in a lot – like you – and it wouldn't do for you to see me lounging around the house, so I stayed out there until he came home. Anne checked on me during the day." She stopped again. "She also kept an eye on you."

"When did you come over here?"

"Yesterday afternoon," she said. "We were going down the coast today, but the storm stopped us."

"I went by the house a couple of hours ago. There was a nightgown on the bed. Is it yours?"

"Yes."

"I told you to put that stuff away," said Mark.

"It doesn't matter," she said. "She can't do anything to us."

I saw Bo, nailed to the ground by a butcher knife. "I looked through the things in the boat, too," I said. "I was especially interested in the black leather bag."

"When you messed up the stock deal for Withers," Regan said, "you screwed it up for Anne, too. She convinced him to pretend that he was the kidnapper and demand a ransom. He promised her a cut of the proceeds." She paused. "We played along with it. It made it easier to get the money and blame Withers."

I looked at Mark. "Did he know that it was all a fake?"

"No. He thought she'd really been kidnapped. By someone else."

"Why did you make me the bag man?"

He shook his head. "That was *not* my idea. I didn't like it, but he insisted." He stopped. "At least you had a gun."

"But not the money."

"No. It was all green and gray paper with a few $100 bills on top. When you told me that it had been destroyed, I almost wet my pants. Nobody would look for the money because it was disintegrating in a waste pool at Deep Creek."

"While it's really in a black leather bag on your boat."

"Yes."

I hesitated. "What would've happened if Withers didn't die?"

"What do you mean?"

"What if he'd opened the bag? What if he thought that Anne had betrayed him? Or that I had taken it?" Neither of them spoke. Anne was a tool, easily disposed of, and so was I. They were all that mattered. "What's the endgame for the kidnapping?"

"Withers will be the prime suspect," said Regan. "It's even better that he's dead. I'll surface somewhere in the next few days and assure the police that he was the kidnapper." She stopped. "It's really worked out very well." We sat in silence. "What are you going to do?"

What, indeed? They needed money, and how else to relieve their poverty than by setting up a phony kidnapping, framing an "innocent" man, and defrauding her mother? The utter lack of scruples – to which they seemed entirely oblivious – was disturbing, but the actual crimes were negligible. The secret that I had longed to share with her caught in my throat. I slipped the gun from my pocket. "I'm going to give the money back to your mother. I owe her that. Anything else is up to her."

"I wish you'd –"

Mark cut her off. "That's fine, Tommy." He sounded relieved. "She won't do anything. She doesn't want this to get out."

He was probably right about that. The old indecision, the refusal to take on the slings and arrows, made me want to walk away. Regan was less than I had imagined her. Why risk the pain to make her better? But – if I didn't act now, this whole sordid mess would be something for them to laugh about tomorrow. They would continue as they were, deluded by their undeserved privilege, until something worse happened. At best, her life would be just like mine. Mark was beyond help, but maybe – maybe she could be redeemed. It was a gamble. Charly and I were damaged goods, too, and the three of us would be hard-pressed to become something different. Still, I had to try. I pointed the gun at him and looked at her. "I want you to come with me."

"Why?"

"Because I'm your father." I recognized the faces immediately – I'd seen them in the mirror a thousand times. The first one was disbelief, not because she doubted me – though she probably did – but because it was always the first reaction. I never took anything at face value, and neither did she. Next came suspicion. Why would I make such an outlandish claim? What was in it for me? The last one, the one I was hoping to see, was thoughtful. It would be easy to verify. Her mother was just a phone call away. I helped her along. "Go ahead. Call Charly. Call your mother."

She looked at Mark. "I – I will. But not yet."

I smiled. She already knew the answer. "You need to leave this place. And him."

"I can take care of myself."

She'd said the same thing to me before. I recognized the refrain because I'd repeated it, too, all my life. The only thing worse than weakness was admitting it. The faux self-reliance would take time to overcome. "Maybe not. Please. Your mother needs you. And so do I."

"I can't. Not yet." She paused. "Tell Mother I'm sorry."

I nodded. "Don't take long. We have lots to do." I turned to him. "Do you have a weapon with you?" He shook his head. I handed her the gun. "Someone cut Bo up with a butcher knife. Be careful." I rose and opened the door.

At the bottom of the steps, I heard her call. "Tommy?" I looked back. She was standing in the doorway. "Why do you call her Charly?"

"It was the only name I knew – once upon a time." I turned away.

"Wait."

She laid the gun on the porch railing, lifted the hem of her gown and picked her way carefully down the broken steps. When she reached me, she stood on her bare tiptoes and threw her arms around my neck.

"All my life I've wished that John Winslow wasn't my father. Thank you."

"You're welcome."

She leaned her head back. "I think Mother will forgive me. Will you?"

I smiled. "I already have." I could see Mark standing on the porch. "Come with me. Now."

She looked back. "I can't leave him like this. He's really in trouble. Some of it's my fault."

So – she was loyal. I wasn't sure that he deserved it, but it was a trait that we could build on. "All right. Come when you can."

"I will."

The storm had passed. I made my way slowly back to the dock, my mind alive with the future. It wouldn't be easy. I was ignorant of my child, and almost as uninformed about her mother. The notion that a young woman I barely knew could give me life was fantastic, the same fantasy I had entertained for the past twenty years, but it was real now. We would all mend together on the island.

I found the bag and tossed it into the borrowed boat. About to crank the engine, I heard the sharp crack of a gunshot, followed quickly by two more. I scrambled back to the dock and turned up the path again.

I paused when I reached the clearing. The old house, awash in moonlight once more, was dark and silent, but as I watched it suddenly blazed with light that surged and dimmed and finally remained. I looked over my shoulder. The Georgetown shoreline was still dark. The restoration of power was selective. I climbed the steps and opened the door.

Every light – lamps, chandeliers, spotlights – was on. Smoke – a few wisps at first, then more – began to fill the room, and I heard a popping noise. Another shot rang out, this one from the direction of the kitchen. I hurried through the dining room and stopped at the door. Flames danced along the countertops, cardboard cartons burned and fell away, and shiny new gadgets turned black. Sparks spewed from overloaded outlets, and bulbs burst in an uneven, stark staccato.

Mark lay face down, outstretched on the stone floor. Anne Clark stood over him holding the revolver I had given Regan. She pointed the gun at him and pulled the trigger again. "Anne!" She turned her head. Her eyes were exactly like Gordon Bell's two days earlier – bottomless holes in a pale, frozen mask that was already dead. She swung the gun around but, rather than turn it on me, she gripped the butt with both hands and fired the final bullet into her chest. Her body fell across his and, momentarily stunned, I stared as the flames caught their clothing and melded them in death.

I raced for the stairs. The century-old wiring inside the walls, overloaded for weeks by the foolish demands of decorators, had failed when the power surged. The entire house was an inferno. Smoke and flames engulfed the landing. I edged up the steps next to the wall and made my way through the door to the gallery. Each of the bedrooms I passed was a conflagration fueled by its new adornment. I opened the last door and plunged inside.

She lay sprawled across the bed, the bodice of her white gown crimson. As I moved toward her, the coverlet caught fire and enveloped her in a blaze like a Viking pyre. I tried to pull her from the flames, but it was no use. The burning gown seared her flesh and the red helmet of her hair was alive, framing the lovely face for an instant before devouring it. I staggered from the room, beating at the fire I carried with me, and fell from the gallery to the ground.

THE VIEW from the bungalow on High Street was unchanged. Traffic – people and automobiles – was sporadic, and no one was in a hurry. Oaks and poplars clad in new green leaves lined the road, and ancient magnolias, surrounded by a riot of lilacs and azaleas, almost concealed the Chancellor's House on the other side. The sun worshippers at Spencer Hall had spread a few blankets on the lawn, and the rhythm of life in our little college town continued as before.

New Hope had barely noticed Gordon Bell's scheme. The usual elements at the College had tried to co-opt it for one cause or another – depending on the source of whatever grant money they were spending at the time – but the town treated it as an inconvenience. Chimneys had been swept, lanterns reclaimed from attics, and everyone but the students went to bed a little earlier. The commercial district – a single long block of High between Division and Anderson Streets – shared the available power during the day and shut down at night. There was less money, and less to spend it on, but few complaints. Some went so far as to suggest that things were better, a notion quickly debunked by the scholars and statisticians at the College.

The rest of the nation had survived as well, though not without more pain. The consequences weren't as terrible as they might have been – the NEA had managed to keep half the reactors from shutting down – but some degree of the chaos that Baldwin had predicted affected every region of the country. The great cities, in particular, suffered. The lack of reliable power impacted every aspect of life there, and large chunks of them were abandoned to those who thrive in the dark. Consumption enabled by borrowed money slowed and, when the power was restored, it was no longer a way of life. Another Great Depression had been avoided – perhaps due to the shifting definitions of a government terrified that it would be dismantled – but the people had emerged from the crisis with a new idea of what mattered.

The finger pointing in Washington continued unabated. A blue-ribbon panel reporting directly to the President was established, and the NEA was replaced by three new agencies whose combined task, stripped of the rhetoric, was the same as that of their predecessor – manage our weapons and grease the way for commercial nuclear power. The pervasive, ever-growing problems with the waste and deteriorating plants – the status quo that Gordon Bell had sought to change – were ignored, while committees on Capitol Hill competed to spend billions to forestall another Deep Creek. The raid on the Cuban missile factory was conducted "quietly," but its details were made public immediately in order to demonstrate that our elected officials were up to the task when it came to a *real* nuclear catastrophe.

I looked at my watch. It was after six, and only now was a drink in order. I was trying to make friends with alcohol, and it was time to renew our acquaintance. A few minutes later, scotch in hand, I returned to my desk and stared out the window. Night was falling, an event that had taken on added significance over the past few months.

I turned my head to the right. New Hope was the same, but I was not. Not long after I returned from Washington, the town had installed a stoplight at my intersection. I thought it was silly – unneeded and oddly extravagant at the time – and said so, but the town fathers ignored me. I was glad for it now. The red and green and amber lights never failed to recall a time when I had stepped away from myself and tried to help someone else. Anger was now regret – regret that we had been denied the opportunity to live the life we had started, regret that I had squandered twenty years being angry about it. The self-pity that threatened again when Regan died was engaged and vanquished.

Her funeral closed the circle. After the mourners were gone, we sat on our benches without speaking. She wept silently, the only tears I'd seen during the long ordeal. The past tugged at me, but I beat it back, and willed my eyes to remain dry. She looked up, finally. "What are your plans?" Charly said.

"I'm leaving for home in a few minutes. If I don't run into any trouble, I'll be there by dark."

She nodded. "What's it like?"

"Slow. Very slow."

"I wish you'd stay a little longer."

"Thanks. I need to go."

She rose and reached for my hand, and we passed through the gate together. "I'm – really a pretty good person," she said, not looking at me. "You should give me a chance."

I shook my head. The island was impossible now. "You're not the problem. I am."

We climbed the back steps and walked through the house. When we reached the front door, she said, "Wait here. I want to get something to write with." She returned a moment later. "I'll probably need to get in touch with you about – something." I took the pad and pen from her and wrote down my address and telephone number. She stared at the pad when I was through, more tears spilling from her eyes. "I wish I'd had this twenty years ago."

"So do I." Thus was born a new regret. I'd picked up the phone a dozen times, but never made the call. Finally, I took up pen and paper and wrote a letter that said the things I'd said to her when we were children, but went unspoken when we met again. I didn't hear from her and after a month or two I began to pack the memories, old and new, away. I had chosen the future over the past, but the future was a secret, uncomfortable and unresolved, while the past unspooled in my head every time I let my guard down. It was potent, and crippling, too, if allowed to gain the upper hand. Like a fine whisky, the past was a pleasure to be savored on special occasions, but a scourge if sampled too often and, just as I was coming to terms with drink, my past and I had to reach an understanding as well.

I was doing better with the booze than the memories. The worst part was the past that I would never have. I had found and lost a child in a matter of days, and the memories I had planned then were stillborn when she died. I wrestled with it, and finally decided that, where Regan was concerned, it was okay to remember things that never were. I closed my eyes and leaned back in the chair, and thought again about the gun, the one I'd left behind to protect her. What if that had never happened? Or what if I'd just thrown her over my shoulder and carried her to the boat? Choices, those decisions I'd refused to make for so many years, came with consequences, and I was learning to live with them.

A sharp knock on the door aroused me. In other times I would have ignored it, but my office hours were more flexible now. I heard the knock again. "Hold on," I called. "I'm coming."

She stood in the doorway in jeans and a white turtleneck sweater. The pale golden hair was pulled away from her face, and the expression was uncertain. It was a woman's face, one that care and the ravages of time had touched though not disfigured, but the image of a girl was just a smile away. She smiled. "Hello, Tom."

"Hello, Charly."

THE END

Also by Alan Thompson

The Black Owls
An Oxford Nightmare

An ocean liner is destroyed and the ruins of an old church blown up, and other parts of England are menaced by unknown "terrorists." The University of Oxford is threatened with a bomb, and the Duke of Aylesbury – Tony Markham to his intimates – calls on Georges St. Cyr, formerly one of America's most ruthless intelligence agents, for help. The Muslim diaspora in London, higher-ups within the University itself, even the government, are suspected, and the two old friends have seven days to avert disaster. It's immediately apparent that the British government, despite acquiescing in St. Cyr's investigation, is engaged in a cover-up. Whitehall's hand-picked Chancellor at Oxford, John Cromwell, comes under suspicion. Other clues point to Ahmed Zhev, Chief of Pakistan's notorious Directorate of Inter-Services Intelligence. England is in turmoil, its most venerable institution threatened and, as time runs out, the future is in the hands of a single man.

Available from
W & B Publishers
www.a-argusbooks.com

Look for more works in the future from
Alan Thompson

www.ingramcontent.com/pod-product-compliance
Lightning Source LLC
Chambersburg PA
CBHW051523260626
47170CB00003B/763